Orfeo Undone

Kathryn Bartlett

Copyright © 2024 Kathryn Bartlett

All rights reserved

ISBN: 9798321223680

Imprint: Independently published

To Steve, Alexander and Daniel, for never doubting.

We read full oft and find it writ
As ancient clerks give us to wit
The lays that harpers sung of old
Of many a diverse matter told
Some sang of bliss, some heaviness
And some of joy and gladsomeness
Of treason some and some of guile
Of happenings strange that chanced awhile
Of knightly deeds, of ribaldry
And some they tell of Faerie
But of all themes that men approve
Methinks the most they be of Love

Sir Orfeo
Author unknown

Prologue

The old Second World War prisoner of war camp, stood on the edge of the forest, around three miles from the village. It seemed like an incongruous setting for such a place, but it had been extremely carefully chosen; its isolation being the main attraction, along with the quietness of the forest. The soldiers who had been responsible for guarding the mainly German prisoners that were housed there were continually surprised that they did not have to discourage the local villagers from entering the forest, in the event of them getting too close to the camp.

The only dwellings nearby were a couple of old cottages on the other side of the forest and a few farms beyond that, where some of the prisoners were sent to work. Stories started to circulate about the locals being scared of the forest, although the soldiers could never quite fathom why that might be. It was not a large camp, one of several in the Highlands of Scotland, housing about two hundred prisoners at any one time. At the end of the war, the camp was left, essentially to fall into ruin, seemingly forgotten by both the authorities and the villagers.

Over seventy years later, the contractors walked around the old camp, peering into the accommodation huts, with their corrugated roofs, formerly green, now mainly rusted and full of holes. There was no furniture in the huts, that had all been taken away at the end of the war. All that remained were the wooden huts and the perimeter fence, with its four guard towers, most of which had by now been choked by nature, overgrown with various climbing and creeping plants.

They had been charged with dismantling the whole site, including the perimeter fence, to make it look as if it had never existed. They did not know what the land would be used for; they did not need to be told that. They were an experienced crew and quickly got to work, setting up their accommodation block, for the duration of the job, which had arrived, not long after them, on the back of a couple of large trailers, before the daylight ran out.

Their sleeping accommodation was spartan, consisting of metal camp beds and lockers for their belongings, but they were used to it when they were on a job like this. They had portable gas stoves for cooking and a mobile generator for electricity, along with plenty of supplies. Self-sufficiency was what they were aiming for, with no need for shopping trips into the local village, to get the job done and leave, as quickly as possible.

Their first night was uneventful, followed by a long, hard day of work. Sitting around, eating dinner that evening, they all felt pretty optimistic at having this job complete within a week. An hour or two of playing cards followed, before they all settled down for the night. The next morning, the team leader had to pull up a couple of the team, for not getting on with their allocated tasks. When he spoke to them, they seemed a bit vague and unable to account for what they had been doing for the past hour or two. This baffled him, as these guys were usually such diligent and hard workers, who had never given him any grief on past jobs.

Later in the day, he noticed another guy looking a bit weary. He asked what was wrong and was told that he had a bad night's sleep, as he kept hearing strange noises outside and then had a really disturbing dream. He did not usually have such conversations with his team and he felt a bit rattled after this. He remembered the dream that he had woken himself up from last night, with a start, one where he had kept falling, into darkness, unable to stop himself. The mood around the table seemed a bit sombre that evening, with a few of them complaining of tiredness and aching limbs and backs. They took to their beds earlier than usual, the team leader being the last to go to bed, after checking everything was turned off. When he climbed into his creaky, narrow bed, he felt sure that sleep would elude him, but he was wrong.

A couple of mornings later, after being unable to get any kind of response from the camp, a small team of soldiers from the Black Watch battalion, based at Fort George, arrived, at the request of the contractors' company. They entered the accommodation block only to find the whole team still in their beds. They felt for pulses and discovered they were still alive but could not be woken up. Medics in unmarked trucks were there within the hour, but still nothing could rouse them, they remained in what appeared to be some form of catatonic state. They took them to a military hospital. A team of Army investigators quickly followed, scouring the site for any clues for what might have happened, but none were found.

The man with close-cropped, grey hair, lowered his binoculars. He had been watching the activity at the old camp for a few hours now. He was alerted during his morning walk in the forest, which was usually so tranquil and undisturbed. As he got nearer to the far edge of the forest, in sight of the perimeter fence of the camp, he became aware of people walking around within the fence. He stopped and concealed himself behind a large tree, carefully peering around. He saw what looked like soldiers, carrying guns, who seemed to be looking for something.

He left the forest fairly quickly and walked up to the hill that stood next to it, where he knew he would be able to see more. Lying flat on his stomach, behind a rock, he trained his binoculars on the camp. He had no idea what he was witnessing, but he distinctly saw stretchers being taken out of the temporary unit that had been put up, their occupants being loaded into an Army truck and driven away.

Chapter One

Don't Want To Know

The sudden thud of the plane's landing gear coming down, jolted Elizabeth out of her daydream. She gazed out of the window and saw Inverness airport beneath them. The flight from Luton had been relatively smooth and uneventful, apart from the demanding passenger in front of her, who obviously had not got the message that they were travelling on a 'no frills' airline and the woman from New Zealand, in her early seventies next to her, who had kept trying to draw her into conversation, from the moment she sat down. She felt a little guilty that she had not engaged with her efforts to tell her about her big trip to Scotland to trace her ancestors and how she had always felt more Scottish than anything else. She was so excited and full of optimism, which had simply not matched Elizabeth's current mood. Eventually, Elizabeth had put on her headphones and switched on some music, John Martyn, whose melancholic melodies and lyrics soothed her. She closed her eyes and leaned her head back on the headrest, her neighbour turning to the man on her other side, who appeared to be more receptive.

The plane touched down and before too long, was taxiing towards the terminal building. She always waited, whether on planes or trains, for other passengers to get up and move towards the exit before she did. She hated the rush of people pressing to get to the exit first, as if that would make a difference to anything. She hated the feeling of impatient people, standing too close behind, their cases pressing against the back of her legs. She wasn't claustrophobic about small spaces, but she had the need for a greater degree of personal space than most other people seemed to require.

When it was clear, she got up and pulled down her small case from the overhead locker. She was tall and had no trouble with this. She had been this height since she was eleven years old. She had hated it then, but actually relished being above average height now, (though did get a little weary in supermarkets, when short people looked at her imploringly when they were trying to reach an item on the top shelf). She didn't mind helping people - she had spent her working life

helping others in some way - but, for some reason, found this really irritating. She embraced her height now and wished it had not taken her so long to realise how looking imposing and statuesque could really work in her favour when she wanted it to. High heels were still not her friend though and she didn't think they ever would be.

She walked down the aisle and said thank you to the cabin crew at the door, marvelling at how they managed to keep those smiles plastered on their faces, and walked down the steps to the tarmac, to make the short walk to the terminal building. It was mid-March and Winter still had its grip on the weather, with foreboding grey clouds, full of rain and nothing gentle about the breeze that whipped her unruly hair around her face. She shivered as she walked and wished she was wearing her thicker, winter coat. Her thin raincoat had seemed quite adequate when she had left North London, but not now.

In the terminal building, she collected her large suitcase from the luggage carousel and wheeled it towards the arrivals gate, suddenly feeling overloaded and a little overwhelmed. People were milling around, as she scanned the crowd for her friend, Louise, who was to pick her up in the car that was to be hers while she was in Scotland. She had known Lou for more than ten years. They had first met when Elizabeth and her husband had made one of their first visits to this part of the world. He had a hobby - model car racing - that had taken them to the Highlands every June, for a race meeting. Her friends in London had never been able to understand why she used to accompany him to these races, imagining her, sitting by the track all day, bored to tears. She tried to explain to them that she barely stayed to watch the racing; she would be off exploring, visiting places like Culloden Moor and other places on the Black Isle, as well as further north to Dornoch and Golspie. She had always felt so much more relaxed and happier when was in the Highlands.

London had never felt like home. She had moved there in her twenties, after leading a safe, comfortable existence in Devon. She had not gone straight to London, having spent a few years in Bristol, studying for an English Literature degree. She had moved to London, like so many others, looking for work and a different kind of life, both of which she had found. Lou was a high school History teacher and the wife of one of the local model car racers and had invited her for a coffee, not long after first meeting her. They found conversation easy and became firm friends surprisingly quickly. Elizabeth knew that she could come over as a little aloof at times, particularly around new people and it always frustrated her that it never crossed their minds that this was a result of the shyness that had trailed her since childhood. People who got to know her, quickly discovered an open, funny and warm person. She was quietly spoken and succinct, never speaking purely for the sake of it. Rather than a wide social circle, she had a small number of good friends, who she could count on and who she trusted implicitly, (Lou being one of them).

Lou was a few years older than her and had led a very different life. She had grown up in the far north of Scotland and living within half an hour of Inverness was as close to urban life as she had ever wanted to be, When Lou had heard she was separating from her husband and planning a move to the Highlands, she had been sad for her having to go through so much upheaval, but glad at the prospect of her friend being more available. Elizabeth heard Lou before she saw her. She could be impressively loud if she needed to be, yelling her name in her slightly shrill voice. She gave her a massive hug when she got to her and took her larger case.

'Where is the rest of your luggage?'

'This is it, the rest is being couriered up in a few days.'

'Would you like to get a drink or some food?'

'No, I think I'd rather get to the cottage as soon as possible.'

'You look tired and too pale.'

'Thank you Lou, for your kind words.'

'Ach, you know that I love you, but it's true. You've really had a tough few months haven't you?'

Elizabeth nodded her head and felt herself starting to tear up. The last few months had indeed been pretty crap. Her husband had, predictably, behaved appallingly when she had told him it was over and had put up barriers every step of the way. They had been together for twenty five years, the last five or six of which had been hard work.

She had felt undermined and belittled by him for most of the time and it took her a while to realise the degree of control he had over her and the toll this had taken on her self-esteem and conviction in her abilities. Covid lockdowns and turning fifty had been a bit of a turning point for her, a cliché possibly, but their two sons were both seemingly settled and happy in their careers and relationships. She never ceased to be amazed at how she had raised two such impressive, compassionate and clever young men and was relieved that they appeared to be able to sustain healthy and supportive relationships. She had spoken to them both, at length, about her plans to move to Scotland. They were both completely supportive of her, as they fully understood how their father had made her feel and were proud of her for ending it and forging a new life. She would miss them, of course, but knew that they would visit her whenever they could and she would make occasional trips to London.

They walked out of the terminal building, into the car park and found the car that would be hers. It actually belonged to Lou's daughter, who was, much to Lou's unhappiness, travelling around

Australia and New Zealand for the next year. Rather than it sitting not being driven anywhere, she offered it to Elizabeth. It was a Volkswagen Golf, something that Elizabeth was quite happy about, as it reminded her of her first car after passing her driving test. It had been an old Golf and had cost the grand total of three hundred pounds, but had been an excellent car. Lou had put her on the insurance, for which Elizabeth would pay her back. Lou offered to drive to the cottage, which she gladly accepted. It was not too far to the cottage, around a forty minute drive, but Elizabeth did not feel quite ready to get behind the wheel, after her long journey.

She had chosen the cottage a few weeks earlier, when she had made a short trip up to look at a few different properties, The estate agent had been very obliging and had met her at the airport and driven her around, He was young, in his mid

twenties, tall and slim, with light blond short hair and bright blue eyes under pale eyebrows. He chatted fairly non-stop on the way to the properties, but asked a few too many questions about why she was planning a move to Scotland. When she had told him she was moving here as she was separating from her husband, he seemed to be attempting to flirt with her, She thought she was imagining it at first, he was about the same age as her eldest son and couldn't think why he would be remotely interested in a woman of her age.

She knew straight away that the first two properties were not right for her, they were too modern and too close to other houses. She was after a bit more isolation. As they approached the third one, a small, whitewashed, stone cottage, up a long drive, off a quiet lane, which the estate agent was quick to point out was built in the sixteenth century, she felt the hairs on the back of her neck stand up and the slightest buzz of excitement coursing through her. This was the one. He let her look around the cottage and the garden on her own. It had two bedrooms upstairs and a small bathroom, with a sitting room and kitchen downstairs. It came fully furnished and the price was surprisingly low for this area of the Highlands.

She stepped out of the kitchen door, into the small, walled garden. On the other side of the wall was the start of the forest and beyond the forest a hill loomed up. It was not a huge forest, but it looked dense and the trees looked old. She wandered over to the wall and opened the wooden gate, making the short walk to where the trees began. She had not walked far, only for a minute or two, before the forest closed in around her and the daylight dramatically decreased, She stood, gazing up at the trees that surrounded her, marvelling at their height, and revelling in the quietness of the place, she couldn't even hear much birdsong or other signs of wildlife, A voice, calling her name, brought her back to reality, It was the agent, She walked back to the garden gate, where he was standing. He looked concerned.

'I thought you'd got lost in the woods.'

'What do you mean? I wasn't gone for long.' He looked at her mildly amused and said that she had been gone for nearly half an hour. She could not understand this as she walked back to the car with him, but was soon distracted by his further chatter and attempts at flirtation on the way back to his office, where she signed some paperwork for the cottage and paid a holding deposit. Elizabeth gazed out of the window,

listening to Lou filling her in on the latest news about her family and the few mutual friends that they had. When they had skirted Inverness, on the A9 and crossed the Kessock Bridge, she could feel a lightening within her, as they entered the Black Isle, passing places that she had become familiar with over the years. Conon Bridge, Contin and then the still, grey water of Loch Garve, before turning off the main road, onto ever narrowing and steepening lanes, flanked by rows of tall, serene Silver Birch trees. As Lou drove up to the cottage, she felt the same way she had when she had first seen it. Lou left her there, after being collected by her husband and made her promise not to shut herself away too much and to be in touch soon.

After Lou left, Elizabeth wandered from room to room. She loved Lou and did enjoy spending time with all her friends and family, but sometimes she really needed to be alone, to have the space to put her thoughts in order or not to think at all. In the kitchen, she looked in the fridge, which already contained some food to tide her over her first few days, including a couple of bottles of New Zealand wine, (Lou knew her so well). There was bread in the cupboard, as well as coffee. She filled the kettle and made herself a cafetiere of good, Italian ground coffee and took her mug out into the back garden, through the kitchen door.

It was midafternoon and the grey skies from her arrival at the airport had lightened, with the faintest trace of sunlight attempting to break through. The garden was not huge; there was a stone patio running along the back of the cottage, with steps leading up to a lawned area. There were no neat, regimented flower beds, which pleased her, there were various shrubs and bushes, which had grown quite large and unkempt, adding a slightly wild quality to the garden. There were not many trees, but that did not matter, as beyond the stone wall, which encircled the garden, was the forest, which had so enthralled her on her first visit. She had thought about this forest fairly consistently over the past few weeks, remembering the sounds and sensations and how she felt both lost and safe there. She had been longing to see it again. The air started to cool a little and, looking up, she saw more grey clouds start to blow in, (she had forgotten how the weather could change in the blink of an eye up here). She had been hoping to take a walk in the forest, but decided that would wait until tomorrow. She felt tired and was not dressed for a woodland walk. As she headed back inside, splashes of rain started to appear on the stones. As she closed the kitchen door, they became heavier until there was a deluge.

She spent the rest of the afternoon and evening quietly. She messaged her sons to let them know she had arrived safely and that she would talk to them soon. She did not feel like talking to anyone this evening. A glass of wine and some music was all she needed. She went to bed quite early and fell into sleep easily. She had the same dream she had been having intermittently for a few weeks now, where she was falling into darkness, but also felt like she was being pulled by an invisible force. She was desperately trying to hold onto branches to stop herself, but had lost the use of her arms. She always woke up, with a jolt, before she hit the ground or whatever it was that she was hurtling towards in the darkness.

Chapter Two
Lilac Wine

She woke up with the dawn the next morning. She felt good, apart from the vestiges of leftover uneasiness from her dreaming. She had experienced vivid, and at times, disturbing, dreams, for most of her life. When she was a teenager and into her early twenties, she used to sleepwalk. Nothing dramatic, she would sometimes walk over to her bedroom window and, after a while, wake up, finding herself staring up at the sky. When she was a lot younger, (maybe three or four years old,) she would wake up in the night screaming, convinced that she had seen a knight in armour in her doorway. Her parents told her it was because she had been looking at lots of story books with knights and princesses, She looked out the window, the day looked promising and the weather forecast last night had not mentioned the possibility of rain. A good day for a walk.

In the bathroom, she inwardly groaned when she looked at herself in the mirror. She had, as she often did, not taken her makeup off the night before and mascara was smudged underneath her eyes, adding to the dark shadows that already lived there. She did not tend to wear a great deal of makeup, only some dark brown mascara to make her eyelashes looks less sparse than they were and some concealer, in an attempt to hide the tiredness and the occasional spot that still plagued her into middle age. Several of her friends had gone down the Botox and fillers route, to try to fight off the signs of ageing, but she did not like the look of their smooth, slightly shiny foreheads or the way that they always had a little more injected than before, when they went back for top ups. She had ever deepening grooves between her eyebrows and lines at the edge of her eyes and did not like the way her jawline was starting to become slightly less well defined, but her eyes were still arresting - the type of eyes that changed colour, according to the light - sometimes golden at other times more green, with a reddish brown circle around her pupils. She had high cheekbones, thanks to her Celtic ancestry, with a straight, fine nose. Her skin was on the pale side, particularly at this time of year, but when she let herself get some sun on it, she developed a golden glow quite easily. Her hair she kept long. She had noticed the texture and thickness changing, but the waves were still there. She did colour it, she was not ready to give in to the grey yet, but she tried to keep this to a minimum. She quickly washed her face, deciding she would shower later and dressed in her old jeans and her favourite, chunky, dark blue jumper.

After coffee and toast, she pulled on her boots and raincoat and set off out of the back door, through the wet grass to the old stone wall that marked the end of her garden. She did not know much about construction, but knew that this was a dry stone wall, which was a fairly common feature in this area. She admired the skill of whoever had built it, the way they had carefully chosen and stacked the stones, now covered in moss and lichen, without leaving any gaps.

The weather worn, wooden gate opened with a protesting creak and looked as if it would not survive the next big gust of wind that came along. She loved how the edge of the forest was so close to her garden, it took less than thirty seconds to reach it. As she walked further into the woods, she felt a real sense of anticipation, tempered with slight feelings of anxiety, the root cause of which she could not pinpoint. As before, she gazed in awe and admiration at the trees; the Birch trees with their uniformly long, straight, silvery trunks, the magnificent Scotch Pines, still with their dark green needles and other trees that she could not identify. She promised herself that she would take some photos and look up all the trees that she did not recognise, but not today.

A small stream ran through this part of the forest, so narrow that she could step over it easily, although she still took care not to slip on the damp, slightly boggy ground around it. She decided she would follow its course one day, to find out where it ran into. She noticed large pieces of stone, at random intervals, some on their own, others in small clusters. They were mostly covered in moss, but on closer inspection turned out to be a yellowish grey colour and had unexpectedly smooth surfaces, as if they had been cut by a human hand.

She thought how different this forest was from those she was familiar with in Devon and in the Home Counties around London. The forests in Devon tended to have trees that grew closer together and, of course, some different varieties, with more Oak trees and Beech trees, as well as Chestnut trees. The ground covering was so different too. Here, there was so much rusty coloured bracken on the ground, interspersed with moss and a green, spiky plant she did not recognise.

Many of the trees here had lichen growing on their trunks, which she had not seen much of before now. She thought about how much her father would have loved this forest. He had always taken her for walks in local woods and let her run and climb as much as she wanted, although also made her find her own way down from trees that she proclaimed she was stuck in. She would invariably return home from these outings, covered in mud and a new array of bruises and small scratches from these climbing escapades, much to her mother's disapproval. He would tell her the names of trees, usually in both English and Latin, (which sadly seemed to have escaped her memory now,) and had told her stories about them. She could remember him telling her about the Rowan tree and how it was meant to offer protection against evil spirits and how some people used to hang Rowan branches over their doorways to guard against them. Her father had died last year, after a fairly short illness, and had left her enough money in his will, to take some time out of work and pay rent on a property for a while, This had been the catalyst for her moving up here, as she could not imagine anywhere else that she would want to live.

She had a deep yearning to live in the Highlands, specifically in this area, since she had started to visit here, She was worried that she had become a bit of a stereotype; a fifty year old woman, coming out of a long term relationship, looking for a bit of an escape, There was an element of this, but she knew there was much more to it than this; the pull this place had on her felt so strong. She would sometimes be walking along a street in London and have the compulsion to find her way to Euston Station and get onto a train that would take her here, a compulsion so strong that it almost hurt and could make her tearful. This was also tied up with the emotions around the ending of her relationship and her dissatisfaction with her working life. Her father had been a gentle, kind soul, always ready with a hug and reassurances when she was upset, never too judgemental when he picked her up in his car from teenage parties and had to pull over for her to be sick, (not telling her mother afterwards, although making her clean up the car if needed).

Her mother had been a more remote figure, a product of her own upbringing by a severe and strict Army Captain father. There was always good food, clean clothes and appointments always made and attended, but Elizabeth had no memory of a hug or being told that she loved her. Elizabeth had been adopted when she was around six months old. Her birth mother had been a young, unmarried woman, from a strict Catholic family, who had made it clear to her that she would not be welcome back to the family home, if she kept the baby, She had felt, like so many other women at that time, that she had no other option but to give up her child, Elizabeth had been adopted by a couple who had already had four children of their own, but felt that they had room for one more. They were financially comfortable and lived in a large, Victorian house, on the edges of Exeter in Devon. Her adoptive mother liked babies and was good with them, but seemed less sure about how to deal with them when they got older and less biddable.

Elizabeth had always been aware of her adoption, but had never been made to feel that it was an open subject for discussion and so simply didn't talk about it at all with her family. She made no attempts to trace her birth parents, until she was in her late twenties and pregnant with her first child. Her birth mother had been relatively easy to find, even in the days before commonplace access to the internet. She had written to her and received a very sad letter in return, full of regret and guilt. She had written back, trying to reassure her that she had a good life and held no anger or resentment towards her. She did not reply for over a year, until she received a letter from her birth mother's sister, telling her that she had died a few months earlier from an aggressive form of Cancer.

She had, naturally, asked her birth mother about her father, but received scant information in return. He had, apparently, been a tourist, who had gone home before she discovered she was pregnant and that she had no way of contacting him. She told her nothing more, no name, not even a country of origin. When her children were older, she had started to look at ancestry websites, to find out about her maternal ancestors and had managed to trace them back a few generations, until brick walls started to be thrown up. They were mainly from Ireland, with one branch having come from Scotland, although there the trail went cold.

When she was younger, she did not feel that being adopted had any significant impact upon her, but now, she could see that it had. She had always felt a little on the outside of life, looking in, that she did not really fit anywhere. She had lived with anxiety most of her life and recognised that her attachment style in relationships was not healthy, often convinced that she would be left. This had made her a little hesitant when it came to letting people into her life. She had friends, who she loved spending time with, but had never had the need to talk to them and see them as regularly as perhaps they would have liked.

Lost in thought, she had walked further into the forest than she had realised. She stopped next to a tree, with a very tall, quite straight, greyish brown trunk. Its large branches spread out far above her and looking up at them, she could make out small, dark buds on the end of the twigs that shot out of the branches. She knew this tree, it was an Ash tree. She remembered her father telling her about its supposed protective and healing properties and was sure there was some tale about people giving ash sap to newborn babies for protection. Apart from the Scots Pines, this looked like one of the larger trees in the forest and Elizabeth found herself reaching out to touch the trunk with both hands. As she did so, she began to experience the same sensations as when she first saw this forest, as if her blood was fizzing, though stronger now. Tiredness also started to creep up on her. She did not understand how she could suddenly feel this tired, so early in the morning, but was quickly overwhelmed by the need to sit down and rest, with the feeling that her legs could not carry her any further. The ground was damp and muddy, but she did not care, all she could think about was sitting down and shutting her eyes, the tiredness was too powerful. She did and let her eyes close.

The next thing she knew, she was waking up from the same dream she had the night before, but the sense of threat within it was even higher. She was lying on the ground, with the side of her face in the leaves and twigs. She sat up, but felt foggy and disorientated. When this had passed, she looked at her phone and was horrified. She had been asleep for hours, it was lunchtime. The need to get out of the woods as quickly as possible, descended on her. She stood and started to walk quickly away, but soon found herself running back to the cottage garden and into the house, locking the door behind her. She took off her muddy boots and coat and went into the bathroom. In the mirror, her hair was dishevelled and she still had the imprint of twigs and leaves on her cheek. She also looked paler and more tired than usual. After washing her face, she went downstairs, feeling the strong urge to get out of there and go somewhere else for a bit.

Chapter Three

Past Lives

She decided to drive to the village to buy some food. In the small shop that seemed to sell everything from fresh fruit and vegetables, to cable ties and sink plungers, Elizabeth browsed the shelves with a wire shopping basket hooked over her arm. She did not need to buy much, mainly a few items for dinner that evening. Her head still felt a little hazy from her extended nap in the forest, so she found it hard to make a decision about what she actually wanted to eat later. She settled on some pasta, along with mushrooms, onions and the ingredients needed to make a light cream sauce. The herb selection was a bit thin, but she managed to find a small glass jar of parsley, hiding behind some tinned sardines, to go with it. As she walked over to the counter to pay, she guiltily picked up a bar of chocolate. The young cashier could not disguise her curiosity about Elizabeth. It being such a small village, they did not get many visitors outside of the summer.

'Just visiting?' she asked.

'For a while,' Elizabeth cryptically replied.

'Are you staying in the village?'

'Nearby, in a cottage.'

Elizabeth felt a little unkind for being so unforthcoming and she could tell that she was not satisfied with these answers, as she turned her questioning up a notch.

'Are you staying in one of the old cottages next to the forest?'

Elizabeth nodded and said politely that she must be going.

'It's good that you don't mind about the stories.'

Elizabeth turned back to her.

'What stories?'

'Ach, nothing, just stupid old tales about goings on in the forest.'

Now it was Elizabeth's turn to press for more information, but, all of a sudden, the cashier seemed to have something important to deal with out the back of the shop. Elizabeth walked out of the shop feeling confused and a bit uneasy. As she was walking along the street, back to her car, she heard her name being called from across the street. It was Lou, who persuaded her to have a coffee in the post office that doubled up as a cafe.

As they sat at a table by the window, Lou looked at her with her wide and disarming blue eyes.

'How are you settling in?'

'Great, the cottage is just what I wanted and I love the peace and quiet'

'No bumps in the night then?'

'What do you mean? You are the second person today who has said something like that to me. What is it about this cottage?'

'Nothing, I was only teasing you. I know you are renowned for your rationality and scepticism.'

'I know, but something odd happened earlier today.'

Elizabeth went on to tell Lou about the feelings she experienced in the forest and falling asleep under the tree. She thought Lou would laugh at her, but she listened carefully and did not say anything until she had finished, Lou started to tell her, quite seriously, about some of the stories that circulated around the village, about the woods. How many of the older villagers, who had always lived here, would not go into them and would warn their children and grandchildren not to either.

The local teenagers would have parties in there, drinking and playing music and leaving a mess behind them, but they had not done this since last summer, when a group of them claimed to have seen a ghost coming towards them, the ghost of a woman in old fashioned clothes, with long, flowing hair.

'Sounds like they had been taking a bit too much of something,' Elizabeth joked.

'These were not the type of kids to be scared like that. Two of them were in my History class and they were different afterwards, quieter and less cheeky.'

'What did they think this ghostly figure was all about?'

Lou went on to tell her about a local history project she had done with a group of her pupils some years ago. She had ended up talking to an elderly woman, who had lived here all her life, who had told her the story of Sir Orfeo and his wife, Lady Isobel. Orfeo had been a local nobleman, a renowned musician, with a castle, somewhere near the woods, long gone, who had a beautiful wife, Isobel had been walking through the woods and had been spied by the ruler of the Elvin realm, known as the Elfin Knight, who had been enraptured by her beauty and vowed to have her.

He used his powers to infiltrate her dreams and to lure her back to the woods, where he took her to his realm. Orfeo was distraught and wandered the countryside, looking for her, for years, until he saw her riding with a group of fairy women. He followed them, into the woods and through the hillside, until he reached the Elfin

Knight's kingdom. He played his harp so beautifully for the Elfin Knight, who ended up being entranced by his music and offering Orfeo anything that he desired as a reward; Gold? Jewels? Other riches? He chose his wife and the Elfin Knight allowed him to take her back home.

'Sorry, but that sounds like a lot of tosh,' Elizabeth said.

'You expect me to believe that all this is somehow related to me and the cottage?'

Lou looked slightly taken aback at this response and Elizabeth softened.

'I'm sorry Lou, that was a bit sharp. Interesting story, but I don't think you need to worry about me being taken off to the fairy kingdom quite yet.'

At this point, Elisabeth noticed two, medium sized dark vehicles driving past the window, which were unmarked, but looked distinctly like military trucks. Surprised, she asked Lou.

'Do you get many military vehicles passing through this village?'

'Not that I've noticed.'

'I didn't realise that there was any type of military base near here.'

'There isn't, to my knowledge. There's an old prisoner of war camp a few miles away, over on the other side of the forest, but nothing has happened there since the end of the Second World War. There's just a load of old huts with an overgrown wire fence around it.'

'But, don't you think that's strange then, for military trucks to appear in the village?'

'I wouldn't dwell on it. Maybe they're finally planning to do something with it, only seventy odd years too late.'.

Elizabeth looked out of the window again, but saw no further trucks, puzzled at Lou's lack of curiosity about their sudden appearance.

They got back to talking about one of their favourite subjects, that is, what an eejit Elizabeth's ex could be and the exciting things that she could do with her life now that she was rid of him. Lou had her laughing in no time and, somehow, promising to come to a dinner party she was having in a few days' time.

Lou walked back to the car with her and gave her a huge hug, telling her to take care. With her mind full of Lou's story and still feeling curious about the Army trucks, she drove back to the cottage. As she approached the driveway, she noticed someone walking in the lane, about ten metres ahead of her. They were right in the middle of the lane and when she got closer, they made no attempt to move over to the side, forcing her to slow right down. She was fighting the urge to sound her car horn, as she would have if still driving in London, but it did not seem to be the right thing to do up here. Suddenly, they seemed to notice her, stopped and turned around.

The face that looked at her was not one she would quickly forget. It was a man, around her age. She couldn't see his face too clearly, as he had his hood pulled up, but she could not miss his eyes, as they stared at her. They were pale and intense and the look he gave her was a mixture of shock and hostility. He moved to the side of the lane and she drove past him, before turning into her drive. still feeling his eyes trained upon her.

She slowly pulled up outside the cottage, feeling very confused about what had just happened. She could not shake off the image of his eyes or the expression on his face or thoughts of where he might have been heading. She did not think she had ever received such a look from a complete stranger before.

There was another cottage, of a similar age to her own, a little further up the lane, which she had noticed on the drive in from the airport. She supposed that he could live there and hoped that she would not bump into him too often, judging by the way he had looked at her. It was starting to get dark before too long, so she walked around the cottage, closing the curtains and turning on lamps. She felt a strong need to hear her sons' voices, so called them both in turn.

Her eldest was a Teacher in a large, inner London secondary school. He loved his job, but it was exhausting and long conversations after work were not his priority. Her call with him was not as long as she would have liked, but at least she felt reassured that he sounded well enough. Her younger son had more time to talk. He had the usual frustrations with work but was otherwise happy.

Talking to her sons, from so far away, was comforting to a degree, but also served to emphasise the huge move she had just made and her isolation. Thoughts that she might have made a mistake started to creep into her mind. To distract herself, she turned on the television and poured herself some wine, but she could not find anything to watch, so turned on some music instead.

She cooked her dinner, pleased with the way it turned out and after eating, she did something she had not done for years. As she danced around the room, to one of her guilty pleasures, Britney Spears, she thought about how some of her friends could not understand why she would be happy with living in such isolation, but she felt more freedom and control now, than she had for many years. Apart from the uneasiness she could not fully shake off after her encounter in the lane earlier, she felt good. When she grew tired, she double checked she had locked the back door. As she tried the door handle, she thought she felt something behind her, like a very gentle pressure in the small of her back. She turned around quickly, not sure what she thought she would find. There was nothing there and she told herself it was likely a muscle twinge in her back.

As she was walking up the stairs, she remembered something from a few years back, not long after her mother had died, when she had been sitting on her bed, looking at some items of jewellery that had belonged to her mother, She found a broach that she had often worn on her coat, a gold oval shape, with an amber stone in the centre, which she had always admired. As she held it in her hand, visualising her mother wearing it, she felt as if someone had touched her lightly on the back, enough to make her turn around and expect to find someone there, though she was alone.

Chapter Four

Female Of The Species

Liam turned into his driveway, He was still trying to make sense of what had just happened out in the lane, how he had felt when he turned around and saw her face. He had been walking along the lane, on his way home, without being aware that he was out in the middle of the lane. It was not until he had heard the car engine, close behind him, that he had realised and looked around. The instant shock of recognition had thrown him. He did not know her, but her face, started something into motion, deep within him, something that he could not put words to. He automatically moved over to the side of the lane and she drove past him, pulling into the driveway of the cottage nearest to him. He had been aware that someone had moved into the place, but had little interest in who it might be.

He still had a head full of what he had witnessed at the old prisoner of war camp, so had not been paying much attention to where he had been walking in the lane or to any approaching vehicles. He did not know much about the history of the camp, but had been under the impression that it was not in use for any reason and had not been for decades. He had never been a member of the Armed Forces and did not have a huge knowledge of the different regiments, but he did recognise that the soldiers he had seen looking around the camp were part of the Black Watch regiment, which he knew were also called the Royal Highlanders. He had met a few people over the years, who had been members of the armed forces and he had always admired their integrity and loyalty, although he would never term himself as a supporter of armed conflict. He had recognised them from their green berets with what looked like a small pom pom on top of it. They had been wearing standard Army fatigues and carrying some form of rifle. He was aware that the headquarters of the Black Watch was at a place called Fort George, which was a twenty minute drive from Inverness, so he assumed that this was where they had come from.

He had been drawn to observe the camp, after hearing something coming from it over the last few nights, a low, rumbling noise, a cross between an animal and machinery. He had wondered if they were demolishing the old buildings that remained there, but could not understand why this would be happening at night. He could have asked around in the village, but preferred to keep it to himself and not reveal his interest to anyone. Seeing people on stretchers being removed and loaded into trucks, was not a sight he had expected and he was finding it very difficult to process. They were being removed from the type of temporary unit that was used for accommodation on large construction projects, a galvanised metal rectangular box that looked a bit like a shipping container with windows. He had counted five stretchers, although some may have been removed before he had reached his vantage point on the hill. His mind was racing over what might have happened to these people. He was speculating about everything from a chemical spill, though he realised this was unlikely, due to the lack of protective clothing being worn by the soldiers and medics, to an attack by something or someone.

He had moved to this place a month ago and his main desire was to get away from people for a while and getting to know his neighbours was not on his agenda. He carried on up the lane until he reached his drive and walked the last eighty yards or so up to his front door. Originally from the Templepatrick area of Northern Ireland, he had spent most of his working life on North Sea oil rigs, starting out as an apprentice, then a drilling worker. The work was hard and he had thought many times about leaving it, but, despite this, he was usually happier during his two week shifts on the rig, than the two weeks he spent on land. He had done well, academically at school, excelling in Maths and Science subjects, as well as in History, and his teachers had encouraged him to apply for university. They had been pushing him towards Engineering, but his true interest lay in Archaeology. He had disappointed them all by leaving school before he had completed his final exams and getting himself the apprenticeship, the main motivation being to get away from home, still in the midst of the Troubles and to be financially independent. After several years of working on the rigs, management started to encourage him to apply for more senior roles, but he had always resisted, not wanting the added stress or responsibility that this would bring.

He had spent his time off the rig, in Aberdeen and eventually met someone he wanted to marry. She had, like so many other spouses and partners of his colleagues, become weary of not seeing him as much as she would have liked to and of him not wanting to go out much with her or go on holiday when he was not at work. Ten or so years ago, she had told him she wanted to end their marriage. He had not been that surprised and did not fight it. Maybe it would have been different if they had children. There had been several, casual relationships since then, but no one he had ever considered as a more serious proposition. He was aware that some people who knew him, considered him to be a bit cold and possibly a bit heartless, where these relationships were concerned.

He would always tell himself that they did not know him well enough. As he reached his fifties, the shift patterns and the nature of the work on the rigs started to take its toll, on his physical and, (only recently acknowledged by him,) his mental health.

He had saved a fair amount over the years, enough to buy a small home and support himself for a while, before having to consider further employment. He did not want to stay in the Aberdeen area, he had always wanted to live further North and this part of the Highlands was somewhere he used to visit when he wanted to get away and clear his mind as much as was possible. He had found this cottage, and the one nearby, up for rent and the decision had been easy, after he had viewed it. He had considered the other cottage, but his had a bigger garden and he planned to grow vegetables and create an outside haven. He had been spending his days since moving in, working on the garden, walking and reading. He was starting to feel more content, but now that was tinged with uneasiness and also slight annoyance that someone had moved into the other cottage, as he had liked the idea of not having neighbours.

When he got inside, he made himself a coffee and sat at the kitchen table. Earlier this afternoon, he had taken a walk up the hill behind the forest, feeling the need for a long, fairly tough walk, after a fractious night's sleep. He had always had what he would term as 'interesting' dreams, but for the last few weeks, they had become infinitely more disturbing and vivid. The hill had a long, gradual incline and no defined path for ascending it. Rough grass and gorse plants covered it, with the occasional yellowish grey rock punctuating it, some large and rough, whereas others looked as if they had been cut by hand. Some locals in the village pub had told him various stories about the hill, usually after multiple glasses of whisky, involving either fairies kidnapping people and taking them to their realm within the hill or of sinister figures with glowing eyes, scaring people in the forest. He had little time for this, having had enough of this sort of superstition where he had grown up, although found them amusing and was willing to listen to them. On his walks through the forest or around the hill, he had felt safe and unthreatened, but had to admit that the forest could send a slight chill up his spine, particularly in the darker, denser spots, where some of the trees looked twisted and petrified. Growing up, he had not heard much about his family's history, but had known of some Scottish ancestry from his grandfather, who was the only one who would talk about such things. His grandfather had made claims that their Scottish ancestors were noble and rich, but had to leave Scotland for some reason, which was never explained to the young Liam. One thing he had learnt, fairly recently, was that these supposed ancestors were from this part of the Highlands, something he planned to research soon.

Chapter Five

Simply Irresistible

Elizabeth fell into a gentle routine over the next few days. On mornings when the weather looked kind she would take a walk, sometimes through the forest, other times skirting the edge of it and heading up an increasingly steep path that took her up the hill that eventually loomed above the trees. This was quite a hard walk, particularly for someone who had spent the last couple of decades living a very urban life, with the main walking being between work and the tube station. How out of breath she felt halfway up the hill disturbed her slightly and she vowed to do more exercise.

    This trek up the hill would take her through swathes of flattened grass interspersed with gorse and heather and the higher she got, the sparser the ground cover became. She looked forward to the later spring and summer when the hill would be covered in yellow and purple flowers. There were also rocks that looked similar to those she had found in the forest. The view at the top of the hill was worth the effort through, as it allowed her to see beyond the forest, to the old camp that Lou had told her about and beyond this to farmland and further hills and wooded areas, Standing on the hill one day she was sure she could see someone in dark clothing, walking around the camp, but without binoculars it was impossible to see more detail than that. She supposed it was all connected to the trucks she had seen and that they were planning to do something with the land. She hoped it would not turn into a big construction site, which would invariably have some impact upon her newfound tranquillity.

She felt so good after these walks, rewarding herself with a strong coffee and some chocolate, when she got home. On the mornings when it was wet, she stayed in and used the time to do some work on her laptop. She was keen to discover more local history and to research her own ancestry, although she was finding this difficult. Elizabeth had always been very adept at whatever type of research she had put her mind to, whether it had been during her university days or as part of her former working life and she would become incredibly frustrated when encountering barriers to the information she was seeking. She usually managed to find a way round this, but not with this family research, which kept eluding her. The intermittent wi-fi did not help and she kept meaning to contact the internet provider, but could not quite bring herself to do this yet. She was also toying with the idea of starting a book, a fictional story, set somewhere mysterious and remote. She had been carrying around stories in her head since she was a child, but had never got further than the first chapter with them. If she had been unable to head out in the morning, she would walk after lunch, as long as the weather cleared up. On this particular day, the morning had been dark and ominous, but not long after lunchtime the clouds had lifted to reveal a pale blue sky. She grabbed her jacket and headed out the door. She felt like walking through the forest today. She loved the denser areas, as she felt as if she was walking in her own private world, (queen of the forest she joked to herself). She imagined herself in a diaphanous white gown, with leaves crowning her head and bare feet. She closed her eyes and stood still for a few moments, but the sound of footsteps nearby, brought her abruptly out of her reverie.

There was a man walking towards her, quickly realising it was the man from the lane the other day. He did not have his hood up this time, so she got a better view of him, not much taller than her, short silver-grey hair and slightly weather-beaten complexion. She had that incredibly awkward feeling that you get, when you meet someone outside, who you do not know, but ignoring them would be weird. As he got nearer, she looked directly at him and said good afternoon. Yet again, those eyes turned on her like lasers and he grunted an acknowledgement and walked on past her. Pretty rude, she thought, but partially relieved that he had not wanted to engage in a conversation, She continued her walk, intrigued by what looked like tracks near the tree that she had fallen asleep under. Too big for an animal, maybe a vehicle of some kind. She came to the conclusion that kids must have braved the woods and been riding their bikes around.

When she got home, she checked her mobile phone, which she had felt vibrate in her pocket when she was out. It was a message from Lou, reminding her not to be late for her dinner party tomorrow evening and not to worry about bringing anything. Elizabeth groaned inwardly. If it was just Lou and her husband, that would have been fine, but she knew that Lou would not be able to resist the idea of inviting a selection of available men for her to peruse. She wished she could come up with a viable excuse not to go, but knew that Lou would be hurt and did not want to do that to her. She also knew Lou well enough to know that she would find it very hard to take no for an answer.

Elizabeth spent the morning and afternoon of the dinner party trying to convince herself that she might actually have fun when she was there, without much success. Attempting to distract herself, she decided to make the half hour drive to Inverness, in order to find something to wear. She had plenty of clothes, particularly now that her boxes had arrived from London, but it had been a while since she had bought anything new. She had visited Inverness a few times before, on previous trips to the Highlands, so had a vague notion of what clothes shops would be available. She was not at all sure what type of outfit she was looking for, she was usually from the 'I'll know it when I see it' school of clothes shopping. She actually hated clothes shopping and only remembered this after going into a couple of shops and finding nothing she liked. A pitstop for a coffee and she felt a bit better, bracing herself to face another clothes shop.

The Sales Assistant in this shop was a woman around her age, who did not appear to have altered the way she dressed or did her make up since the mid-1980s. Elizabeth distinctly remembered doing her own eye makeup like that when she was about fifteen. Even her hairstyle was classic 1980s, with its backcombed Bananaramaesque style. Elizabeth had been listlessly flipping through a few rails of clothes when she pounced.

'Can I help you with anything?,' she asked, in the most refined local accent she had so far encountered.

'No, thank you, I'm not really sure what I'm looking for yet.'

She must have noticed Elizabeth edging towards the door, so persisted.

'What is the occasion you are dressing for,' she asked Elizabeth in her rather stiff and formal manner

'It's a dinner party.'

The woman's eyes lit up.

'Informal or formal d'ye think?'

'Oh, definitely informal. Really, it doesn't have to be that smart, a casual dress would be fine. I like this one,' she said, picking up a fairly shapeless, black, longish dress off the rail.

'I think we can do a bit better than that,' and she proceeded to walk around the shop, picking hangars off rails as she went, with a ruthless efficiency. She chivied Elizabeth over to the changing room at the back of the shop, hung up about six or seven dresses on the changing room hooks and drew the curtain across. Elizabeth had not even been planning on trying a dress on, getting undressed and dressed in changing rooms being one of her least favourite activities, but she had come to the realisation that this woman was not going to give up until she had found her dream outfit. Wishing she had worn matching underwear and that there was not a small hole in the front of her sensible, flesh-coloured knickers, she reluctantly started to try the dresses on. Much to her surprise, the second dress that she tried felt really good as she slipped it over her head and smoothed it over her body. It was simple, made of deep red woollen jersey type of material, with long sleeves and fitted bodice, flaring out slightly to a little below her knees. She would have been a bit happier, if her stomach was flatter, but would try not to eat too much before this evening.. This coincided with the Sales Assistant coming in and asking how she was getting on. She stepped out of the dressing room and said that she liked this one,

'Oh yes, that's perfect on you. The colour brings out the green in your eyes.'

Goodness, thought Elizabeth, she's more observant than I gave her credit for. Relieved that her shopping expedition was now over, Elizabeth walked back to the car and drove home, thinking that, if nothing else, she would look good tonight,

As the dinner party drew closer, Elizabeth was really regretting not finding an excuse to turn it down and was seriously considering whether Lou would believe that she had been struck down with a sudden bout of something unpleasant, (probably gastric). Thoughts of how disappointed Lou would be had got her into her new dress and into the taxi, to make the fifteen minute drive to Lou's, who lived a mile or two beyond the village, in a relatively new house that they had designed and had built themselves. Thankfully, she had already been promised a lift home with Lou's husband, Sandy, who was not drinking alcohol at the moment, as he was in training for a two hundred mile cycle challenge, called the Caledonia Way. She admired him for contemplating such a feat and for being able to face a dinner party without wine.

As the taxi pulled into Lou's driveway, she saw a few cars parked already and lamps glowing in the downstairs rooms. The taxi driver wished her a good evening. She had already told him, on the way here of her reluctance about this evening, sitting in a taxi could be like a confessional at times.

'How do I look?' she asked him, as she stood next to the open car door.

'Right bonnie. Now you go and have a good time and don't fret about anything.'

Elizabeth smiled and thanked him. She walked up to the front door and rang the bell. An already merry Lou greeted her with a hug, pulling her into the hallway and taking off her coat, before she could protest. Holding her hand she led her into the sitting room, where Sandy and about four or five others were already sitting on large, squashy sofas that looked like they would swallow you. Lou announced to the room

'This is Elizabeth, my friend who has just moved up here from London, who I was telling you about.'

She introduced the other people in the room.

'This is Graeme and Janet, who work with Sandy at the hospital,' a short balding man with eager eyes and his red headed, slightly sour looking, wife. They looked safe, if not a little dull. Elizabeth wondered where Lou found these people sometimes.

'This is Ralph who has just moved in next door.' Ralph was handsome, conventionally so, with dark brown hair, an unnatural looking tan and very white teeth, which he flashed at her more than was necessary. She went on to introduce another couple, Alistair and Catriona, who gave her a cheery greeting, in unison, but she didn't quite catch where Lou knew them from. They appeared friendly and looked quite wholesome, as if they spent their days striding across the countryside, with their pink and white complexions and sensible, tweedy clothes. The last person Lou introduced was an attractive woman of about forty, who was poured into an extremely tight black velvet dress and would have had a really pretty face, but for the amount of makeup she had trowelled onto it. Lou introduced her as Joanna, who was an English teacher at her school.

'We're waiting on Tony then we'll all be here.'

The doorbell rang and Lou rushed to greet the mystery Tony.

When he walked in, Elizabeth knew straight away that this was the man that Lou had lined up for her. He was exactly what Lou would describe as her type; an inch or two taller than her, about ten years older, long, grey hair, tied back in a man bun, twinkling grey green eyes, an aquiline nose and a slightly mysterious air to him, A musician, Elizabeth thought.

'This is Tony, everyone. He's a writer and moved up here last year, from Edinburgh.'

Oh, I'm wrong, thought Elizabeth to herself.

'He has this marvellous band that I heard playing not long ago and got chatting to him after the gig.'

Yep, a musician, I knew it, Elizabeth thought. I'm going to have words with Lou later on. She loved music, particularly listening to live music and certainly had nothing against musicians, (Indeed, she wished she was a better one herself,) but her former partner had been a musician and for some reason unknown to herself, she had proved incapable of resisting them from about the age of sixteen. She was sure it must have been possible for some people to have successful romantic relationships with musicians, but not for her.

Lou had placed Elizabeth in between Ralph and Tony, with Joanna on the other side of Ralph.. She tried to look at her appealingly, but Lou was too busy playing hostess and trying to get the food out, at the same time as making sure everyone had a full glass. She had always admired Lou's ability to make cooking and entertaining look relatively effortless and she really was an excellent cook. Tony was directing all his twinkling charm towards her during dinner, asking her lots of questions about her reasons for moving up here and whether she was here on her own, although she got the distinct feeling that Lou had already furnished him with this information. She started to find his questions a bit intrusive, particularly from someone she had just met and tried to deflect his inquiries by asking him about his writing, which fortunately turned out to be one of his favourite subjects. He had written two books that had been published, both set in Edinburgh and with a horror theme and both, according to him, had sold extremely well. He seemed a little put out that she had not read either of them, even though she had told him that she had not read many books of that genre. He told her that he had wanted to set his next book somewhere else, so thought that he would immerse himself in the Highlands, to gain inspiration.

'Will it be more horror fiction?,' asked Elizabeth.

'I'm thinking of moving away from that and trying my hand at historical fiction this time, maybe with a touch of romance,' he replied, looking meaningfully into her eyes.

She was saved by Janet, who asked her from across the table.

'Don't you miss London; all the shops and the places to eat? You must be finding it so quiet and dull here?'

'No, it's perfect, exactly what I wanted. I have had twenty five years of the people, the traffic and the pollution and it's only getting worse.'

Janet looked at her as if she had just said something truly heinous or threatened to steal her husband and turned back to Lou's husband to continue talking about how local house prices were rising.

'I can completely understand your need for a change. That's how I felt when I decided to leave my wife,' said Tony

'That wasn't the reason for the ending of my relationship.' Elizabeth was about to try to explain to him why this had happened, but then stopped herself, as she did not want to have to justify herself to this slightly arrogant and unempathetic man sitting next to her.

She turned to Ralph and, like most of the others, started to ask his opinions on what appeared to be safe subjects, such as the state of the local roads. Joanna, who clearly fancied her chances with Ralph, sensing a threat, turned her seduction technique up a notch. Leaning forward a little more, so that her ample cleavage was on maximum display, she diverted Ralph's attention back to where she wanted it. Elizabeth had tentatively asked him and some of the other guests if they had noticed anything going on at the old prisoner of war, only to be met with blank looks and shrugs. She somehow got through the rest of the meal and thankfully, it did not go on too late, due to a few of them having early starts.

Elizabeth's heart sank, when she realised Sandy had been unable to resist a few glasses of wine and, after not having drunk alcohol for a few months, was currently dancing around the sitting room, singing along to the Proclaimers. Lou attempted to look embarrassed, but failed miserably, as she too had downed a fair amount of wine by this point. She tried to persuade Elizabeth to stay the night in their spare room, but Elizabeth really wanted to get back to her own bed. Tony appeared by her side, as if by magic.

'Don't worry Lou, I can drive her home, it's not too far out of my way.'

Elizabeth protested.

'I can get a taxi, please, I don't want you to put yourself out on my account.'

'It would be a pleasure and I doubt you'll find it easy to get a taxi at this time of night around here,' was Tony's reply.

As they left the house, he called back to Lou.

'Thanks for a lovely evening and I'll make sure she gets home safely.'

Lou happily waved goodbye and then got back to dancing around the room with her husband.

Tony's fairly new, dark blue SUV with its blacked out windows, pulled away from Lou's house and he put on some music, something smooth and soulful that she did not recognise. He asked her how she had enjoyed the evening and what she had been doing with herself since she came up here. Their conversation was fairly safe and innocuous, but as they got nearer to her house, she started to feel a bit anxious, despite still feeling fairly mellow from the effects of the wine she had drunk. She did not want to invite him in, even though she got the distinct feeling that this was what he expected. She started to steel herself to get out of the car quickly, when they reached her house, to avoid any attempts at good night kisses. Maybe this would not be too bad, but she really did not want this tonight and definitely not with him. They turned onto the lane that led to her house and he surreptitiously placed his hand on her thigh and she felt it drift up her leg. She froze for a moment as he slightly turned and smiled meaningfully at her. Her reaction surprised her. She grabbed his hand and pulled it off her leg, saying in a voice that she hoped was firm and assertive, though she suspected it was more shrill and panicked.

'Stop the car, I want to get out!'

He laughed incredulously and said,

'Don't be ridiculous, I'm not stopping here, I think you're overreacting a bit.'

'I'm not joking, if you don't stop now, I'm going to jump out while you're moving.'

He slammed on his brakes and brought his car to a violent, screeching halt, angrily telling her to get out. As she rapidly got out of the car and before she could slam the door, she heard him call her a frigid bitch. Elizabeth stood in the lane, looking at his car speeding away, stunned, and started the ten minute walk back to the cottage. She shivered and pulled her thin coat as tightly around herself as she could. It was really dark, the new moon, barely lighting the way and cold, with a light drizzle in the air. Using the torch on her mobile phone, she carefully picked her way along the potholed lane, occasionally stumbling, in shoes that were not designed for this type of activity. She had been walking for about five minutes when she heard footsteps behind her. She was not sure what to do for a moment, but then slowly turned around to see who was there, shining the torch towards them. It was him again. He had seen her and did seem thrown by her presence there. As he got closer, she said.

'Bit late for an evening walk, isn't it?'

As she said it, she realised that she sounded rude and abrupt. She didn't even know who he was. The response she received surprised her a little.

'I could ask you the same question. At least I'm dressed for it!'

His tone was defensive and, to her ear, a bit hostile. She reacted in a way that was unusual for her, by blurting out that it was none of his business and storming off up the lane and into her driveway. She slammed her front door behind her and leant against it, breaking into big, convulsive sobs. A fitful, dream-filled night's sleep followed.

Chapter Six

Open Your Eyes

Elizabeth woke up later than usual the next morning, with a bone dry mouth and a sore head. As the events of last night came seeping back to her, she cringed. Small waves of nausea hit her as she stumbled to the bathroom and tried to avoid her reflection in the mirror, as she felt pretty sure it would not be good. She could not even face coffee this morning, which was pretty much unthinkable for her. She managed a small glass of tepid water and decided that a blast of fresh air might help, so opened the kitchen door and stepped outside, kicking something over as she did so. She looked down, only to see that it was a small plant in a ceramic pot. She picked it up and examined it, having no idea what type of plant it was, but it was very pretty. There was a small white envelope stuck with tape to the side of the pot, which she opened with slight apprehension. Written on some plain white paper, in a sloping, old fashioned hand was something very unexpected.

'My behaviour last night was unnecessary, which I would like to apologise for. Please feel free to knock on my door if you would like a coffee some time. Liam, (your neighbour).'

Elizabeth was not quite sure what to do with this. At first, she had thought it was a peace offering from Tony and if that had been the case, she would have been likely to throw the pot across the kitchen, (though on second thoughts, why should an innocent plant suffer because of the actions of a clueless dinosaur). She found it very hard to equate this gesture with the irascible and borderline rude man from last night. The idea of knocking on his door taking up his coffee invitation seemed unlikely at this point and she hoped he would not be waiting expectantly for her.

Before she could think too much about this, her phone rang. It was Lou, asking her if she had got home alright last night and whether Tony had just dropped her off or been invited in for a late night coffee. Elizabeth gave her the whole sorry tale, including what she had found on her doorstep this morning and Lou could be heard stifling a giggle,

'It was not funny at the time,' Elizabeth insisted.

'I'm sorry, I didn't mean to laugh. It's just the idea of his confusion as to why you wouldn't fall for his charms.'

'Oh come on Lou, you should have known better than to set me up with someone like that. Give him an English accent and he could have been my ex.'

'I thought you liked that type of guy, you know, the creative, silver fox type.'

Elizabeth went quiet on the phone and Lou said.

'Don't be cross with me, I just don't like the idea of you being lonely up here. I'm sorry if I messed up.'

Elizabeth told her she was not angry, but definitely not ready to be set up yet, particularly with any more ageing, silver haired musicians, whatever their nationality. Changing the subject, Lou asked her if she was going to knock on her neighbour's door.

'I don't think so, do you? What would that achieve?'

'It's always useful to get on with your neighbours, particularly around here, you never know when you might need their help with something.'

'What sort of help are you talking about?'

Lou laughed, which always made Elizabeth happy.

'I better go. I've got a few things I want to do in the village.'

'That sounds intriguing, although, there is not an awful lot you can do there.'

'I'll tell you about it later.'

'Okay, I'll let you go now, but please reassure me that you're not upset with me about Tony.'

'Of course not, but I'll be quite happy if I don't clap eyes on him again.'

'That might be difficult in such a small place,' was Lou's parting shot.

Elizabeth drove into the village after this with the intention of trying to increase her knowledge of the history of the area. She had noticed a tiny tourist information office the other day, which she was happy to find open, outside of peak tourist season. When she gently pushed open the dark green wooden door, the room that greeted her was empty, apart from a few revolving stands; one full of leaflets about local places of interest and another with postcards to buy and another that stood empty. There was also a square table with a yellow formica top, that had two old wooden chairs on either side of it and framed pictures on the pale yellow walls that had probably been up there for at least forty years. Elizabeth looked around; some of the pictures were beautiful, likely to be collector's items now. Images of smiling and laughing nuclear families in clothing from the 1950s and 1960s, standing by the side of lochs and on top of hills, looked back at her, next to steam trains storming through the Highlands and rosy cheeked, rotund men blowing into bagpipes.

'Can I help you?'

Elizabeth had not noticed the very small woman come out from behind the door at the back of the room. She was at least eighty years old and not much more than five feet tall, with an extremely wrinkled face that looked as if would be capable of withstanding whatever the elements threw at it. She had a large, slightly hooked nose, much too big for her face, but the eyes that looked at her were dark and bright and full of curiosity and the mouth was kind, despite the curtness of her tone.

'I'm very interested in local history and wanted to come in to see if you had any information I could look at.'

She gestured towards one of the chairs by the table and Elizabeth obediently sat down. The woman sat opposite her.

'What type of information are you looking for?'

'Anything really; local stories and legends, old families, lost houses and castles, that sort of thing.'

'Oh, so are you wanting to research your own family history? Do you have ancestors from around here?'

'I'm really not too sure, they could be. I don't have much information about this. What I do know is that my maternal ancestors are mainly from Ireland, but a branch of them supposedly went over there from Scotland, from somewhere in this region.'

'Do you not have any ancestral names?' asked the woman.

'Nothing definite, I've really only just started my research, though Stuart, Grant and Mackenzie are names that have cropped up so far.'

Elizabeth was sure that she noticed a change in the woman's expression at this point, almost indiscernible, but definitely there. She stood up and started to walk back towards the back room, turning to Elizabeth as she went.

'You wait there now and I might have something for you in the back.'

Elizabeth sat there pondering this change in the woman's demeanour. Had she offended her in some way? She found it hard to imagine how she could have, but that was how it felt. She came back after about five minutes with a small stack of very dusty looking books, which she placed on the table in front of Elizabeth.

'These might be of interest to you.'

She picked up the top one, saying,

'This one is about grand houses and castles in this part of the Highlands, including those that no longer exist and this one talks about local folk stories.'

'That's wonderful, Can I look at them here for a while?'

'No this isn't a reading room. please take them with you and bring them back when you are done.'

'That's very kind of you. I won't keep them too long. I'm living in one of the cottages near Cnoc Lag forest, so I am not too far away.'

Elizabeth noticed another fluctuation in her expression, although this one was more pronounced. This one looked more like worry and concern. Elizabeth continued.

'One thing I was wondering about is the name of the forest. Am I right to translate Cnoc Lag as Hollow Hill? I'm intrigued by that name, do you know anything about its origins?'

The woman made her jump a little by placing her wrinkled hand upon her arm and saying

'You take care up there. Best not to go into the woods, not even in the daytime.'

'Why do I keep hearing this from people around here? What is supposed to be so bad about the woods. I've been walking there most days, since I have been up here and have not encountered anything strange or dangerous there. Is this to do with the legend about the Elfin Knight? My friend was telling me about this. Do people actually believe it around here?'

The woman abruptly took her hand away and wished her luck with her research and told her not to rush back with the books, making it clear, without words, that she had used up enough of her time.

'I'm sorry, I didn't mean to offend you in any way.'

The old woman did not respond, so Elizabeth gathered up the books, sending a cloud of dust flying into the room and left the office. As she drove home, she could still see the shining, bird-like eyes of the woman looking at her, as if she could see right through her. Elizabeth had found her reactions very disconcerting, but tried to shake this off, putting it down to an elderly local woman, who was not too keen on recent arrivals to the area.

Once home, she pretty much dived straight into the books, which were fascinating and contained some beautiful illustrations and photographs. She was particularly struck by the book on old houses and castles, according to which a castle called Coille Dorch, used to stand very close to where her cottage was. Using a translation tool on her laptop, she discovered this meant Dark Forest in Scottish Gaelic. She could not quite work out where it would have stood exactly, but presumably somewhere near the forest. The castle was built in the 1300s for a son of the Mackenzie family. It did not say much about why it fell to ruins and eventually disappeared. She was surprised that there were no ruins at all in the area. It said that the family left for another part of Scotland. She decided that soon she would have a thorough look around the garden and the surrounding area, to see if she could find any evidence of this. The local folklore book she also found engrossing, but due to her general scepticism about all things supernatural, it was hard for her to swallow tales about Banshees, Kelpies and the like. To her, they were interesting stories with foundations in superstition and no more than that. She had grown up with a mother who had a strong belief in the spirit world, who was convinced that she could sense ghosts. Elizabeth had always found it difficult to relate this side of her mother's character with the stiff and undemonstrative woman she had known. She remembered, when she was a teenager, rolling her eyes at her mother going to a Spiritualist meeting one evening and trying to convince her that it was a rip off, that they were purely after their money. Her mother had come home bright eyed and animated, absolutely adamant that her dead mother had been trying to reach her, only serving to increase Elizabeth's frustration and cynicism.

There was a story about the Elfin Knight and his realm supposedly being somewhere around this area, beneath the hills; a realm of unimaginable beauty, with buildings made of gold. Apparently, he would work his way into the dreams of mortals to get them to do his bidding, including abducting some to his kingdom, never to be seen again. She shut the book with some contempt and decided to take a break from reading. The print in the books was tiny, causing her eyes to strain and her stomach was rumbling, so she made some cheese on toast and poured a glass of wine. She really should cook proper meals more often, she thought to herself, adding a slice of tomato in an attempt to make her food healthier. She ate her food standing up at the kitchen counter, thinking about what she had been reading. Despite the disturbing dreams and the uneasiness she had felt in the forest, as well as the whole falling asleep incident, she could not bring herself to believe the idea of some supernatural force at work.

She considered calling Lou, but it was quite late and she did not want to disturb her. After her food, she went back onto her laptop, trying to find more information about the old castle, without too much success, until her wi-fi connection dropped out yet again. Time for bed, she decided. Tonight she felt virtuous, removing her makeup and moisturising her face and hands. Despite her tiredness she didn't think she looked too bad, her eyes were bright and her skin looked clearer than it had in London, which she put down to all the walking she had been doing lately and the clean Highland air. She had been asleep for an hour or so, when she was woken up by a low, rumbling noise coming from outside, not an animal, more like a noise from underground. She got out of bed and looked out of the window, towards the woods, but could see nothing unusual. As she stood there, the noise stopped, nevertheless, she could not prevent herself from feeling spooked and suddenly felt very isolated and a little vulnerable. She dived back into her bed and threw the duvet over her head, like she used to do when she was a child and was scared by a sound or something she thought she had seen in the night.

Chapter Seven

If You Could Read My Mind

The next morning, Elizabeth was still feeling rattled and wrestled with the idea of knocking her on her neighbour's door, to find out if he had heard anything last night. She wanted the opportunity to discuss this with someone, but was not convinced that the man who she had so far only met when he seemed to be angry about something, was the right one to talk to. After a few false starts, she started walking down her drive and the short distance up the lane to his cottage. She had annoyed herself before she left the house by looking at herself in the hallway mirror and checking her hair and face. Why would I care what he thought of me? She said out loud to no one. As she approached his door, her heart quickened and her stomach started to feel a little turbulent. She knocked and waited, but nothing happened. She knocked again, after a bit of deliberation and still nothing. She had started to walk back down his path when she heard a shout.

'Hey, I'm round the back, sorry I didn't hear you knock.'

Elizabeth, suddenly seemingly incapable of lucid speech, said.

'Uh oh, it's okay, I don't want to bother you if you're busy,' and kept walking.

He ran around the side of the house and down the path behind and stopped when he had caught her up.

'No bother at all, Please, come back, I'll make you that coffee.'

Elizabeth studied him, he was wearing a T-shirt, pale blue and worn thin in parts and his eyes, still pale and striking, held a different expression today, not hostile, gentler and softer.

'I make really good coffee,' he said, when she did not respond straight away.

She gathered her senses and thanked him, saying she'd love a coffee and he gestured for her to follow him into the house. He led her into the kitchen, which was similar, in layout, to her own and invited her to take a seat at the kitchen table. She watched as he made the coffee, ground coffee in a cafetiere, and noticed how strong and well-toned his arms were, but he did not look as if spent lots of time in the gym, they were the sort of arms you got from years of physical work. She idly wondered if he was a builder or some form of engineer. She noticed his upright posture and his broad shoulders, as well as the curve of the back of his head. She had been slightly taken aback by his Northern Irish accent, which she had not been expecting, an accent she had always liked listening to. He turned around to ask her if she would like milk or sugar and she felt self-conscious that he had caught her staring at him. She felt some warmth creeping into her face. Dammit, she thought to herself, women my age are not supposed to blush like this. She said no to both. He brought over a couple of mugs and placed them on the table, followed by a plate of rather delicious looking chocolate brownies.

'Did you make them?' she asked.

'Yes, one of my many talents. Please, try one. I promise, they don't have any added extras.'

Elizabeth smiled at this and took one. It really did taste good. After she had finished her mouthful, she felt awkward again, not really knowing where to begin the conversation. He sat there, across the table from her, apparently comfortable with the silence between them.

'Thanks for the plant,' she blurted out, 'that was thoughtful, you really didn't have to.'

'I know, but I realised I had possibly been a little unwelcoming to a new neighbour. Did you like it? It's a Jade Plant, usually called a Money Tree Plant, so you don't need to water it too much, but put it somewhere with a bit of natural light, but not too much.'

'You can bake and keep plants alive. I'm impressed!' Elizabeth had not meant that to sound sarcastic, but as she said it, she realised that it probably did. He seemed unphased and said

'Any horticultural advice, please don't hesitate to ask me. To be honest, I didn't know much about plants or gardening until I moved in here. I'm learning as I go.'

She asked him how long he had been living here and where he had been living before that. He told her about his years of working on oil rigs and how, when he had reached the point when he needed to stop, he knew that he wanted to live somewhere like this, where he could work on a garden and have good walks on his doorstep. She had not been expecting such openness from the scowling man she had met in the lane and felt disarmed. He did not ask her the usual question that she had been asked, by most people she had met since she had been living here, that is, 'why did you move here?' He gave her room to tell him as much as she wanted to about her reasons for coming here and how she was finding it. She ended up telling him about her former life in London, her family, the work she had done, helping young people with their issues and problems, for many years, and the area she had lived in. She also told him about where she had grown up and how she had ended up living in London. He listened well. Elizabeth had spent most of her working life listening to other people and recognised good listening skills when she encountered them, which was sadly all too rare. She was all of sudden, conscious that she might be prattling on too much about herself.

'Sorry, I'm talking too much. I should let you get on with your day.'

She made a move to stand up from the table and was surprised when reached his hand across to her and touched her hand.

'No, not at all, I've enjoyed hearing what you've said. Please, don't feel that you have to go.'

Something had happened when he had touched her hand, more than the warmth from someone's touch. She had felt a sensation running from her hand up her arm that she did not recognise. Not unpleasant, but, at the same time, not familiar and a bit disconcerting. She sat back down and said.

'There was a particular reason that I came over today. I wanted to ask you if you had noticed anything strange at all happening around here, particularly in the woods, over the past week or so.'

'Strange in what sense?'

'This is going to sound a bit ridiculous, but,' and she went on to tell him about how she had felt in the woods. However, she found herself holding back on telling him about falling asleep in the forest and her persistent dreams. She did go into some detail about the elderly woman in the tourist information office and how she had changed when she told her where she was living. She also told him about Lou's story of Orfeo and his abducted wife and how this supposedly happened somewhere nearby. Liam was fairly dismissive of all this and put it down to local superstition.

'It's rife in isolated areas like this. I grew up with a lot of it back home. There were some people who believed in fairy folk, who lived under thorn bushes. They would never cut down a thorn bush, even if it was growing in the way, for fear of angering the fairies, who would wreak revenge on them. Those wee fairies could be pretty nasty. You'd be amazed at how many people still believe this and not just the older folk. To my mind, it's a very convenient way of blaming misfortune on something else.'

'Yes, I get it. Devon has loads of folk stories or myths, whatever you want to call them. The Hairy Hands of Dartmoor, to name one.'

'The Hairy Hands?' repeated Liam with a look of bemusement.

'Honestly, look it up later. Your mind will be blown. My mother was convinced that the woman who lived down the lane from our house was a witch and used to take extra care checking all the doors and windows were closed properly on Halloween. She used to tell me to not look out of my window that night, or the witch would see me and try to steal me away. You can imagine the impact of that on a five year old. I still get a bit anxious on Halloween night.'

This seemed to amuse Liam.

'Oh dear, you're going to love Halloween up here, You know that they take it very seriously.'

Switching the subject, Liam asked.

'Something I am a little puzzled about though, and please tell me to mind my own business if you like, but what were you doing in the lane so late the other night?'

Elizabeth rolled her eyes, replying.

'No, I don't mind you asking, I was being driven home by someone and let's just say, they were being a bit familiar. I demanded to be let out of the car and they, eventually, obliged, hence my late night walk.'

Liam took a moment and then said.

'They sound like an arsehole, whoever they are. Sounds like you definitely did the right thing.'

'Hmm, it was the result of a well-meaning friend thinking I needed matchmaking, which I really do not.'

'How about yourself, what took you out so late that night?'

'I was just having a job relaxing, so thought a walk might help.'

His response was unconvincing, but she did not press him further.

Liam asked her a bit more about her family. She told him about being adopted, something she had never had difficulty talking to people about, and how far she had got with tracing her birth family. She did not tell him how it had made her feel when her birth mother could not bring herself to meet her before she died or the impacts it had upon her self-esteem and her attachment style in relationships. She had been fairly oblivious to all this until the last few years, but after doing a fair bit of research into the long term impact of adoption on adults, a lot of how she had behaved during her life had started to make more sense, She certainly did not know him well enough for that. He seemed interested in what she had managed to find out so far about her maternal ancestors, particularly the bit about the branch of her tree that came out of Scotland. Liam said that he also had ancestors from Scotland and how he was interested in finding out more, but that research was not his strong point, as he found it frustrating after spending too long looking at a computer screen.

She was expecting him to ask her about her marriage, but he did not, asking her instead about her children and what they were doing now.

'Your sons sound like they are pretty grounded. You must have done a good job with them.'

'I haven't always felt like I have and I was worried that they'd see me moving up here as some sort of desertion, but I needn't have worried about this, as they have both been incredibly supportive of my plans.'

She wanted to ask him about how he had not ended up having any children, but she never liked to ask anyone that question. She knew how much it rankled her childless friends when they were asked this and she did not want to make anyone feel like that.

Liam made another pot of coffee and offered her one.

'A small one. I drink enough of the stuff as it is. I don't need anything else to disrupt my sleep.'

Liam looked at her sharply and asked.

'Have you been having a lot of trouble sleeping since you have been here?'

She hesitated, as she found this quite an intimate question, but said.

'I've had some of the most vivid and disturbing dreams since coming here. Lots of falling into darkness and sensations of floating. Not seeing anything, but sensing danger and threat.'

He looked pensive.

'You've had them too haven't you? Dreams like this?'

'Yes, similar, but dreams about falling are very common.'

'These are different. It takes a long time to shake them off and I've never had the same dream night after night. My dreams haven't felt this real since I was a child.'

She omitted to tell him how she used to wake up screaming about dark, shadowy knight-like figures in her room or how she used to wake up standing in front of her bedroom window, with no memory of getting there. When this used to happen in her twenties, she would put it down to stress and anxiety, as it seemed to occur more often when she was experiencing a degree of this in her waking life.

'Have you experienced anything else, apart from the dreams, since you have lived here?' Elizabeth asked.

She started to feel a coolness from him at this point, but she carried on. Liam definitely did not want to engage with this conversation and she sensed him starting to shut down. Elizabeth got up from the table and this time, he did not stop her. As she walked out of the kitchen, saying she would see herself out, she turned back to him and said.

'I meant to say, did you hear anything odd last night, coming from the woods?'

'I did hear a noise, but it could have been a sonic boom from a fighter jet. They come out of RAF Lossiemouth and fly over here sometimes.'

'In the middle of the night?'

'Not impossible. They need to practise flying at night too.'

The sarcastic edge to this comment triggered something in Elizabeth, an unwanted reminder of the tone often used with her by her ex, causing her to stand up and abruptly announce she needed to go. She left his cottage and walked home, fighting the annoyance and frustration with him, that she could feel rising within her.

Chapter Eight

Only The Ocean

Liam went to his front door, after she had left and watched her walk down the drive, towards the lane. There was a bit of a flounce in her step, causing her chestnut waves to bounce as she walked. He did accept that his tone might have sounded a little terse and this could well have been the reason that she had vacated his kitchen so abruptly. He regretted upsetting her, but really did not think that telling anyone about what he had seen at the camp would be wise right now. He had no idea what had been going on there or what the implications for himself or others might be, from discussing this.

He had enjoyed talking to her before that; he liked the way she spoke with her soft voice, that had the slightest hint of an accent, which he supposed was a west country accent, one that he was not particularly familiar with, and the way she made eye contact and made you feel like she was listening really carefully to what you were saying. Her eyes were arresting and he had tried not to stare too much at them, but he could not quite make out what colour they were, sometimes greenish and almost golden at times. She did not smile often but when she had her face was transformed. He had not spoken to someone like her for a long time. He was not convinced he had ever spoken to someone like her. He had found aspects of their conversation disconcerting, particularly the dreams, but he refused to let himself consider anything other than pragmatic, rational reasons for this, although he of all people knew that not everything could be explained away.

He had been quite surprised when she turned up at his door, as he had started to assume that the plant offering was misjudged, when she had not come yesterday and that she had no desire to get to know her neighbour, either that, or she was not in a forgiving mood yet. He could have just knocked on her door and apologised and he did usually prefer to take the direct approach, but his instincts were telling him that this would not be the best course of action in this situation. His years of experience working on the rigs had occasionally thrown up difficult situations with colleagues and management, which he had usually managed to successfully navigate his way around, but his track record of dealing with conflict in his personal life was not so good.

His ex-wife had frequently pointed out to him that he did not communicate his feelings to her enough and that she had no idea what he was thinking half the time. She would get frustrated with him, leading to her becoming angrier with him and, in turn, him retreating further. He had truly loved her when he married her and he still held some positive feelings for her and he acknowledged that his work had been a major factor in the breakdown of their relationship. Many of the relationships of the people that worked around him had failed. Towards the end of his marriage, trust had pretty much eroded between them, not helped by his wife's suspicions that he was too close to some of the few women that worked on the rig. There had been nothing going on, but she would not be convinced and, in the end, her insecurity and frustration with him was the end of them.

Later that day, Liam gave his old friend Iain a call. He had not expected him to answer, as he was usually out and about somewhere and did not have a mobile phone. He did however pick up after a few rings and Liam was heartened that he sounded so pleased to hear from him.

'To what do I owe this pleasure? I know your dislike of talking on the phone, so it must be more than a friendly catch up.'

Liam was a little abashed and said.

'You know me too well my friend and I am sorry for not calling more often. You're right though, I have something I'd like to run past you.'

Liam knew this would pique Iain's interest; he could never resist a request for advice, particularly from an old friend.

Liam had met Iain twenty years ago, whilst working on a rig. It was one of the older types; due to be decommissioned the following year and had been a good crew to work with. A few members of the crew started to express uneasiness at entering certain parts of the rig. They claimed that the air temperature would change suddenly and they could hear a noise like a low moan. All this had initially been dismissed by the Rig Manager, who was a man in his late fifties, generally fair, but hardened by years on the rigs, as so many others like him.

Liam did not experience any of this himself, but was concerned as the crew members that were making these claims were usually so outwardly tough and unbothered by the rigours of life on the rig. One night, a crew member, a woman, was found shaking and rambling incoherently outside, afterwards claiming she could not remember going outside, but woke up to see a huge dark form looming over her, with glowing eyes. The Rig Manager found this hard to ignore and a few days later, the talk of the rig was the slightly odd looking man who had been flown in from the mainland.

No one seemed to know who he was or what he was supposed to be doing there and the Rig Manager remained tight lipped. Liam found this man later that day, wandering around a part of the rig that was not safe, particularly for someone without training or appropriate clothing and equipment. This was how he met Iain. He had asked him to come away from where he was to a safer part of the rig. Liam was intrigued by this short man in his mid-forties, with a balding head and thick rimmed glasses. They introduced themselves and Liam found out that Iain was a lecturer at a university, where he taught History, with a specialism in Scottish folklore and mythology. He told Liam that he was often asked to investigate situations like this, where unexplained occurrences were happening. Liam asked him whether he had discovered anything here. Iain said he needed to look around a bit more and talk to some more of the crew members. Liam pressed him on whether he had heard about anything similar happening on any other rig. Iain said no, this was the first time he had been invited to an oil rig. Iain's findings were inconclusive, but Liam had noticed him the next day, in the area where the crew member had been found, reading out loud from a large book. He had no idea what language he was speaking, it was not one that he recognised. He wanted to ask him, but the look on his face told Liam that now was not the time to disturb him. Iain left the next day and life went back to relative normality on the rig.

Liam had looked up Iain's name and found some of the books he had written and ordered a couple. A few months later, he noticed he was doing a book reading and signing for his latest work at an Aberdeen bookshop. This coincided with his leave, so he went along and spoke to him after. They went for a drink and talked about his writing and some of his experiences. They stayed in sporadic contact after this, not seeing each other that often, but always with lots to talk about when they did. Iain had never married and Liam noticed his shyness around women. He could talk to hundreds of students in a university lecture hall, but stumble over his words, when talking to a woman on a one to one basis. Liam's interest in Iain's work and his admiration for his depth and breadth of knowledge was genuine and Liam assumed that it was this that enabled him to gain his trust to allow him into his life.

Occasionally they would meet up at Iain's house, which was a good three and a half hour drive from Aberdeen, outside the town of Brora. The house was old and large and stuffed full of dark wood furniture and a vast number of books, which lined shelves in the majority of the downstairs rooms and a few of the bedrooms upstairs. Liam loved Iain's study. It was painted a deep red colour, with a beautiful Kilim rug on the floor and large, mahogany, Victorian desk, always piled high with books and papers. Iain's books covered many different genres, although there was a distinct lack of romantic novels. They passed many happy evenings talking and drinking good red wine in that study. The subjects they discussed were wide; their upbringings, families, education and the topic that Liam liked to talk about most with Iain; his investigations and his understanding of what lay behind them. Iain was aware of Liam's scepticism of some aspects of this work, but seemed to appreciate and enjoy his enthusiasm and thirst for knowledge. One thing puzzled Liam. There was a door leading off the study, that he knew was locked and had never seen Iain go into. He had asked him about it and he had said it was only a store cupboard, full of empty crates. This sounded feasible, but Liam always felt that there was more to this locked room than Iain had implied.

'You have my attention. What has been happening?'

'There's an old prisoner of war camp, that appears to have been completely neglected since the end of war, near my cottage. Not long after I moved in, I noticed some very strange activity there. A couple of unmarked military trucks were there and I saw five people being stretchered out of the place into the trucks. A small unit of soldiers, from the Black Watch regiment I think, has now moved in and seem to be guarding the place. I haven't been talking to anyone around here about any of this, it doesn't seem that it would be a good idea to do so, but it's very hard to ignore and pretend it didn't happen. They obviously don't want people to come near the place and there's no talk about it in the local village and certainly nothing in the media.'

'I know the camp you're talking about, I read about it a long time ago, in connection with a case I was called in to, at another former World War Two prisoner of war camp. My understanding is that they did not treat the prisoners at all well and several of them could not be accounted for at the end of the war, Locals assumed they managed to escape. Have you noticed anything else going on nearby?'

Liam paused, not wanting to hand in his sceptic's badge quite yet.

'I haven't seen anything there, but I have heard noises, a low, rumbling noise.'

'Describe this noise.'

'Like a cross between the wind and a large animal, or maybe a machine.'

'Where did it come from?'

'At first, I thought it was from the forest, but I think it was actually coming from the hill next to it, from inside the hill.'

'What else?'

'Only dreams, where I'm somewhere dark and I'm falling and then floating through this strange blue light.'

'How often have you had this dream?'

'Every night, pretty much.'

Liam considered telling him about Elizabeth, but held back, he wanted to hear his initial reactions first.

'There's something else that you're not saying?'

Liam should have known better than to try to withhold anything from Iain, it never worked.

'My new neighbour has just told me that she also heard these noises and that she has had some strange experiences in the forest.'

'Goodness, you've been talking to your neighbour, you must be softening in your old age.'

'I've only had one conversation with her and that was at her instigation,'

'What's she like?'

'Recently separated, obsessed with the Highlands and her family ancestry research, seems very interested in the local area and superstitious tales the locals are feeding her.'

'Attractive?'

'You could say so, but that's not the point here.'

Iain told Liam that he would do some digging into what he told him and let him know if he found anything. They said goodbye. Liam felt better after his phone call with Iain, he usually did after any interaction with him. However, he found it hard to settle down to anything for the rest of the day, he felt more restless than he had in months. He considered going for a walk, but came to the realisation that he needed to go to the coast. Even though he had spent years on the sea, it was still in his blood and he craved the smell and the power of it now and again. He took a long drive out to the Black Isle, to the coast at Rosemarkle and sat on the harbour, looking at the still, grey water, trying to get her eyes and her voice out of his mind.

Chapter Nine

Damn Your Eyes

After her coffee with Liam, Elizabeth felt more restless than she had for a long time. She wanted to do some work on her laptop, to do more research into local history, but she did not have the focus. She remembered something she had read the night before, in one of the books from the tourist information office. There was a castle not far from her, which was one of the seats of the Mackenzie family. This castle would have stood around the same time as the one that supposedly stood here. She had read that there was an impressive library there, stocked full of books relating to the local area. She had no idea how she would get to access this library, but she knew the castle was open to the public at this time of year. She decided to take a drive there, if nothing else, to look around and get a feel for medieval Scottish life, (at least, for the nobility).

After driving for nearly half an hour, she pulled into a long, straight, tree lined driveway, at the end of which the castle could be seen. It was not what she would describe as a massive, austere castle, it was more like the type of castle that a child would draw, with tall towers on either side and turrets along the top. It was made of a pale greyish pink stone and the windows were relatively small. A flagpole reached up from the top of the building, with a flag raised on it. She was too far away and her eyesight was too bad to be able to make out what was on the flag. There was a car park halfway up the drive, to the right of the castle. She was relieved to see that the car park was not too full and there were only a few other cars.

She paid her entrance fee at the small wooden hut, in front of the main castle entrance and was handed a small leaflet, which contained information about the castle and the special events they were running this year. She noticed that they were advertising an easter egg hunt for children in April and a May Day Bank Holiday Classic Car show. She walked through the grand, arched entrance way, into an inner courtyard. There was an antiquated signpost, in the middle of the courtyard, pointing in different directions. She did not really mind where she started, so headed in the direction marked Great Hall. She stepped through a wooden door, into a large, empty space, with a high, vaulted ceiling and a stone flagged floor. It was chilly in this space, hardly surprising considering the cold, stone floor, the thick walls and no apparent source of heating.

There was a vast stone fireplace on one side of the hall, large enough for several people to stand up in comfortably and was furnished with a dark wooden table that must have been at least fourteen feet long. There were chairs on either side of the table, with a grander, throne-like chair at one end. Weaponry was hanging on the wall on one side of the hall, a frightening looking array of swords and axes, interspersed with shields with different insignia marked on them. She kept seeing the same symbols, stags' heads, what looked like a hill on fire and three legs joined together. Suits of armour also stood guard against this wall. She walked through the entirety of the hall, imagining how it would have been full of people, conversation and music, with plotting and intrigue taking place in the dark corners.

She walked through a door, into another room, a smaller room, which offered something a little more comfortable than the great hall. She admired the hardiness of the people who had inhabited castles like this, which must have been so cold in the winter. This room contained some portraits, as well as various chairs and side tables. Recognising the age of furniture was not her strong point, but she guessed from the fine, elaborately carved, legs of the tables, they were probably from the eighteenth century. A baby grand piano, covered with a piece of green cloth, fringed along the edges and embroidered with red and gold flowers, stood to one side of the room. She walked over to one of the portraits, which depicted a woman in an elaborate dress and headdress, with a very fine ruby and gold necklace hanging from her neck. Her eyes looked cold and hard and her mouth thin and angry. Mind you, she thought to herself, it probably wasn't much fun for women, even noble women, at that time, so she could be excused for her dour expression.

She walked past a couple more portraits, both variations of the previous one, but the next one stopped her in her tracks. It is a man, dressed in what she surmised to be Medieval clothing. His face is long and fairly solemn in expression, but his eyes, pale blue-grey, with a fierce intensity, were what had made this portrait stand out so much for her. She had seen those eyes before, on Liam. She told herself not to be so ridiculous, but she could not stop looking. There was nothing written on or near the portrait to indicate who this was. She was about to move on when she heard a voice behind say.

'It's a remarkable face isn't it?'

She turned around to find a tall, thin man of about eighty, with white hair and long, solemn face similar to the man in the portrait.

'Yes, it's a fine painting, I was wondering who this was?'

'That is a very good question that I wish I could answer for you. He's not an ancestor of this family, so it has always been a bit of a mystery how his portrait ended up here. In those days, it was not uncommon for items of value to be taken from neighbouring castles, in exchange for debts of some kind. Several of my ancestors were notorious gamblers, so it could well have been part of someone's winnings.'

'Your ancestors, oh, I'm sorry, I didn't mean to bother you.'

'You are most certainly not bothering me and it was me that spoke to you.'

He introduced himself as Roderick, omitting any title that he possessed, although Elizabeth assumed he must have one. and offered to show her around some of the other parts of the castle.

'I'm sure you must have something more important to be doing?'

'It would be a pleasure.'

He led her into the next room, which was another sitting room, more femininely decorated than the previous one, which he said, held more portraits and some other items she might find interesting. There were portraits of his ancestors, more recent ones than in the previous room, ranging from the eighteenth century to a portrait of his wife from the 1950s.

'She looked beautiful, ' commented Elizabeth and she really meant it. She had bright blue eyes and artfully arranged fair hair, with a gentle smile and wore a stunning pale blue ball gown.

'She was and she was still the most beautiful and generous woman I have ever met, right up until she died.,'

'Oh, I'm so sorry. How long ago did she die?'

'Two years ago now. I was sure she would outlive me. I thought I had smoked too many cigars and drunk too much whiskey, to reach this age.'

Elizabeth noticed that he had gone somewhere else in his mind for a moment or two and let him.

As they continued to look around, he asked her what had brought her here today. She was not too sure how to explain this, but told him about her recent move to the area and how she had heard that a castle used to stand near her cottage, which had sparked her interest. He told her that there were some old maps in the library, that he could show her, if that helped. She said that this would, but said she felt very conscious of using up his time.

'My dear, if I don't have time for a beautiful woman, what is the point?'

Elizabeth felt herself blushing a little and smiling. As they left the room, she noticed a small cabinet and looking into it she noticed a bracelet, made up of pale blue gemstones, held together with gold.

'What a lovely bracelet,' she said.

'Yes, it is, I've always liked that piece. It's actually rumoured to be part of a set, but we've never been able to locate anything similar. Its origins are a bit of mystery, again, I suppose it originally belonged to another family.'

'What are the blue stones?' asked Elizabeth.

'Blue Topaz. Quite rare for jewellery from this period. We've had an expert examine it and he estimated it was from the fourteenth century. He said that he had never before seen blue topaz of this quality.'

'I'm giving you a very bad impression of my family. I promise you we don't 'acquire' things anymore and fortunately, are not prone to gambling, unless you count the odd flutter on the horses.'

He led her into the library, which to Elizabeth, was her dream room, lined with books, from floor to ceiling, with a big desk, as well as comfortable reading chairs and padded window seats. He gestured for her to sit down in one of the more comfortable chairs, while he opened up a cupboard and rifled through rolled up maps. She was a little surprised at his casual handling of them, but supposed they were his, so he could do that. After much muttering, he brought two over to the table in the middle of the room and unrolled them, weighting the corners down with glass paperweights, which were already on the table. She went over to him, but was not sure what she was looking at. He explained the various landmarks and places. He pointed out the village near her cottage. It then made more sense to her and she could make out the forest and the hill next to it. There was some writing where her cottage now stood.

'What does that say?'

'Coille Dorch.'

'So there was a castle there. Do you have any information about the castle or the family that lived there?'

He went over to a bookshelf and peered at the spines of the books there, eventually pulling one out. He brought it to the same table and gently turned some pages. He stopped and asked her to look at She found it hard to decipher the archaic script that was written there, so he told her that this page was describing the castle and those who lived there. Sir Orfeo and his wife, Lady Isobel.

'This is very interesting, it goes into some description of Sir Orfeo's character and personal qualities. He was, apparently, a fine musician and poet, his harp playing having the ability to send people into some sort of rapture.'

'Does it say anything about what happened to them?'

'Not really, only that they moved from the castle to one that belonged to an Uncle, near Inverary, on the west coast of Scotland.'

'That's so interesting, as that lines up with the story told to me by a friend. Would it have been usual for such a family to up sticks and move like that, from the area where they were the Laird and owned great swathes of land?'

'It would be rare for such a thing to happen. Land was so strategic and valuable. To leave this behind and to allow the castle to fall into ruins, would indicate to me that something fairly dramatic had occurred.'

He glanced at his wristwatch and said that, sadly, he did have to make a telephone call soon and would have to leave her. He suggested a few other parts of the castle that she might find interesting and took his leave, formally holding her hand as he said goodbye. He said that she would always be welcome there and handed her a card with his telephone number, so that she could let him know if she needed anything. Elizabeth was touched by this and knew that he was serious. She did not spend too much longer looking around the interior of the castle. She was more interested in the family history aspect of the place, than looking at a recreation of an Elizabethan kitchen or the warren of cellars that ran beneath her. She could see there was still a lot of renovation going on, making much of it inaccessible to visitors.

She thought about Roderick and what an unusual existence he must lead here. She hoped he was not lonely and had some family and friends around him. She remembered how low her father had been in the year or two after her mother had died. He did not do well on his own and stopped caring for himself and about himself. She still carried the guilt of not having spent more time with him in the months before he died. She had been so tied up with her life in London, her children and her failing relationship, she had not been there for him. Of course, she regretted this now and was sometimes almost floored by the grief that occasionally still came out of nowhere and the realisation that she would never talk to him again. Being a parent was tough and she thought it would get easier as her children became adults and started careers and settled into long term relationships, but this brought different anxieties with it. The fear that they would grow away too much and be too taken up with their lives and that contact with them would dwindle away. She tried to console herself with the knowledge that the relationship she had with her sons was so different from that she had experienced with her own mother. Elizabeth shook herself out of her introspection, which she was well aware would only lead to going down rabbit holes and spiralling thoughts.

Chapter Ten

Here You Come Again

Heading back to her car, she debated whether to go straight home or not. She was still not quite ready for home, so gave Lou a call to find out if she was at home. She, sadly, was not, being at her mother's house, but they arranged to meet for lunch, in the village cafe, the next day. On the drive she listened to some music, Etta James was suiting her mood today and sang along, wishing that she had such a voice. The information she had gleaned from Roderick at the castle had created more questions, but she felt motivated to carry on with her research, more motivated than she had felt in a while. She had managed to partially satisfy the restlessness she had felt after her conversation with Liam, although she was left wondering whether he now thought of her as a bit of a flake.

She pulled into her drive and entered the cottage. She had not had the opportunity to eat much today and felt her stomach growl.

Opening the fridge, she could not find anything that called to her and had a sudden pang for the ease and speed of having takeaways arriving at your door in London. She made do with tinned tomato soup and toast, whilst imagining Thai food. She went to bed early that night, taking one of the tourist information office books with her.

She had been in bed reading for about half an hour, when she heard a car pulling up outside the cottage. Puzzled, she looked out the window to see a taxi outside. Someone got out and headed for her front door, she could not make out who it was, and started knocking loudly. Her heart was beating fast and felt like it was in her throat. She stood at the top of the stairs and the knocking continued. Then she heard a male voice shouting her name and realised who it was Tony from the dinner party.

'Elizabeth, it's Tony Let me in! I just wanna talk to you. Go on, let me in, I won't stay long. We can have a drink.'

He sounded drunk, his words slurring a fair bit.

'Go home, Tony. I'm not going to let you in.'

'Oh, please, c'mon now, just a little drink. I know you want to really.'

'I really don't. I want you to go home and leave me alone.'

At this point, she had moved halfway down the stairs. She did not want to go any further, as he would be able to see her then, from the letter box.

'Don't be a bitch, I don't know what's wrong with you. We had a good time the other night.'

'If you don't leave now, I'm calling the police.'

He snorted.

'Good luck with that one; they'll take forever round here.'

More banging on the door and shouting her name, then, another male voice.

'Okay mate, time to go home,' followed by sounds of scuffling and plant pots being knocked over and much posturing from Tony. Then it went quiet and Liam was calling her from the door.

'Elizabeth, are you alright? It's okay now, you don't have to worry about him, You can come out.'

She walked slowly to the front door and peered around it.

'What have you done to him?'

He gestured towards the flower bed. There was Tony, sitting on the ground with something tied around his legs and his arms behind his back. He was muttering to himself, but otherwise seemed unharmed.

'Who is this charmer?'

'That is Tony. the one I told you about from the other night, that night I met you in the lane.'

Liam seemed to understand and said he knew a local taxi driver who would come and make sure he got home.

'Go inside, I'll wait with him'

As she went inside, she heard Tony drunkenly apologising to her, but shut the door without responding. She went back upstairs to the bathroom and splashed some water on her face and ran her hands through her hair. Pulling on a jumper over her pyjamas, she went down to the kitchen to make a coffee. Before too long, she heard a car pull up and a loudly protesting Tony being bundled in and a car door firmly shutting.

There was a knock on the door, this time a gentle one. She opened it and Liam stood there, looking at her thoughtfully.

'I don't think you'll be bothered by him again. Are you okay?'

'I'm fine, but don't really understand why he came here. I thought I'd made it fairly clear to him that I wasn't interested in him.'

'Some people need it spelled out to them a bit more.'

'I think I did let him know pretty clearly.'

Elizabeth felt a surge of anger rise inside her, but instead of arguing with him about this, it came out as a sob and, much to her embarrassment, she found herself starting to cry and shiver uncontrollably. Liam came in and shut the door and put his arm around her, leading her gently into the sitting room. He got her to sit on the sofa and put the blanket around her shoulders.

'Here, sit down, I'll get you something to drink.'

He came back with whisky and the tissue box that had been on the kitchen table. Handing her a glass, he sat next to her and watched as she took a couple of sips and dabbed at her eyes and nose.

'I'm sorry about all this. I feel so stupid.'

'Why, you met an eejit at a dinner party, who couldn't take no for an answer. It happens. I'm glad I heard him and could help.'

'I shouldn't need rescuing. I am grateful, but I need to be able to deal with this sort of thing on my own.'

She started sobbing again. He took the glass from her hand and placed it on the coffee table and found herself being held by him and crying noisily into his chest. He felt warm and strong and smelled of soap. When the crying subsided, she pulled away from him and once again apologised. She suddenly realised that she must look a fright, she always did when she cried, red puffy eyes and a red nose, so buried her face in a tissue. She started to feel incredibly self-conscious and all too aware of his closeness and the way that his eyes made her feel.

'I've taken up too much of your time, I should let you go home. You must be tired.'

'I'm absolutely fine. I'm happy to stay a bit longer if you'd like me to.'

'No, I'm better now. As you say, he's unlikely to come back.'

Liam stood up and said she knew where he was if she needed anything. When he had gone, she remained on the sofa, wrapping the blanket further around her and curling up on her side. She fell asleep like this and before long was falling into a dream, not the usual one about falling and falling into darkness, but of a woman's face, saying something to her, but not being able to make out what she was saying. She had skin so pale and a crown of white flowers and leaves around her long, flowing hair. In her dream she was shouting at the woman, begging her to speak louder and let her know what she was trying to say, but she began to fade into a mauveish light until she was gone.

Chapter Eleven

Flowers

She woke up on the sofa with a stiff neck and some initial confusion. When the embarrassment and discomfort from last night started to come back to her, she groaned and put her head in her hands. She remembered something that her ex-husband used to say to her, a little too frequently, that shame was an emotion that she seemed to do really well. She, unfortunately, tended to agree with him on this one. She had always wished that she did not care quite so much about what other people thought of her and whether anything that she said had upset them or offended them. Her ex had always made it fairly plain that he viewed shame as a pointless feeling, (and possibly he was right,) but she thought that it went hand in hand with empathy and being caring towards other people.

She started to feel annoyance, verging on anger, rising within her, at the thought of her ex-husband's vindictive nature and before this could overtake her, she got off the sofa. Bringing the blanket with her and pulling it around herself like a cloak, As she did so, she was caught by a scent on its edge, his scent. She walked across the sitting room and was about to open the door when her attention was caught by something on the floor in front of her. She bent down to pick it up, only to find that it was a white flower petal. She had no idea how it might have ended up there. She had no flowers in the house and there certainly weren't many outside at the moment, that she could have brought in with her unknowingly.

She looked at her reflection in the full length hall mirror, resembling a more primitive, ancient woman, with her dishevelled long hair and long cloak, and wished she could feel a bit more warrior-like. After a coffee in the kitchen she started to feel a little more in control of herself. She thought about the day that stretched ahead of her. When she had been working she would have been out of the door by 7.30 on most mornings, without too much time to think of anything other than the tasks and appointments facing her that day. A day that would usually be taken up with the problems and anxieties of other people. This could, of course, be traumatic at times and her friends would often ask her how she coped with this, with some of the incidents she would hear about. She could not really explain how she managed this, but she was innately able, somehow, to remain calm and not reveal any judgement or shock to the young person in front of her. She felt a huge amount of empathy for them and tried her best to help them, probably down to the way she had always felt through her life, that is, looking in on life, feeling like a spectator, not quite feeling part of everything. She was in a position now that she had longed for, on those working days, to be able to set her own agenda and felt cross with herself for the self-pity. In the shower, she had a flash of inspiration. She wanted to go back into the village to talk to the lady in the tourist office again. She was sure that she had more useful information to impart; she just needed to approach it in a different way.

Dressing in her newer jeans, a black, long sleeved top and her black ankle boots, with some subtle make up applied, she felt a little more ready to face the day. When fastening her jeans, she noticed that she had lost a little weight, which she put down to the amount of walking she was doing and the reduction in snacking that occurred in her previous workplace. The day held the promise of sunny intervals and the occasional rain shower, so she pulled on her raincoat. As she left the house, she looked in the direction of Liam's place, getting an unbidden flashback of how his arms had felt last night. Apart from her early encounters with him, he had been nothing but kind and concerned towards her, but she could not stop herself from feeling something akin to anger towards him.

She had no idea where this was coming from, but was sure that Lou would be able to enlighten her once she told her about him.

She had arranged to meet Lou in the cafe, but when she walked in she was not there. It was quiet, with only one table being occupied by two women, who might have been a mother and daughter. Elizabeth sat down at the same window table from her previous visit there; the lace tablecloth as pristine as ever had a small ceramic pot in its centre, resting on a rattan placemat, containing a purplish blue hyacinth plant. She leant forward and breathed in its sweet scent, instantly transporting her to her childhood home. Her mother had loved these spring flowers and had always planted several of them each year and positioned them around the house. She acknowledged that she was usually pretty hard on her mother, when she remembered her or when she described her to other people, which did make her feel guilty and ungrateful. She could excuse her for being damaged by her own background and experiences of being parented, but not for her lack of warmth and affection, or seeming inability to instil self-worth and self confidence in her daughters. Her sister claimed to never understand when she spoke of their mother in this way, but Elizabeth recognised the insecurity and doubt that also plagued her sister's life.

A man, maybe in his seventies, came over to her with a notepad and asked if she was ready to order. She said she would order when her friend arrived, but would have a glass of orange juice while she waited. Lou came bursting in about ten minutes later, full of apologies for being a bit late, citing a traffic jam and temporary traffic lights, (though Elizabeth guessed it was more likely a case of her being late leaving home, due to being distracted by something). She leant down to kiss Elizabeth's cheek and sat opposite her. Eager to find out her news, she pressed Elizabeth for information, but the man came over to hand them the menu, so Elizabeth waited until he had gone. She glanced over her shoulder, to make sure he was not within earshot. Lou noticed this and said.

'You have to tell me what is going on, the way you're behaving you must have stumbled across some state secrets!'

'Not quite, but I don't want the whole village knowing my business.'

'Will you just tell me. I don't want to have to force it out of you.'

Elizabeth started to tell her about the last couple of days, pausing when the man came back to take their order. They both chose baked potatoes, as it seemed like a comfort food sort of day.

Lou was horrified at Tony Showing up at her door like that.

'He'll be hearing from me later on.'

'No, leave it, I don't think he'll try anything like that again, or at least for a while. Maybe don't try to fix him up with anyone again.'

'I'm so sorry, he seemed okay when I first met him. I would never have introduced him to you if I'd had an inkling of what he was really like.'

'Lou, please, don't feel bad. He's a classic Narcissist and would have turned on the charm when you first met him, fooling you into thinking he's a reasonable, well-adjusted man.'

She wanted to hear more about Liam and what she knew about him.

'He doesn't sound like your usual type. More rugged and physical.'

'It has no bearing on anything, whether he is my type or not. I have absolutely no interest in him like that,' said Elizabeth a little too adamantly.

'Not even with those big strong arms?' teased Lou.

Elizabeth hoped she was not going to regret telling her about what had happened. She had not provided her with every single detail. She did not know how good he smelt or how safe and content she had felt, for a moment or two, in his arms. She found it hard enough to admit this to herself, let alone to anyone else, not even Lou.

Lou's expression changed and a look of real concern grew on her face as she said

'I have been really worried about you, basically for the last few years. I knew you had issues with your marriage, but wish I'd known sooner, quite how unhappy you were and that I had been there more for you. I get it that you're not ready for a relationship yet and I promise to fight the urge to introduce you to every decent single man that I meet, though there are some really attractive doctors working with Sandy.'

Elizabeth opened her mouth to object, but was silenced by Lou continuing.

'I just don't want you disappearing into some kind of hermit-like existence up here, which I know you are quite capable of.'

'I won't, I just need some time before I start even contemplating new relationships. Anyway, far more interesting than that, I had a very enlightening day yesterday, with an octogenarian.'

Lou laughed. 'I know you've always had a thing for older guys.'

Elizabeth described Roderick and what he had shown her. Lou was fascinated, the historian in her taking over.

'So your Roderick must be an Earl. He sounds pretty amenable for a member of the aristocracy.'

Elizabeth felt defensive about him and said, trying not to sound too curt.

'He was a charming man and very generous with his time. He must get fed up with people tramping through his home, gawping at things.'

Lou was not to be deterred.

'Hmm, and paying to get in and buying overpriced tea and cakes in the cafe and twee tat from the gift shop,'

'They don't have a gift shop.' was Elizabeth's indignant reply to this.

'Anyway, what have you got against places like that? Is it not important to keep a record of social history?'

'But it only depicts a certain type of social history. Whenever I walk around castles and grand houses, I just think about the poor buggers who had to work in the kitchens and stoke the fires and pander to the whims of their mistresses and masters.'

'I did not know you were such a republican. You'll be calling me a Sassenach soon and start chasing me out of Scotland.'

'Never, I've only just got you here!'

Elizabeth rolled her eyes at Lou and went on to tell her about her idea for the woman in the tourist information office.

After they had eaten lunch and after having to convince the man in the cafe that they did not want a pudding, they headed towards the place. Before they entered, Elizabeth turned to Lou and said.

'Are you ready?'

'I don't know what you're so worried about. She's just a little old biddy, volunteering a few times a week. She's hardly going to chase us out of the building for asking her a few questions!'

They walked in and the room was as quiet as before, which, of course, Elizabeth understood was perfectly normal for a Highlands village at this time of year, Lou looked around in wonder

'This place is like a time capsule. I love those posters.'

They heard a movement behind the door at the back of the office, so Lou called out.

'Hello, is anyone there?'

The old lady appeared in the doorway behind the counter. Elizabeth saw a faint look of surprise on her face, which she quickly changed to an almost welcoming smile.

'Good afternoon, ladies, how can I help you today?'

Elizabeth took the books out of her bag and said.

'I didn't introduce myself properly the other day. I'm Elizabeth and this is my friend, Lou.'

Elizabeth paused, waiting for the other woman's name to be proffered, but all they got in exchange was a neutral expression, with the same half smile. She continued.

'I wanted to bring these back and ask you some questions about a few things I read about.'

'What sort of things are you talking about? I'm sure I don't have anything further to add to what's already in those books. You're very welcome to keep those books for longer.'

'I was reading about the story of Sir Orfeo and Lady Isobel and am really interested in where this might have taken place, I think their castle was very close to where my cottage sits now.'

'Ach, that's a fairy tale. Pay no heed to it.'

Lou spoke, as Elizabeth had asked her to.

'I'm a History teacher at the high school and we did a project a while back on the folklore of the local area. I did quite a lot of research into this story, amongst others. The whole Fairy King idea might be a bit farfetched, but Lady Isobel and Sir Orfeo did exist and there were stories written at the time, that she disappeared for a long time and how he searched endlessly for her, living like a hermit and leaving a steward in charge of his castle and lands.'

Elizabeth had hoped that Lou's presence, as a local and a history teacher, might give some credibility to her inquiries and make it more difficult for her to politely fobbed off again. For a moment, she thought that she was wrong and that the old woman was going to get a bit snarky with them. After a moment's silence, the old woman sat down at the table and invited them both to do the same. The story she told them was remarkable.

She described how there had indeed been a grand castle next to the woods, where Sir Orfeo and his bride lived. Writings from the time talked about her behaviour changing and becoming erratic, with her waking from violent dreams and being nearly impossible to comfort. She disappeared after heading into the woods, despite being in the company of others, with accounts of her being taken by the Elfin Knight. As she recounted this tale to them, she became so animated and seemed tearful at one point, as if it had only happened yesterday. When Elizabeth pointed this out, she held her with her dark, shining eyes and said.

'I can trace my ancestors back to the Steward who was left in charge by Sir Orfeo. He was devastated and felt responsible for her loss and vowed to protect the castle and the land until his master returned.'

'That was such a long time ago, Why do you still feel so strongly now?'

'That I can't answer. My father and my grandfather were the same. Fiercely protective of the names of Orfeo and Isobel and what happened here.'

Lou asked her whether she believed in the idea of the Elfin Knight taking Isobel and why many of the locals were so scared of the woods.

'I've never set eyes on him myself, but others claim to have.'

She looked directly at Elizabeth again, putting her hand on her arm as she did.

'You should take care. I felt it when you came in before and it's stronger now, I don't know what it is, but just be careful.'

Elizabeth did not really know how to respond to this, but turned to Lou and said they ought to be going. Lou seemed quite happy to stay, but Elizabeth needed some air. They were almost out of the door, when they heard the words.

'I'm June, by the way.'

As they walked away up the street, Lou laughed.

'Wow, I've heard stories about her, but she's something else in the flesh.'

'What stories and why have not you not mentioned this before now?'

'Because they are ridiculous, that she's some sort of witch. I hear it from the kids at school, who won't go near her house on All Hallows Eve.'

Elizabeth didn't have her pegged as a witch, but with those eyes it wasn't that surprising that she had such a reputation

Elizabeth drove home, despite Lou inviting her back to her place. She had a strong desire to be on her own and needed headspace to order her thoughts about what she had learned today. In the car her mind had been full of Liam and tales of Orfeo, Isobel and the Elfin Knight, but it was all muddled and intertwined. When she got back she had the fleeting idea to knock on Liam's door, for some reason, she wanted to tell him about today, but this quickly passed. Instead, she fired up her laptop to read more about the old story of Orfeo and Isobel. She had not paid too much attention to the role of the Steward before, but now this had new meaning. The Steward played such an integral role in the story, without him, Orfeo's lands and riches would most probably have been taken by another nobleman. His loyalty had been impressive. She was still baffled by the remaining strength of this loyalty within June, She heard her mobile phone ding and saw a message had come in from her eldest son. She called him and he told her that he had been thinking about her today and had been a little concerned about her.

'No need to be. I'm honestly okay here.'

'You sound distracted. Has something happened?'

'Nothing bad, I've been with Lou today, doing a bit of digging into some local history.'

'Ah, that will explain it, if I know one thing that my mother loves, it's a bit of digging!'

He went on to tell her that he was hoping to come up next month and that he was looking forward to seeing the place. She felt sad when he ended the call, but went to bed, happily making plans for his visit.

Chapter Twelve

Blues In The Night

Liam had found it impossible to sleep after he had dealt with the eejit on Elizabeth's doorstep. After years of working with predominantly men on rigs in the middle of the North Sea, he was not fazed by having to get physical with someone. Alcohol was strictly forbidden on the rigs, but that did not mean that the odd fight was out of the question. When some of the guys were back on shore, they could go a bit too far with the drinking and Liam would find himself in the midst of a few of his colleagues and some unhappy locals, on more occasions than he would like to remember. He was not as strong or quick as he used to be, but he had a good understanding of his physical capabilities and situations that he would be able to handle alone.

He had been standing, looking out of his back door, breathing in the brisk night air, taking a break from reading a book on Medieval Scottish history, recommended to him by Iain, when he had heard a commotion from Elizabeth's place. He walked out of the house to get a better idea of what was happening and could hear the slurred speech of a man and increasingly loud knocking on her door. He didn't hesitate in going over there and when he got closer to the man, he could see he was not particularly large, so would not cause him too many problems. He had been right; after a few firm words from Liam and having his arm held behind his back, he stopped shouting. Liam had told him to sit down on the ground, but he had refused and started trying to throw punches at him. This led to Liam taking out one of the extra-large cable ties he had grabbed when he left his house, getting the guy on the ground and tying his ankles together and his wrists behind his back. All this being done quickly and pretty deftly, before the guy, with his impaired faculties knew what was happening to him. When he did realise that he was tied up, he started to loudly complain to Liam, telling him all the things he would do to him, when he got out of this and how dare he assault him like that. He said he was going to do everything from beat him up to sue him. Liam took no notice of anything that he said and was more concerned with checking that Elizabeth was alright.

When he was safely bundled into his friend's taxi, with strict instructions that he was not to cut the cable tie until he guaranteed he would not set foot at her house again, (the size of his friend, meant that he was unlikely to argue with him,) he let Elizabeth know it was safe to open the door. He was met with the sight of her standing in the doorway, with the light behind her, long chestnut hair falling all over her shoulders, wearing her pyjamas and an old jumper. For a moment, he felt mesmerised, as there was something ethereal about the sight of her. He gathered himself and went in. He had not been surprised at her being upset, it would have been a shock to most people, but he had not expected the way he would feel when she was sobbing into his chest. He instinctively stroked her soft hair and felt something close to emptiness when she pulled away. She seemed in a hurry to get him out the door, so was concerned that he had overstepped the mark by holding her like that. He had not really felt comfortable leaving her so soon, but it was her choice.

When he got home, he had tried to get back to his book, but could not, so sat at his kitchen table trying to write down some of his thoughts on what had happened since he moved in here. Sitting in the quiet kitchen, he could keep an ear out for any further sounds from next door. He admitted to himself that he found her attractive; he could still feel the damp patch on his shirt, into which she had cried, but he did not want to change it. He did not think that she needed protecting, to the contrary, he got the sense of an inner strength from her, that she probably was not even aware of, but he wanted to be near her. It was not how he had felt about other women in the past, this was different.

Since his divorce, he had seen a few different women, mainly who he had met through friends, when he was on the mainland, He had enjoyed spending time with most of them, except for the one that talked about her cats nonstop and got upset with him, when he forgot all their names and was not as interested in their latest exploits, as she thought he should be. He had nothing against cats, he quite liked them, but he preferred people with a bit more range to their interests and conversation. He found that after a few months of dating someone, they would invariably want more from him, in terms of commitment, than he was able or willing to give. He would begin to see their frustration with him and the time they spent together started to become more fraught and less light hearted, He hated hurting them, when he ended the relationships, but to his mind, it seemed to be better for them, in the long run, to know where they stood and try to move on. Of course, they did not always see it that way. One of his friends told him he was becoming a bit of a cliché, a divorced, middle aged oil rig worker, with commitment issues, which he found hard to argue against. Now that he was off the oil rigs and aiming to put down a few roots, his mind occasionally turned to relationships and whether he was ready to contemplate something a bit more serious. When he did have such thoughts, he would tell himself that he would not actively seek someone out, but if he met someone along the way, maybe. He started to feel tiredness creeping up on him and wearily took himself off to bed, fairly quickly falling into a deep, for once, dreamless sleep.

The sound of his mobile phone ringing gradually dragged Liam out of sleep. He groaned and reached for it, but it was not on the bedside table as usual. Peering over the edge of the bed, he realised the sound was coming from under the bed, but the ringing stopped by the time he had grabbed it. He banged his head on the side of the bedside table as he brought his head and cursed, gently rubbing his head. He recognised Iain's number as the missed call and immediately called him back.

'Hope I didn't wake you?'

'Yes, but it's ok, I need to get up.'

'Not like you to lie in. I thought you'd already have been out for a walk by this time.'

'It's a long story, but I had a bad night.'

'Talking of long stories, I thought you might be interested in hearing what I've managed to find out.'

'Go on.'

'I've been talking to a friend with military connections.'

This did not surprise Liam one bit, as Iain seemed to have so called connections all over the place. He often wondered how, but thought it best to not press him too much on this subject.

'Seems you're right to be dubious about what is going on at that camp. When I mentioned the place to my old friend, he was quite tight-lipped at first, but with a little gentle questioning, I managed to get out of them that something unexpected happened to the original team of contractors working there, that ended up with a specialist Army unit having to go in to investigate.'

'What happened to them, were they hurt?'

'Not entirely sure, but my friend has it on good authority that there was a big flurry of activity at the military hospital near Aberdeen, with a section of it being more or less placed into quarantine.'

'Sounds like they've been infected with something? Or uncovered some dangerous substances?'

'I'd agree with you if it weren't for the nature of some of the professionals that have been spotted there. Not sure why you would need a renowned expert on mythology and folklore for a supposed case of hazardous substance exposure.'

Sounds like they should have called you.'

'I'm not so popular within certain circles. Seen as a bit of loose cannon by some, apparently.'

'Do you think this might account for the noises I've been hearing lately?'

'Possibly, but I'm also looking into something else.'

'What do you mean?'

'You're going to need to open your mind up a bit now. Have you heard of the story of Sir Orfeo and his wife, Lady Isobel?'

'As a matter of fact, I have, but how has this got anything to do with what has been happening at the camp?'

Iain explained his theory to Liam, that the team at the base had been overcome, somehow, by a risen Elfin Knight. Iain's research had shown him that he was alleged to have the ability to cast people into a dream-like state, from which they could not be woken and the story did supposedly take place in the area close to the camp. Liam did not immediately say anything in response to what Iain had just said, which was, in the circumstances, quite understandable.

'Liam, you've gone very quiet on me. You're making me nervous. I could be way off the mark here, but my instincts are telling me that I'm not.'

'I know that your instincts have rarely let you down,' said Liam tentatively. 'But to hear that this story which I assumed was nothing but an old myth, cooked up by suspicious locals, might actually be true. It's a lot.'

Before Iain could speak, he carried on.

'Why now? Why the sudden increase in activity from your Elfin Knight?'

'That I don't know, but certainly want to find out. I've got my best research assistant, Fred, helping me on this.'

'What about your lovely neighbour, has she noticed anything else?'

'No more than I have, but she's also got hold of this story of Orfeo and as far as I can make out, has been listening a bit too much to some of the locals' nonsense about it.'

'I have to go now, lots to do, but I'll stay in touch.'

'Thanks Iain, I appreciate it.'

'One more thing, I know you won't like hearing this, but be careful and think about avoiding the woods and near the camp for a while.'

Liam, of course, paid no heed to Iain's advice and went for a walk later that morning. His curiosity about what might have taken place at the camp was too strong for him to ignore. He entered the forest and took the now familiar path towards the perimeter of the camp. When he was about halfway there, he had to kneel down to retie his bootlace, as he did so, he noticed something shining on the ground next to him. Partially covered by some mud, was some sort of gemstone. Liam had no idea what stone this was, but it was blue and teardrop shaped, about half an inch in diameter, at its widest point. He picked it up and placed it carefully in his pocket. He walked in the direction of the camp and skirted the perimeter fence for a bit, looking out, unsuccessfully, for any gaps in it. He was about to turn back when he heard voices from inside the fence. Instinctively, he concealed himself behind a tree, peering around to see two fairly large soldiers, carrying what appeared to be automatic weapons. Liam was no expert on guns, but he could tell that these were serious bits of kit. The guards looked like they were on a routine perimeter check and soon disappeared.

As Liam walked back through the woods, Iain's words were whirling around in his head. He could not bring himself to believe that some incarnation of this Elfin Knight had somehow been resurrected and was causing havoc in this place. However much he tried to rationalise what he had just seen, he could not come up with any ideas that sounded less unbelievable than Iain's theory. The conclusion that he settled on was that they had accidentally uncovered a stash of toxic chemicals that had knocked them out, though he accepted that still did explain the presence of a mythology expert at the hospital. As he passed Elizabeth's place, he toyed with the idea of telling her what he had seen and warning her to take care in that part of the forest, but decided that this could wait until tomorrow. Back at his cottage, he remembered the gemstone in his pocket and took it out, to gently clean it up. After he done so, he help it up in the light and was stunned by its beauty and the clarity of the stone. He would look up what type of stone it was, but not now, he was hit by a wall of tiredness, so decided to lie down on the sofa.

It was three hours later when he woke up, feeling rough but slightly more rested. A shower and a strong coffee helped him to feel a little more human. He opened up his laptop and looked up gemstones, holding up the stone to compare it to those on the screen. He concluded it was a blue topaz and spent some time reading about this stone. He had never read into this area before, but found it interesting, particularly that it was thought to have been discovered by the Romans, more than two thousand years ago, on the island of Topazios in the Red Sea. There was a lot of information about it mythical properties, it apparently being a gem of peace and healing, that would protect its wearer from enemies and bring reconciliation. To Liam, this all seemed to be a bit of a tall order for a blue stone, albeit a very pretty one. It was also the birthstone for December, which he believed in about as much as horoscopes. He had no idea whether this stone was the real or not, but his instinct told him to look after it, so he found a small box in a kitchen drawer and put it in the drawer of his bedside table.

He needed a physical distraction, so decided to do some work in the garden before he lost the daylight. It was nearly five o' clock, so he reckoned he had about an hour left. Digging in the hard ground of the neglected flower bed was exactly what he needed and after an hour of this, his back started to ache and he felt ready to go inside and relax for the evening. After cooking himself some pasta, as usual, way too much for one person, and berating himself for eating too much of it, he got out his laptop and started to run searches on any sightings of army activity in the area and the military hospital that Iain had mentioned, He found nothing, which he supposed was hardly surprising, but nonetheless found it hard to believe that he was the only person who had noticed anything strange going on.

He started to feel tired at around ten, which was early for him, but considering his lack of sleep last night was to be expected. He checked he had locked the cottage doors and shut all the windows, turned off the lights downstairs and went up to his bedroom. Sitting on the side of the bed, he took the topaz out from the drawer and admired it in the light of the bedside lamp. As he was doing so, he heard something outside, not close to the house, in the distance, near the forest. He turned off the lamp and went to the window. Looking towards the forest, he saw nothing, but could distinctly hear a low, rumbling noise, similar to what he had heard before, but it sounded nearer. It stopped, but rather than getting into bed, he went downstairs and pulled on his boots and jacket, grabbed his phone and house keys and went outside.

As he walked towards the trees, there was a very loud inner voice telling him that this was potentially a bad idea, but he could not stop himself. The noise started again, but this time, on top of it was what sounded like trees rustling in the wind. Looking upwards he could see the tops of some of the trees swaying. What happened next stopped him in his tracks, as he began to hear what could only have been something very large making its way through the trees, causing them to part in its wake. He unfroze and his next instinct was to run as far away as he could from whatever this was. He turned and ran, not to his cottage, but to Elizabeth's.

Chapter Thirteen

Drive

Elizabeth had drifted off to sleep happily, with thoughts of her son coming to visit, when she was abruptly woken up by the sound of banging on the door. This made her heart leap into mouth, surely Tony had not come back for round two? She quickly realised the banging was coming from the back door of the cottage and stood in her bedroom, trying to gather her wits and think about what she should do. She pulled on a jumper, picked up her phone and for the second time in a week, she found herself cautiously walking down her staircase. She headed towards the kitchen, pausing as she reached for the door handle. More banging, but this time she heard a voice, but it was quiet, too quiet for her to hear. Opening the door a crack, she could hear more and realised it was Liam's voice. She opened the door more confidently and walked towards the kitchen door.

'Liam, what on earth is it? Why are you here so late?'

She hoped he wasn't drunk, although instinct about him told her that this was unlikely.

'Elizabeth, open the door, now, you have to let me in!'

'I'll do no such thing, not until you tell me what is going on.'

'Elizabeth, please, we need to get out of here, as quickly as possible.'

'Don't be ridiculous, go away, we'll talk about this in the morning.'

'If you want to live, you need to come now!'

'Go home Liam, what on earth are you being so melodramatic about?'

At this point, she heard something else outside, a loud, whooshing noise, like trees swaying in a strong wind.

'You hear that? That's why we have to leave now!'

She opened the door and he rushed past her, with a look on his face that she had never seen before, a look that told her that everything he said was probably true.

'Grab a coat and some boots, nothing else, where are your car keys?'

She pointed towards her keys, lying on the kitchen table and then rushed into the hall and did what he said, without question. When she came back into the kitchen, he looked at her and said

'Are you ready?' and reached out his hand to her. She took it, without any hesitation, and he ran with her, out of the kitchen door and towards her car, which was parked along the side of the cottage. As they did so, the noise was getting louder and nearer, the sound of something crashing through the trees, something large, He got into the driver's seat and started the engine

'You haven't turned the headlights on.'

'I don't think that would be a very good idea right now,' was his quick response.

'What the hell is that? It sounds like some kind of large animal.'

'I don't know what it is, I just know that we need to get as far away from here as we can.'

He drove fast, too fast for someone without lights, down the dark driveway, and told her not to look back, but, of course, she did and what she saw terrified her. A dark shape loomed over the back of the cottage, taller than the roof. She could not make out details. As Liam turned onto the lane, she turned back again and saw the figure turn towards them and she could clearly make out two eyes, glowing like fire, looking directly at the car. She screamed at him to drive faster and he did.

They drove for more than half an hour in stunned silence. She kept turning back, to look out of the rear window, but there was no sign of it following them. He pulled the car over into a layby and turned off the engine and after a minute or so, he turned towards her. What followed was him telling her everything that he had sighted at the old camp and what he had heard about it since. He told her about the strange noises he had been hearing, coming from the forest and what had happened just before he ran to her, She listened to him without interrupting and when he stopped talking, she asked him

'So, where are we heading?'

'I have an old friend, Iain, who lives an hour or so from here. He's an academic and a bit of an expert in all things strange and unusual. He's the one that used his military connections to find out what had been happening at the camp.'

'What else did he tell you? That still doesn't explain what that was.'

'Well, it might, he has a theory, with origins in local folklore.'

She interrupted.

'Don't tell me, he's talking about the Elfin Knight!'

'Yes, that's one of the stories that he mentioned.'

'This story of the Elfin Knight and his supposed abduction of Lady Isobel is following me around all over the place. That lady I told you about, from the tourist information office, June, wholeheartedly believes in it all and claims one of her ancestors was involved. You should hear how she talks about it, as if it only happened yesterday. She even warned me to stay out of the woods and seemed horrified that I had been walking in them.'

Liam looked at her, pensively.

'Iain warned me off going into the woods too and he has no connection to this area or these stories at all.'

'And you believe him? Do you think that thing was actually the Elfin Knight?'

'Unless you have any other explanation, then yes. I'm inclined to believe it and, trust me, I'm not usually taken in by fairy stories.'

Elizabeth did not respond to this comment, looking straight ahead into the darkness, Liam started up the engine and said they should get going.

'Won't it be a bit late to land on your friend. Shouldn't we call first?'

'No, I don't want him to worry while we are on the way and. to be honest, I don't think he'll be that surprised to see us.'

She sat right back in her seat and felt suddenly cold. Reaching into the back seat, she grabbed the blanket she kept there and covered herself with it. He glanced at her, but said nothing. After a while, she turned on the car stereo and started to play the CD she still had in there and let the sound of Black Books wash over her.

'This is good, who is it?' asked Liam.

She told him and remembered when she had first heard this band, coming back from one of her first dates with her ex, full of promise and probably a bit too much wine. Whenever she thought about those times, it was quickly tempered by what had happened between them the past year or so and how his early, apparent, all-consuming love for her had so easily turned into the coercive, emotionally abusive relationship she had ended up with. This brought her back to the present moment. The image of that thing was seared in her mind, along with the pure terror she had felt. She started to think about her sons and tears started to fall. He noticed, but did not say anything, simply covering her hand with his for a moment.

Chapter Fourteen

Confusion

They drove up the A9, heading north, until they reached Brora. As they drove through this coastal village, passing by houses mainly in darkness, but a few with some lights still on, Elizabeth stared out of the car window, envying the people that were safely asleep in their beds or curled up on their sofas, watching television. Past the village, they headed west and after turning off a quiet lane, reached Iain's house not long after midnight. Elizabeth liked the large, solid-looking, double-fronted Victorian house and hoped the inhabitant was as reassuring as the house. At least he was still up, judging by the light that glowed from some of the downstairs windows. Liam had been right, after initial exclamations of surprise, he ushered them into the house, as if he had been expecting them. The entrance hall was warm and softly lit with lamps. He led them into a sitting room and invited Elizabeth to sit by the log fire.

'You look like you need to warm up. Please sit and I'll get you something to drink.'

She sank into the old armchair, covered in tapestry patterned fabric, slightly threadbare in parts and Iain took a blanket from the chair on the opposite side of the fireplace and offered it to her. She gratefully took it and wrapped herself in it, shivering despite the warmth of the room. Iain left the room, exchanging an indecipherable glance with Liam as he did so. Liam, who had been quietly standing near the door, watching her, sat down in the other armchair and leant forward towards the fire, staring at the flames. Iain came in with a tray and placed it on the low coffee table in front of her. There was coffee, sugar, milk, biscuits and a bottle of brandy with two glasses next to it. Iain brought over a wooden chair and sat down next to Liam, saying to them.

'I'd recommend starting with the brandy. You both look like you need it.'

Liam poured two glasses and handed one to Elizabeth, which she took and sipped. She didn't really like brandy but after taking a few sips, understood why it was recommended for shock.

He looked at Iain.

'You're not having one?'

'No, I feel that a completely clear head might be in order.'

Liam described to him what had happened to make them flee. As he did so, Elizabeth studied Iain, trying not to look like she was staring at him too much. He was quite small, both in height and frame, with unusually small hands for a man. His head was practically bald and slightly shiny and his dark rimmed glasses, with fairly thick lenses, obscured his eyes, so that she could not make them out too well. He was dressed in a warm looking, dark green jumper, with a shirt collar visible at the neck and beige coloured cord trousers. On his feet he had, to her surprise, burgundy, velvet slippers, with the letter I embroidered on the front in gold thread. These slippers intrigued her, as every other aspect of his appearance shouted eccentric academic to her. She tried to gauge his reaction to what Liam was telling him, but there was not a flicker of surprise or incredulity; he kept a completely serious expression, intently listening to what was said.

When Liam had reached a natural pause, Iain surprised Elizabeth by turning to her and asking her a question.

'Would you add anything to this, do you feel that Liam has missed a detail that could be important?'

'No, I'd say that was a pretty accurate record of events. I don't know what it was that I saw tonight, but it was real and I can't imagine what would have happened to us if we had not left when we did.'

Elizabeth shuddered at this point and Liam leant forward and placed his hand on her arm.

'It's okay, we're safe here.'

'Are we? How can you possibly know that?'

Iain interjected.

'I have much I need to ask you both, but I think now is not the time to do that. I want you both to rest a while, to recover from the shock a bit more and then we'll talk.'

Iain left the room and they both sat gazing into the fire. Elizabeth drank a bit more brandy and felt herself drifting.

The next thing she knew, she was waking up in the chair, but Liam was no longer there. She needed the bathroom, so left the room, wondering where on earth it would be. She tried a couple of the doors off the hall; one was a dining room and the other a store cupboard. The third door was a small lavatory. She looked at herself in the tiny mirror above the hand basin, unimpressed by her tousled hair, paler than usual face and haunted looking eyes with purple-grey shadows beneath them. Washing her face and smoothing down her hair helped a little. Back in the hall, she heard muffled voices from behind one of the doors she had not tried. She knocked on the door and Iain opened it and gestured for her to come in. The room she entered, she presumed was his study. All but one of the walls were covered in books, reaching right up to the ceiling, with a tall wooden ladder leaning against one wall. There was a large, dark wood desk in the middle of the room, covered in books and papers, with Liam sitting in one of the chairs. Iain pulled out another chair for her.

'Please sit here'

Iain sat and looked at her. He had taken off his glasses allowing her to finally see his eyes. She could now see they were dark and shone with intelligence and sharpness. She tried to think whose eyes they reminded her of and then realised it was June.

'I don't think Liam has told you much about me or the areas that I specialise in?'

'He told me that you were a Historian, but also an expert in mythology and folklore'

'That's a flattering description, but yes, that's true, but has he told you how we met?'

Elizabeth shook her head and Iain described the events on the oil rig and how he had been called into similar situations.

'I've always been aware of Liam's sceptical nature, even after I've shared with him some of the investigations that I have been involved with, but I have a long held belief that there is still hope for him, as he has a very open mind and an innate desire to learn. That's why I have let him into all this and trust him implicitly.'

Elizabeth understood what Iain was leaving unsaid here, that he was trying to find out whether he could trust her, but did not know how to let him know that he could.

Iain went on to ask her if Liam had shared what he had found out about the military activity at the camp and the reaction of his connections when he had brought up this subject.

'I knew it was strange when I saw those trucks going through the village.'

'You were right to think it unusual. I still have not managed to find out what those people are being treated for. The military hospital basically seems to have the wing that they are in on some kind of lockdown.'

'The stories about the Elfin Knight imply that he has the power to infiltrate or influence peoples' dreams and to send them into some sort of dream-like state. Are you saying that you believe this and think that this is what has happened to these people from the camp?'

Iain explained that, for centuries, there have been stories around the area, of people being taken in the woods and children being warned by their parents not to go into the woods after dark, or the Elfin Knight will send them to sleep and take them. He told her that there were versions of this story throughout the British Isles and beyond, including in Norse mythology.

Elizabeth told him of her conversation with Roderick and what she had found out from him about Orfeo and the location of his castle and also about June, with her ancestral connection and fierce loyalty. Iain seemed extremely interested in all of this and said,

'I would be very keen to meet these people, particularly June.'

Elizabeth carried on.

'In all the information I have looked at so far, there is nothing said about their reasons for leaving the area and allowing the caste to fall into ruins.'

Liam spoke, sounding a little terse.

'You can hardly blame him for wanting to get away from the place, I imagine the threat of her being taken again, hung over them or maybe it was Isobel wanting to get far away from there, after her ordeal.'

Iain added.

'There is another part to the legend that you might not yet be aware of. It states that the Elfin Knight vowed to stay away from Isobel and her family, a pact, if you like, with Orfeo.'

'So despite that, they were still too afraid to stay there,' said Elizabeth.

'She was gone from him for so long, I doubt that Orfeo wanted to risk a recurrence. Something else I read was very intriguing. That the only way to truly defeat the Elfin Knight and stop him from harming humans, is for the blood of a descendant of Sir Orfeo and Lady Isobel to be shed under the tree where Isobel originally was taken.'

Liam, said

'This still does not explain why this has happened now, what could have caused the Elfin Knight to come back after centuries, It makes no sense.'

'You're right, it doesn't, maybe it has something to do with the camp, maybe not, I have a theory, but I need to find out more about your family history for it to have any credence.'

'My family history? I can't see how that affects anything.'

Iain looked at Elizabeth.

'You too, I'd like to find out about your ancestry.'

'That could be tricky. I'm still trying to find out about this myself.'

She explained to Iain about her adoption and her Scottish roots, but that all she knew was that they had left Scotland for Ireland, maybe around the 1600s and that the surnames Stuart and Mackenzie were possibly connections, but she could not be sure about that.

Iain turned to Liam.

'What about your family? Weren't you planning to research your Scottish forebears?'

'I was, but haven't spent much time on this yet. My parents rarely spoke about anything related to our ancestry, whether this was out of disinterest I don't know, quite possibly with the way that they were. There was too much going on in Northern Ireland, in the present, for them to think too much about the past. My grandfather used to talk about it a bit, regaling me with tales about our supposed noble Scottish ancestors, but that was the extent of his knowledge.'

'You're both lucky, I do relish a challenge and I have just the person to help me.'

Elizabeth looked at Iain with concern.

'Is it a good idea to involve someone else in all this?'

'Fred is my regular research assistant, I'm assisting him with his Doctorate and, trust me, I would not give him my time if I didn't think he was worth it.'

What Iain neglected to tell them was that Fred was brilliant and, as loathe as he was to admit it, could outthink him most of the time. He had first met him as an Undergraduate student at the university he lectured at. He had been brought to his attention by a colleague, who had been so impressed by his first piece of writing, on the subject of Medieval Scottish Witchcraft, that they had given it to Iain to read. Iain had been stunned at the insightfulness and originality of his work, not something he often found in undergraduates and invited him to his office for a meeting. Iain questioned him further on what he had written and what he discovered was someone with a deep interest in the subject, outstanding research and analytical skills, but also something that he couldn't quite fathom. Iain had needed an assistant on an investigation he was called into and Fred was the first person he thought of. He was always concerned at bringing in others to these situations, as you could never be quite sure how they would react, but Fred was completely unphased and was a massive help to him.

After time and a few more investigations, Iain began to gain a better understanding of Fred. He had other abilities, harder to define, that enabled him to see through certain situations and foresee potential dangers, which had been extremely useful when they had been called in to find out what was terrorising the staff at the Highland Estate of a Saudi Arabian Prince. It turned out to be a Bean Nighe, a form of Banshee, that took on the form of a beautiful woman and lured some of the male staff towards it, turning into a terrifying form as they got nearer, forcing them to run for their lives. Much to Iain's embarrassment, he had succumbed to the power of the banshee and was making his way towards the loch on the estate, where it stood. Fred had been in his room on the other side of the house, but had a vision of what was happening and rushed to Iain's aid, preventing him from being killed by it, shouting out the correct incantation with seconds to spare. Iain would not consider any investigation without Fred after that. Liam chimed in.

'Are you seriously going down the route that one of us could be a descendant of Orfeo and Isobel?'

'It is one line of inquiry I'll be exploring.'

Iain stood up and said firmly.

'It's very late, you two are exhausted and I have a lot to do. I'm going to suggest that you go to bed and we will resume this when you wake up.'

With no argument from either of them, Iain led the way up the stairs and showed them to his spare bedrooms. Elizabeth paused in the doorway and said to Iain.

'There's one thing I haven't told either of you. When I first moved in, I took a walk into the forest and was drawn to a certain tree, a pretty old looking Ash tree. It's probably nothing, but I was overwhelmed with tiredness and could do nothing else but lie down and sleep. When I woke up, I thought I must have only drifted off for ten or fifteen minutes, but it turned out to be a few hours.'

Iain looked at her intently.

'Did anything else happen near this tree? Liam, do you know the tree Elizabeth is talking about?'

'I do, I haven't felt tired there, but have felt something, like a sudden drop in the air temperature"

'Thank you for sharing that Elizabeth and if you think of anything else like that please tell me straight away.'

Elizabeth took in the room, it was large and painted a deep red, with thick curtains that looked like tapestry. It contained a double bed with carved bed posts, a large dark wood wardrobe, a chest of drawers and a writing table with a chair. She turned on the lamp on the bedside table and pulled back the bed covers. She had no toothbrush and no bed clothes, but did not care. She lay down on the bed and brought the covers right over her head, feeling almost safe, and fell into a very deep, unusually, dreamless sleep.

Chapter Fifteen

Give Me Your Hand

A thin shaft of light, piercing through the gap in the partially closed curtains, pulled Elizabeth out from sleep. She covered her eyes with her arm, momentarily confused about where she was. As she came to, the events of last night had her sitting up in bed and reaching for her phone. It was out of charge and she groaned when she remembered that she had no charger with her. She looked down at herself, still wearing her clothes from yesterday, but this did not bother her as much as it usually would. In the circumstances, she thought, this was probably the least of her worries. She longed to call her sons, but, at the same time, had a strong desire to keep them away from all this and not to worry them. She looked around the room and noticed a neatly folded pile of clothes on the chest of drawers. Curious, she went over to them to find a cream fisherman's jumper, a pale blue t-shirt and some dark blue jeans. She picked them up and left the room in search of a bathroom. Iain had most probably told her where it was, last night, but she honestly could not remember.

The first door she tried was another bedroom, furnished in a similar way to hers, but with two single beds, the next door was indeed a bathroom, with a white, claw footed bath and tiles that looked as old as the house. She found a new toothbrush, still in its packet, toothpaste, face wash and some deodorant, on the glass shelf above the sink. There was even a comb and a hairbrush. She longed for a shower, but there was only the bath. She ran herself a fairly shallow one and quickly washed herself with the vanilla scented soap on the side of the bath. The idea of a long, hot soak was usually very appealing to her, but she was keen to get downstairs to the others, as soon as possible. The large towel that had been folded over the wooden rack, next to the bath, was soft and fluffy and smelt of lavender fabric conditioner. The clothes she had been left fitted surprisingly well, although the jeans were a little short and the jumper was pretty big on her. She really wanted to find out how Iain was in possession of a pair of women's jeans, as there had been no mention of a partner or a daughter. The thoughtfulness of Iain, at providing her with things she might need in the morning, was touching and unexpected. She wished she had clean underpants though, in fact any underpants at all would be good right now. In the mirror, her face still looked pale and tired, but slightly more rested than before. She wished she had some mascara, but then scolded herself for being vain. Back in the bedroom, she pulled on her socks and boots and went downstairs, hoping to find good coffee and a phone charger.

She felt slightly nervous as she walked down the stairs; she usually felt like this when staying in the home of someone she hardly knew. The smell of ground coffee led her to the kitchen, where she found Iain and Liam sitting at a wooden table, which stood in the middle of an impressively large kitchen, which looked like it had not changed much since the house was built. Iain greeted her cheerily

'Good morning! I hope you managed to get some sleep?'

'Surprisingly, yes, I did. That bed is very comfortable. Thank you for the clothes and the toiletries.'

'No problem at all. They were left behind by my niece from Canada, who stayed here, with a friend last year. I think they found it a little quiet for their taste here and decamped to London after a while.'

She sat at the table and glanced across at Liam, who was already eating a plateful of eggs and toast. His face covered in stubble, which she could not help but think suited him. Iain poured her some coffee and offered her some food. It looked good, but she could not contemplate it yet, at least not until after coffee.

'I don't suppose you have a phone charger?' Elizabeth asked Iain.

'I have several, I don't have my own mobile phone, don't trust the things, the last thing I want is to be tracked, but I keep a few just in case.'

He wandered over to a drawer and pulled out a tangle of chargers, placing them in front of her.

'I hope one of these will do,'

Elizabeth examined the jumbled mess in front of her, trying not to speculate how Iain had acquired them all, eventually finding one that looked like it would fit her phone. Walking towards a socket she had noticed, she turned to Iain and asked,

'May I?'

'Of course, although finding a signal might be another issue altogether.'

Liam, who had been silent the whole time, said, rather abruptly she thought.

'Never mind about mobile phones, Iain has got a lot to tell us. We were waiting until you came down.'

'Liam, give the poor girl a break, she was done in last night; she's not on oil rig time like you still are.'

Looking at Elizabeth he said,

'If you are ready, I will tell you.'

'Yes, please do,' shooting what she hoped was a slightly defiant look at Liam, who did a good job of ignoring it.

It transpired that Iain had not been to sleep at all, but was in his study, working away until dawn. He told them that he had taken what little family ancestry information they had given him and had traced their family trees as far back as he could.

'You also have Fred to thank for this. He's usually up all night anyway and without his outstanding research skills, we would not have found out so much information.'

Elizabeth had noticed the two large rolls of paper next to Iain, one of which he now unfurled and laid on the middle of the kitchen table, weighting the corners down with spare coffee mugs and a sugar bowl. On the paper was a large family tree, written out in an antique looking hand. Iain pointed to the bottom of the tree.

'Here are you, Liam.'

With his finger, he traced up several levels of the tree and stopped.

'Here are your Scottish ancestors, who migrated to Ireland in the mid-1700s. If we go further back, in fact right to the top of the tree, we have these two names.'

Liam leant over, taking a little time to decipher Iain's elaborate writing.

'Sir Orfeo and Lady Isobel" he read out loud.

It seemed to take Liam a moment to realise what he had just read, after which he looked at Iain with a mixture of confusion and incredulity.

'You're kidding, surely? This must be some kind of mistake.'

'With the combination of Fred and myself having done the research, I very much doubt that. We have checked and rechecked our information sources and are confident that all this is correct and accurate.'

While Liam digested this revelation, Iain then turned his attention to Elizabeth, placing the other rolled up piece of paper next to Liam's family tree.

'You, my dear, are here.' pointing her name out.

Elizabeth could not help noticing that her family tree was a fair amount shorter than Liam's, which was not a huge surprise to her.

'Your ancestors were, as you predicted, harder to find, but all the way up here, we have your Scottish ancestors, who were indeed Stuarts, who also went to Ireland, around the same time as Liam's ancestors. We were able to trace the Stuarts back a few more generations, but, much to our frustration, did not manage to go any further back than that. We hit the proverbial brick wall around 1600.'

Elizabeth devoured the information laid out in front of her. She had never succeeded in tracing her ancestors as far back as this and ran her finger along some of the unfamiliar names that rested upon the various branches of the tree. Iain misreading her silence, said,

'I hope this is not too disappointing for you. Fred and I will keep working away at it today, to see if we can go back another hundred or so years.'

Elizabeth looked up at him.

'I'm not remotely disappointed, You and Fred have done, in one night, what would have taken genealogists months. I'm staggered at what you have found out.'

Liam, who had been sitting, staring at his family tree, with an expression on his face, that could have been either fascination or horror, (or more likely both,) looked at Iain and said,

'So this is all because of me, that this has happened? The Elfin Knight is after me?'

'That's a definite possibility,' replied Iain, "But, let's not be too quick to jump to conclusions. There could be other factors that have led to him reappearing.'

'Maybe, but it's too much of a coincidence, that this all starts not long after I move into the cottage and if what you're saying is right, I'll be the one that needs to go back to try to get rid of him.'

Before Iain could respond to this, Liam abruptly stood up and headed out of the kitchen, followed by the sound of the front door slamming shut. Elizabeth stood up and started to walk towards the door.

'Leave him,' said Iain. "He'll be looking for a bit of space. I've known Liam for long enough, to realise that he needs to process and rationalise things in his own way. It won't help to go to him.'

Elizabeth reluctantly sat back down at the table, distracting herself by looking at more of the names on her family tree, whilst Iain took himself off to his study.

The sound of a car approaching the front of the house, brought Iain back into the kitchen, as he announced that Fred was here. Elizabeth was intrigued to meet him and was slightly taken aback by this man, of average height and build, in his late twenties, with short reddish blond hair, glasses and an open and friendly face. Elizabeth was not sure how she had expected him to look, but it was not like this. He could have been one of her sons' friends, rather than the brilliant mind that Iain had described. She felt a strong pang for her children, an overwhelming urge to hug them and for the first time in weeks, she wished she was back in London.

Iain's pleasure at seeing Fred was clear, but there was none of the usual small talk that would pass between people on greeting one another, as Fred immediately pulled a laptop out of his rucksack. He asked Iain if he could have a private word with him, saying that he wanted to run a few bits of information past him. Iain looked at Elizabeth, slightly apologetically, and ushered Fred out of the kitchen. She did not think she could drink another cup of coffee quite yet, but had started to feel a bit hungry, so decided to look in Iain's fridge. She found the remains of a quiche and had just taken a mouthful when Liam walked back into the kitchen. As she attempted to guiltily swallow the quiche, without choking, he gruffly asked,

'Where's Iain?'

'He's with Fred, in his study I presume. Fred had something he needed to talk to him about. Are you alright?'

'I'm fine, just needed a bit of air.'

Elizabeth was not too sure what to say to him next. He really did not look as if he wanted her to ask him any further questions about how he was feeling. Much to her relief, Iain and Fred chose that moment to come back into the kitchen and after quick introductions, Iain announced that Fred had discovered something quite significant. Elizabeth felt a bit concerned, when Iain turned towards her with a look that she could only describe as troubled.

'Elizabeth, I'd like you to take a look at this.'

He was gesturing towards Fred's open laptop, which he had turned towards her, enabling her to see the screen. Leaning forward, she saw what looked like another family tree.

'What am I looking at?'

Iain pointed at a name at the bottom of the screen.

'This is a continuation of your family tree. Fred has traced your Stuart ancestors back a few more generations, to this person, Marie Stuart, who married a Kenneth Mackenzie. If you look at the parents of Kenneth …'

Iain tailed off as Elizabeth looked in bewilderment at the two names on the screen.

'What is it?' asked Liam, as he got up to look over her shoulder, only to see the names Sir Orfeo Mackenzie and Lady Isobel Mackenzie in bold type.

'So, we're related? Cousins of some kind?' was Elizabeth's initial reaction to what Iain had just shown her.

'Very distant ones. We are talking about five hundred years ago and about fourteen or fifteen generations ago.'

'You're sure about this? I don't understand how you worked all this out in such a short time.'

'For goodness sake, Elizabeth,' Liam said sharply.

'If he says this is right, then it is. You heard what he said about the care they took to check their information.'

Iain, unphased by this interaction, carried on.

'I know this seems incredible and unlikely, but it does explain a lot and does substantiate my theory.'

Which theory is that?' asked Elizabeth, although she already suspected the answer.

'I strongly believe that the reason the Elfin Knight has reappeared is due to him sensing descendants of Orfeo and Isobel in close proximity to where they used to live. I think it began when you arrived Liam, but Elizabeth's presence in particular seems to have escalated events.'

'What does he want and why would me being here have speeded things up?' asked Elizabeth.

'That I don't know for sure, but if the legend is to be believed, he could be wanting his revenge on Sir Orfeo by taking one of his descendants and you, being female would, of course, be more of a replacement for Isobel.'

'Do you honestly suspect that he wants to somehow abduct me and take me off to his kingdom and keep me there?! Do you know how ridiculous that sounds?'

Liam looked very directly at her, with his pale, intense eyes and said,

'No more ridiculous than being compelled to fall asleep under an ancient tree and losing a few hours, or being plagued by the same dreams, over and over, oh and the small matter of seeing a large dark figure with glowing eyes last night?'

This silenced Elizabeth for a minute. Iain continued.

'If you remember what I told you last night, as descendants of Orfeo and Isobel, you also have the power to send him back to his realm. I think that we need to seriously consider this as an option now.'

Elizabeth looked at him with what could be described as a mildly horrified expression as she said

'You're expecting me to go back there and drop some of my blood under a tree? That is, assuming that he does not get me first.'

Trying to make it sound less awful, but failing, Iain said,

'You wouldn't be alone. Liam would be with you and we would make sure that you were as well prepared and well protected, as you could possibly be.'

'Oh, that sounds perfectly fine then! What could possibly go wrong?'

Now it was Liam's turn to shoot her a look.

'I need to step outside," Elizabeth said, as she stood up and left the table.

She walked out of the front door and continued around the side of the house, breathing in the still cool air, taking in the view that she had no idea about last night, when they had driven here in the dark. The house was on a hill, with a clear view of a small loch, which looked perfectly still and reflected the hills and trees that surrounded it like a mirror. She walked at quite a fast pace, for ten or fifteen minutes and then stopped and sat on a low stone wall, trying to process what she had just been told. She had always found it frustrating when she had tried to research her ancestry, as she had such a small amount of information and no one to ask about it, within her family. Her birth family, that is. Her half sisters and her aunt did not seem to have any interest in it and she did not feel entirely comfortable asking them questions about their ancestry. She had noticed that when people were not adopted like her, they often seemed to take their ancestry for granted and lacked the curiosity needed to look into it, For Iain and Fred to have the capability to find out so much, when it had taken her ages to just go back a few generations, was a bit overwhelming. As for going back there to try to face up to that monster, she could not even contemplate that. Iain and Liam must be deluded to think they were capable of succeeding.

She was pulled out her thoughts by the sound of someone approaching her. It was Liam. He sat next to her, in silence and a few minutes, he said, with a much gentler tone than before.

'I realise this is a lot to take in, but I believe Iain. I've never known his instincts to be wrong.'

'You honestly expect me to go back there and seek out that thing? Why would I risk my life? I have my family to think about.'

'If we don't go back and at least try to send this thing back to its own realm, we really have no idea what it will do, what it is capable of or what kind of destruction it could cause,'

'Iain said the legend states it was confined to the forest and the immediate area, it can't get anywhere near the village or any other populated areas.'

'We don't know that for sure. It is possibly waiting for us to come back, but given time, how do we know that its power and ability to travel further will not increase? Surely, we owe it to people to try to do something.'

'There must be someone who can be contacted. Iain seems to have connections everywhere, he must know some sort of shady organisation or covert government department that can deal with it.'

Elizabeth knew she was grasping at straws by saying this and expected Liam's tone to sharpen again. She was wrong, as he continued to maintain his gentle tone as he said in response,

'I talked to Iain about this and he feels that if we can deal with this ourselves, without drawing the attention of the authorities to it, the outcome will be better.'

'I don't understand why it would be better to keep it quiet and Iain must realise it's very unlikely that the soldiers at the camp are unaware of what happened last night. They must have heard it too.'

'That's true,' agreed Liam, 'But, I'm with Iain on this one, the more people that are involved, the more could get hurt.'

Elizabeth fell silent again. She knew what he was saying was right and that they should return and try to defeat it, but she was scared. The sight of that thing looming over the cottage kept intruding on her waking moments. She had always thought of herself as a brave person, willing to jump to the defence of anyone who needed it. Once she had seen a young teenaged boy getting beaten up by three grown men and had intervened, with no regard for her own safety, This could have badly backfired on her, but she had found it impossible not to do anything. She had always had a strong sense of justice and hated the idea of anyone being wrongly accused or mistreated. However, she had never thought of herself as physically strong and had never had any type of physical altercation with anyone, apart from the odd scuffle with her sister, when they were younger.

Liam, as if reading her thoughts, said,

'I understand, this is out of the realm of any type of experience I have ever had too, but I think that you are stronger than you realise and from what Iain says, all we have to do is shed a few drops of our blood, under that tree, for this to be over.'

'That is a myth, how do we know that will be enough?'

'What else do we have?'

He stood up and held out his hand to her. She hesitated for a moment, looking up at his face, from his proffered hand and again, something in his eyes held her and she found herself taking his hand and allowing him to pull her up from the wall and lead her back to the house.

Chapter Sixteen

Weapon Of Choice

As they approached the back of the house, she could see Iain standing just outside the back door and as she got closer, she could not fail to notice the anxious look on his face,

'Iain, I owe you an apology,' were her first words to him, followed by, 'I was scared and overwhelmed, I still am, but I do understand how important it is for Liam and I to do this.'

'Thank you and as I said before, you won't be alone.'

When they went back into the kitchen, she was distracted by the fairly large, slightly grubby. Leather holdall that Iain placed on the kitchen table. Asking them to sit down, he opened it and looked at them with a more serious than usual expression.

'Fred and I are usually the only people who are party to the contents of this bag. The details of what I show you now cannot be talked about with anyone outside of this room.'

Elizabeth thought he was joking for a moment and almost had to stifle a giggle, but soon realised he was not. The first thing he pulled out was a book. It was thick and bound in a reddish brown material that looked like leather and was battered in places. There was a symbol in gold, on the front that she had never seen before, an inverted triangle over a circle, with what looked like a frog skeleton in the middle of it.

'This is a Grimoire, more specifically a Svarteboken. There are many versions of this book around the world, the general name for them being Cyprianus, but this one originates in Scandinavia. The label Cyprianus originates from Saint Cyprian of Antioch, a Medieval practitioner of magic, before his conversion to Christianity.'

Elizabeth had heard of Grimoires before, but knew very little apart from it supposedly being a book containing spells. The last time she had heard one mentioned was back at university, when one of the girls she shared a house with would talk obsessively about it. She had told them all she was a Wiccan and practiced magic, but Elizabeth certainly had not seen any evidence of this. She remembered when the poor girl had been collected by her parents in the middle of the night, after she and her other housemates had found her staring blankly at the television screen, not responding to any of them, seeming to be in some kind of trance. She did not come back to university. Elizabeth had occasionally wondered what had happened to her. People at the time had said she was taking drugs, but Elizabeth had not been convinced by that. She could not keep the slightly sceptical tone of her voice when she said to Iain,

'A book of spells. Do they really work?'

Iain looked at her with a troubled expression.

'It contains much more than just spells and in the right hands, the answer to your question is yes, but used by the inexperienced they can make a situation much worse.'

Liam said,

'Worse in what way?'

'It could lead to increasing the strength of an entity or indeed summoning other entities unintentionally.'

Elizabeth noticed Fred glance at Iain at this point and say,

'Maybe you should tell them about the incident at Manstone?'

'Good idea,' said Iain in agreement.

Iain described to them being asked to go to Manstone, a boarding school in the North of England. The Head was an old university friend of his, who was aware of Iain's specialist knowledge. Some pupils had reported sightings of a shadowy figure in the grounds of the school, which had been dismissed as the product of vivid teenage imaginations by the staff. However, these sightings suddenly started to escalate and a few boys began to display worrying behaviour, with one boy attempting to strangle another, a usually well behaved and good natured young person. After this incident, the Head became seriously worried, in fact more scared than worried. Iain said he and Fred became aware of more than one entity within a very short time of being at the school and upon talking to the boys, learnt that one of them had got hold of a Grimoire from the internet. A group of boys had tried to use some of the spells and in doing so had summoned a couple of rather unpleasant demons, one of whom had the ability to affect the behaviour of the boys.

'What did you have to do?' asked Liam.

'We used the correct spells from this book, combined with a few other rituals and succeeded in ridding the school of their unwanted guests.'

'If this type of thing is going on in a school, there would be uproar amongst the parents as soon as they heard what was going on. How has this been kept quiet?'

'You're quite right,' Iain said to her.

'We were able to use another part of the Grimoire to help the boys to alter their perception of what had happened.'

Elizabeth looked at Iain in disbelief.

'You mean you erased their memories?!'

'That makes it sound a little harsh. We are very careful when using such incantations, so as not to take away other memories.'

Fred interjected.

'Think of it more like a form of hypnotism.'

'That doesn't sound much better,' Elizabeth replied, thinking of how livid she would have been if this had happened to one of her sons. Liam sounded a little impatient when he said,

'Can we move on please, I don't think we have time for a debate on the ethics of all this.'

Elizabeth could not suppress the glare that she threw in his direction.

Iain took out a few more items from the holdall, the first being a necklace, a gold circular pendant on a gold chain. The pendant had what looked like the sun on it.

'This amulet has the Greek God Apollo's symbol etched on it, the sun, or at least one of his symbols. He is also known for music, poetry, truth and healing, but the sun and light are by far the most powerful.'

He turned to Liam and handed him the amulet.

'Liam, I want you to wear this. It will offer you some protection from the powers of the Elfin Knight and allow you to see the truth and reality of a situation, if he is attempting to confuse you and create a fog around you.'

Liam carefully placed the amulet around his neck, tucking the pendant underneath his t-shirt.

Iain took out another object that appeared to also be a necklace and looked at Elizabeth.

'This is a charmstone, very unique to Scotland. They are used for many reasons, from stopping toothache to preventing disease in livestock. This one is a flint arrowhead charmstone.'

Elizabeth could see a small piece of flint, roughly arrowhead shaped, suspended within a clear, oval, crystal container, hanging on a gold chain.

'The flint is prehistoric and was believed to be an elf bolt, part of an arrow fired by elves. This would act as a counter charm for the wearer, a form of protection from elfin powers.'

'You want me to wear this?'

'Yes, please. I'm not saying that either of these necklaces will give you both complete protection, but they will help.'

Elizabeth picked up the charmstone and undid the clasp of the chain. As she struggled to refasten in behind her neck, Liam stood up and helped her, momentarily feeling his warm fingers touch the back of her neck, as he managed to fasten the clasp.

The last item that Iain showed them was a knife, a small knife, with a curved blade and a white handle.

'This is a Boline and it is used in rituals, such as inscribing symbols onto objects or cutting herbs to be used in rituals. It can also be used for ritual cutting.'

It dawned on Elizabeth what he meant.

'You want us to use this knife to cut ourselves?'

'Yes, for the blood that you will need to draw.'

She looked at Liam.

'You take that, I don't want to hold it.'

He took the boline and the leather sheath it came with and placed it in his jeans pocket.

Iain carefully put the Grimoire back in the holdall and shut it. There were obviously more items inside it, but that was all he was sharing with them for now. Elizabeth said,

'If drops of our blood, amulets, talismans and spells have no effect on this monster, what next?' Iain looked at her with an unreadable expression.

'I have every faith this will work. You both have very special and unique blood running through your veins. Sir Orfeo got his wife away from the Elfin Knight when it looked impossible. If anyone can do this, you two can.'

'I hope you're right. Do you actually know what might happen if you're not?'

With great conviction, Liam said,

'If Iain says it will work, then I trust him. You seem to be forgetting that he has faced other situations like this before and succeeded. If we don't follow what he tells us, what else do you suggest we do? I think we should leave here soon and try to get this done as quickly as possible.'

'Yes,' said Iain, 'I think we mustn't delay our departure any longer. We can discuss this a bit more and make some more preparations when we get there.'

Elizabeth stood up, without a word and went upstairs to the bathroom, to splash some cold water on her face. She had to get away from the kitchen and had started to feel unwell, as if she was going to either faint or be sick and certainly did not want to do either of those things in front of them. As she dried her face, she looked in the mirror. Her eyes were more gold than usual, the reddish brown circle that outlined her pupil seemed darker. As she stared at her reflection, the lightheaded feeling she had felt at the table, was replaced by something else. She felt as if the blood running through her veins was tingling and surging, so much so that she needed to hold onto the side of the basin, to steady herself. It passed, but instead of feeling shaken, she felt stronger, more upright. As she walked down the stairs, she saw all three of them waiting, looking concerned, at the bottom, in the wood panelled hallway, hung with mysterious men and women from various periods of history. They looked up at her and she saw something else on Liam's face, apart from the usual intensity of his eyes.

'Are you ready?' he said, 'I thought you might have made a run for it?'

'Then you don't know me very well.'

They all headed out the door, Iain locking it carefully behind them. Elizabeth noticed him saying something quietly to himself as he did so. Iain and Fred were going to follow behind in Fred's car.

Iain hugged them both, taking her slightly by surprise, whilst saying,

'When this is over, you must come back here, we have lots more to talk about.'

Not understanding what he was referring to, she walked over to her car. She watched as they put the holdall in the back seat and got into the car. She had not had a discussion with Liam about who would drive, but he automatically got into the driver's seat.

'Do you realise you're not insured to drive my car. What if we are pulled over?'

'Feel free to drive. I just thought you might prefer not to.'

'Well, you're wrong. I'd like to drive.'

He shrugged and got out and walked around to the passenger door. She felt better driving, than she would have as a passenger, as she paid careful attention to the road and the few other drivers they encountered. Whenever she caught sight of Fred's car in the rear view mirror, she felt reassured.

For the first ten or fifteen minutes of the journey, they did not speak, but then Elizabeth said,

'What did he mean when he said we have lots more to talk about?'

'Oh, I don't know, Iain always has a lot going on. He probably didn't mean too much by it.'

Elizabeth was not convinced by this, having the feeling that Iain was unlikely to say anything that he did not mean, but let it go and, moving onto another aspect that was concerning her.

'We haven't discussed what our plan is when we get there. Do you not think we should?'

'Iain seems very hopeful that our blood will be enough to make it disappear. He's not usually wrong.'

'You keep saying that and I admire your faith in him, but I still think that we need a contingency plan. I don't rate our chances at outrunning that thing.'

'That's why they are coming with us, with that book. They will already have an idea of what spells will be needed and I'm sure they will be discussing it more in the car.'

Driving through the village near the cottage, Elizabeth remembered the coffee she had with Lou a few days ago and how different her life felt then. She longingly thought about evenings she had spent with Lou and other friends, drinking wine and talking for hours. She had assumed she would feel more scared than she did, as they got closer to the cottage, but the thing that scared her most was the thought that she might not see her sons again. Yes, she was frightened and full of apprehension about what they were about to do, but this was combined with a strong conviction that they had to do this, a feeling from very deep within her. As they drove up the lane that led to their cottages, she felt as if all the hairs on her body were standing on end and she felt cold, despite the relative mildness of the day. She turned to Liam.

'Do you feel that?'

'Yes,' was his short reply.

Apart from these physical sensations, as they turned up the drive to her cottage, everything appeared as if nothing had happened,

'Maybe it's gone,' she said.

Liam did not reply. He stopped the car and as she put her hand on the door handle, he put his hand out to stop her.

'Wait. I'll get out first and look around.'

'No way. We're in this together and we stay together. I think we should wait for the others. They might have some more ideas or information for us.'

They waited for Iain and Fred to pull up and get out of the car. Elizabeth noticed Iain quickly scanning his environment in all directions.

'It looks as if nothing has happened here, like he was never here' were her first words to Iain.

'Don't be fooled, it might look as if all is well here, but that is part of the Elfin Knight's powers, to create an illusion, a smoke screen if you like. He will be around and he will be waiting.'

Elizabeth rolled her eyes

'So, he can make himself invisible too?!'

'No,' Iain said, 'Not in the literal sense, but he can alter your perception of what you see. Of course, he will have caused damage to the trees and the ground the other night, but none of that is visible now. That is what I mean. Fred and I will wait here, for you to come back.'

'What if we don't come back or we come back with the monster in hot pursuit?'

'I think it might help if you stop thinking of him as a monster, ' said Iain.

'You could actually argue that he did not have any malevolent intent towards Isobel when he took her; he had simply fallen in love with her, seeing her walking and singing in the woods. There was no evidence that he mistreated her when she was in his realm.'

Elizabeth found this hard to contemplate, but persisted.

'That does not help at all. I can't think of the thing that I saw the other night, as anything other than a monster and that also doesn't answer my question, about what happens if we fail.'

'Then Fred and I will be here with spells and incantations at the ready.'

Liam's growing impatience was very evident when he said,

'We need to get on with this.'

'I was under the impression that you had more preparations to make, before we actually did this?' Elizabeth directed at Iain and Fred.

'Fred and I are ready and I believe you two are.'

Elizabeth suddenly felt more scared than she had ever felt before. No, actually, she thought, that's not true. This fear did not compare to what she had felt when she thought she had lost her eldest son, after he fell and was in an induced coma due to a head injury. She started to think about her sons again and how they would feel if anything happened to her. She found herself backing away, towards the car.

'I don't think I can do this. I need to get away from here.'

Liam held out his hand to her.

'Here, take my hand.'

Yet again, she found herself looking down at his proffered hand and hesitating, but it was not long before she took it, the need to hold onto something real outweighing everything else. They followed the gravel path which led around the side of the cottage, into the back garden and then walked across the lawn, towards the wall that marked the end of the garden and the start of the forest. Opening the wooden gate, Liam passed through it first, closely followed by Elizabeth.

Chapter Seventeen

I'm Gonna Be

Lou generally slept pretty well. Of course, she dreamt, but unless she was having a stressful time at work or it was one of the rare occasions when she had fallen out with her husband, the nature of her dreams did not tend to be too traumatic. She occasionally had anxiety dreams about her daughter, who was so far away, but last night's dream had left her really rattled and she was having a job shaking it off, even after a shower and breakfast. Her dream had Elizabeth in it and was really quite a literal dream, with her trying to reach out to Elizabeth and grab her hands, as she was falling away from her, into darkness. Elizabeth, strangely, did not look scared as she was disappearing into the dark hole or whatever it was, but she was trying to tell her something, which she could not hear. She was screaming at her, telling to speak louder, but, at this point, woke up, breathing rapidly, confused and scared. Her husband had stirred next to her, but was otherwise undisturbed.

She was very relieved that today was not one of her working days. A year or so ago, she had made the decision to reduce her hours at the school. She had been very doubtful that the Head would permit it, as his previous track record of allowing flexible working was not great, but he did, telling her that she was a valued member of the school and he would hate to lose her. Working part time had such a positive impact on all aspects of her life, she wished she had decided to do so a few years earlier. Her husband was a Consultant at the hospital in Inverness, which was, naturally, a consuming role, but, thankfully, he seemed to have the ability to separate his work and personal life. They had been married for nearly thirty years, but had known one another for longer, since their university days, but she was still happy with their life together. They were able to communicate, even when the subject was a difficult one and both of them could compromise if necessary. He was still the person that she would go to if she was upset or overwhelmed by anything and the person that she wanted to share adventures and joy with. She was very aware that their relationship was rare, she only had to think about Elizabeth and how the later stages of her relationship with her ex had created so much sadness and misery for her. She loved Elizabeth, but admitted to having moments of frustration with her and had been quite frank at times, telling her that if she was that unhappy, she should end things with him, years before she actually had. She was not naive, she knew how difficult it was for her to extract herself from him and had been so proud of her when she had phoned her to give her the news. When she had gone on to tell her that she was considering coming to the Highlands, she was so excited at the idea of having her friend close by and being able to see her more than a couple of times a year.

She picked up her phone and called Elizabeth, despite the early hour. She was probably fine, but she wanted to reassure herself of that. There was no answer, so she sent her a text, asking what her plans were for the day. When there was no reply within half an hour, she started to feel anxious. Her rational, inner voice was telling her not to worry, that she was out for a walk without her phone or in the garden, but her anxiety continued to build. She could not understand why she felt like this. Yes, the dream was disturbing, but just a dream. When her husband had left for work, she had found it impossible to settle down to anything, her focus was non-existent, so she reached the decision that the only course of action was to drive to Elizabeth's place.

When she got to the cottage, she saw her car was gone, which slightly alleviated her concern, but she still knocked on the door, trying again, when there was no reply. She would not usually try someone's front door, but when she did, the door opened, which she found odd. Even in the Highlands, they locked their doors if they went out. She called into the house, before she entered and walked through the hall and into the kitchen. Nothing looked wrong, but then she noticed Elizabeth's handbag on the table. She would usually have taken this with, even for a quick visit to the local shop. She tried the back door, leading from the kitchen, which was also open and saw a couple of plant pots knocked over, their earth spilling out. She picked them up, scooping as much of the fallen earth as she could, back into them with her hands and went back into the kitchen. Standing there, in the middle of the kitchen, she considered what to do next and, much to her surprise, it did not take her long to reach a decision. Hurriedly getting back into her car, she drove towards the village.

June let herself in the back door of the tourist information office. It was a mild morning with a blue sky punctuated with tufts of fair weather clouds. On a day like this, her mood would usually be lifted on the short walk from her small, terraced cottage to the village high street. She would be thinking about how she would sit outside, after work, in her back garden, with a cup of coffee, feeling the spring sunshine on her face, admitting to herself that spending a little too much time like this had led to her wrinkled and slightly leathery complexion. Today, all she felt was the same underlying anxiety and sense of foreboding that she had been experiencing since last night.

She was hoping for a quiet day, with few visitors to the office, which was the likely scenario at this time of year. She rarely felt like this, her pride in the area she lived in and her enjoyment of seeing visitors discover its beauty, was her default position. Instead, this was a day for sitting quietly and trying to process what she was feeling. She wished she had someone to talk to about this. She had friends, but the sort of friends she would have lunch with or go to the theatre with, not to share her feelings with. Her husband had died about ten years ago and the pain of missing him still had the ability to stop her in her tracks, but she had learnt to cope a little better when this happened. She would have been able to talk to him about this, he understood her ancestry and how this impacted upon her. He would not have made her feel remotely foolish.

She knew full well that there were some in the village who were wary of her, suspecting her of everything from being mildly eccentric to a full blown witch. She did not really care what they thought of her, she loved her village, but some of the people who had lived there all their lives, were prone to closed minds and quick to judge and mistrust anything or anyone a bit different. She had never felt like this, always trying to expand her mind through reading and learning as much as she could about subjects that fascinated and intrigued her. She would have loved to have gone to university when she was younger, but her family had not encouraged her to do so and she lacked both the self-confidence and the financial means to simply take herself off to somewhere like Aberdeen university.

Her husband had been like her, full of curiosity and eager to learn, which was one of the main aspects of him that had attracted her in the first place, that, along with his beautiful green eyes and thick dark hair. They had many discussions, in the early part of their marriage, about whether they should move away, but, despite the attitude of some of those around her, she could not imagine living anywhere else, the forests, the hills and the loch still had the power to fill her with joy and make her soul soar.

She had come to learn, in time, that her father and her grandfather had been treated with a similar suspicion, by the villagers, in their time. She had been an only child and she knew that if she had a brother, he would have been fed with the stories of Sir Orfeo and their ancestor's loyalty to him, rather than her. She had no children, had never been able to conceive, occasionally feeling sad that she had no one to pass on these stories to or to whom this sense of duty could be conveyed.

Once inside the office, she locked the back door behind her. She did not usually do this, but today it felt instinctive. She had half an hour before she needed to open to the public, so turned on the kettle and made herself an instant coffee. She had no milk, but did not care this morning. There was no tidying up to do, she had done all that when she left yesterday, so she sat with her coffee and thought about last night. The start of her evening had been uneventful. After closing the office, she had gone to a friend's house, a few doors away, for tea. This was a friend she had gone to school with and they had both lived there all their lives, who she liked as she was an artist and more non-judgemental than most. She had also been very kind to her when her husband had died, unlike some of her so-called friends, who had melted away for a while. She had never married, but had a mild obsession with the local vicar, (which June did not have the heart to tell her was not at all reciprocated). After a couple of hours of listening to her friend speculating about what it had meant when the vicar had smiled at her and said good morning the other day. June was tired and was craving her own company. She extricated herself and walked to her house. She felt the tension leave her as she shut the door behind her.

Her house was small, but, in her mind, perfect. It was full of furniture and other items that had belonged to her parents and grandparents. She had bought her own furniture along the way, but she by far preferred the older pieces. Her husband's absence was the only thing that marred her happiness at living here. She went into the kitchen and poured herself a small whisky and sat in her armchair to savour it, remembering how her father had taught her about whisky and how to drink and really taste it. This was a particularly good one, from a relatively local distiller. It was expensive, but one of the few things that would treat herself with every year. She did not feel like watching television, so decided to read. She always had a couple of books on the go, usually one fiction and one non-fiction. An avid reader since childhood, her main frustration now was her eyesight. She needed fairly strong reading glasses, but also needed a bright lamp trained over the book, if she was hoping to be able to read for an extended period. Picking up the non-fiction book, she looked at the beautifully illustrated cover. It was a book about the battle of Culloden, about a particular Clan that had fought there. She had chosen it as it was her mother's clan and she hoped that it would make her feel more connected to this side of her family. Growing up, it had always seemed to be more about her father's side, with her mother's being a bit of a mystery. Her mother's mother had died when she was relatively young and father had been a severe man, who had disapproved of his daughter's choice of husband, which had led to them becoming estranged. As a result, her mother had rarely spoken of her own family history and June had not wanted to upset her by asking too many unwanted questions about it.

She must have been reading for about an hour, when she fell asleep in the chair. She was jolted awake by a low, rumbling noise. Still drowsy from sleep, she was confused at what this was. It sounded like she had always imagined an earthquake would, but there was no shaking. It stopped and she looked out of her window, but all appeared to be in order. She went upstairs to look out of the back bedroom window, from which she had a fairly good view of the forest and the hills that surrounded it. At first, all she could see was darkness, until her eyes had become accustomed and she could start to make out what she was seeing. She kept looking towards the forest in particular and started to see the trees swaying, but there was no wind tonight. She looked away, shaking her head in disbelief, then looked back. The trees were definitely moving, as if being pushed to one side, to make way for something large.

As she stood there, she began to feel very strange, as if her blood was rushing through her veins. This scared her, she thought she was having a stroke or a heart attack. It took her a minute or two to realise that she felt fine, no light headedness, no pain anywhere, just a feeling of something rising up within her body.

Her attention was caught by something coming out of the forest, a dark shape that she could not make out. At first, she thought it was an animal, but as it moved away from the forest, it grew in size until it looked like a huge figure, like a man. She shut her eyes and opened them again. It was gone. She kept looking for about half an hour, but was nothing more and heard nothing again. The tales that her father and grandfather had instilled in her, were screaming out to her and she began to realise that this was what all that had been building up to all her life, but she had no idea what she was supposed to do now. She thought about going outside, but decided that was a bad idea. Instead, she dug out her father's old notebook from the drawer of her bedside table and read, as she had so many times before, his writings on the Elfin Knight. Her father had never claimed to have seen him, but he had made drawings of how he might look. He had been pretty accurate, if what she had seen outside was him. She had managed very little sleep after this, but had, of course, fallen asleep a couple of hours before she had to get up.

Walking to the office she had felt very tense and edgy and had looked over her shoulder more than once. The main street of the village looked as it always did and the handful of people that she met on the way, greeted her as they did most mornings, all seeming untroubled by anything. She found it hard to understand how these people could not have seen or heard anything last night. She toyed with the idea of calling the friend she had tea with last night, to ask if she had heard anything, but she felt the need to keep this to herself, at least for now. She was about halfway down her coffee when there was knocking on the front door of the office. She walked over to the door and said loudly,

'We don't open for another five minutes.'

A voice that was vaguely familiar to her came back.

'I know, I'm sorry to disturb you so early, but I really need to talk to you. It's Lou, I came in here with my friend, Elizabeth, you were telling us about Sir Orfeo.'

June hesitated, but then opened the door to her, knowing that she needed to have this conversation. Lou thanked June and came into the office. June gestured towards one of the chairs and she sat down.

'Would you like a coffee?'

'No, thank you.'

'Well, you won't mind if I finish mine.'

June sat on the other side of the table and looked at Lou with a direct and steady gaze, as Lou started to speak.

'I'm not sure where to start, but I'm really worried about my friend Elizabeth. I think she's in some kind of danger.'

'What makes you think that?'

'This is going to sound strange, it's nothing concrete, I just have a very strong feeling that something is wrong. I had the most disturbing dream about her last night and when I woke up I really wanted to speak to her, to check she is alright. I've tried calling and messaging, but nothing has come back from her.'

'Maybe she's just having a quiet day and doesn't want to talk to anyone?'

'She would usually let me know that. If she didn't want to talk, she would send a message to that effect. I have just been up to her place, her car is gone and she's not there, but both the front and back doors were left unlocked and some of the plant pots by the back door have been knocked over.'

'Did you go inside?' asked June.

'I didn't know whether I should, but I did anyway. There was no sign of her and everything looked in order, but I found it off that her handbag was still on the kitchen table, as she would definitely take that with her if she had gone out in her car. I know, I'm probably worrying about nothing, but something does not feel right.'

'I'm sorry you're worried about your friend, but I really don't understand how you feel that I might be able to help you with this'

'I'm sorry, I'm not sure, Our conversation the other day has really stuck in my head and, for some reason, I think ...,' Lou paused, but June encouraged her to continue.

'What is it that you think?'

'That this is somehow connected, that Elizabeth is in some kind of danger. I know that sounds a bit farfetched, but I can't shake off the feeling that something is very wrong.'

June did not say anything straight away. She looked at Lou sitting there with her furrowed brow and her anxious blue eyes and could feel the genuine desire that she had to help her friend and this touched her. She also knew that Lou was thinking along the right lines. She started by asking Lou,

'Last night, did you hear anything strange, any kind of noise?'

'No, nothing unusual. Why, what did you hear?'

June described to Lou what she had seen and heard last night. She found it hard to believe that she was recounting this to someone she barely knew and found it hard to make eye contact as she spoke. When she had finished, she looked at Lou. There was no doubt or disbelief in her face, only anxiety tinged with a fair amount of fear.

'Are you suggesting that it was this Elfin Knight that you saw?'

'I can't imagine what else it could have been, can you?'

'No, but how can it be, it's just a myth, I didn't think anyone really believed that the Elfin Knight was real or that Sir Orfeo's wife or anyone else for that matter, was taken by him.'

'Do you not remember what I told you last time? About the role of my ancestors in the story?'

'Yes, of course I do, I found that so fascinating, but mainly in the context of history and how stories are passed down the generations.'

June started to feel impatience and frustration with this younger woman. She was obviously an intelligent person, with a passion for history, but she seemed a bit closed-minded. Maybe she had made a mistake and told these two women too much about herself. Lou sensed her mood and apologised.

'I'm sorry, I didn't mean to diminish your family history or beliefs. I'm just finding it difficult to understand how what you have told me connects to my friend.'

Lou answered her own question.

'Oh my god, you think that he has taken her, don't you?'

'It's a possibility, her cottage is near to where I saw him. I doubt she could not have heard it last night.'

'Why would he want to take her?'

'That I can't answer. Maybe she was the first thing he saw?'

Lou looked visibly upset and June patted her hand gently.

'I might be completely wrong about that. Maybe she has just gone out for the day. Please try not to worry too much. I could have been seeing things last night.'

'You don't really believe that, do you?'

'Admittedly, it was a bit too real for me to have imagined and it's not just that, I've been feeling pretty strange in myself today as well.'

'I'm definitely going to go back to her house and if she's not there, I'm going to talk to that strange neighbour of hers. He must have heard something too.'

June surprised herself by saying,

'Would you mind if I went along with you?'

'Of course not, as long as you feel up to it?'

June stood up purposefully and said,

'Give me a moment and I'll be ready to go.'

She wrote a note and stuck it the front door of the office, saying it would be shut today, grabbed her coat and bag and turned to Lou,

'What are we waiting for? Come on!'

Chapter Eighteen

Stop The Cavalry

He should be used to wearing this uniform by now, but today it felt uncomfortable and awkward. He sometimes wished that he could take it all off and walk around in a soft t-shirt and a pair of shorts, but then his well ingrained sense of duty would kick in and he dismissed such thoughts. He pulled the strap of his gun further up his shoulder and continued patrolling the perimeter fence. He could see his colleague further ahead and wondered whether he ever felt the same.

They had been guarding this place for nearly a week now and had not been told much about why they were here or what they were guarding against. Of course, there had been talk amongst them about what had happened here, about why whoever had been here before them had left in such a hurry, leaving all their kit and equipment behind. The rumour was that the team of contractors who had been working here had all been taken ill and were now convalescing in hospital. There was speculation about everything from food poisoning to something toxic being unearthed. Their orders were to regularly patrol, day and night, and to not allow anyone into the camp. There were twelve of them here, working in shifts. They had been told not to touch any of the equipment left behind, which had been locked away, and that another team would be there next week, to relieve them. When they got there, this all sounded a bit odd, but not particularly difficult, compared to some of the other missions he had been sent on during his time in the Army.

The first few days had been uneventful, but then the atmosphere seemed to change. At a certain part of the perimeter, where it bordered the forest, they all reported that the air would inexplicably change, getting colder and noises could be heard from inside the forest. They teased each other about this back at the mess, telling lurid stories about werewolves and vampires. More likely, it was local kids, hanging out in the woods and partying. They knew that this did not explain away the temperature change, but they tried to ignore this. The forest was usually quiet, a bit too quiet he thought and he had been surprised when he noticed someone walking through it the other day. He had kept an eye on them, to make sure they did not get too close. They had hidden behind a tree when they saw him, thinking they were invisible.

When he observed him trying to creep stealthily away, he carried on with his patrol. One of their orders was to not engage, if possible, with civilians in the area.

This was their second sweep of the perimeter this evening, one more and they would be relieved by another patrol. He was looking forward to this, definitely feeling the need for a break after the events of last night. Yesterday had been more of the same, patrolling, resting, cleaning their kit, eating and repeating. It was his turn to sleep from ten o' clock, for six hours, but when he had got into bed, sleep evaded him and he turned on his bedside lamp and picked up the book he was reading. It was a detective novel, part of a series that he had been enjoying over the past couple of years. He had always been able to immerse himself in a book and was lost in the world of the seedy underbelly of Los Angeles, when he heard a very loud noise outside. He and his sleeping colleagues jumped out their beds and they all started to quickly pull on their uniforms and boots. One of them tried to contact the patrols on the radio.

'All patrols Come in, over, what are your positions, over?'

When there was no response after the fifth attempt, they were ordered to all pick up their weapons and head outside.

The noise continued, he could only describe it as sounding like something large crashing through the forest, but it was not moving towards them. Wearing their night vision goggles, they rushed to find the two patrols. When they did, they were alright, but said they could not hear anything on their radios, just static.

Each team was ordered to fan out around the perimeter.

He said,

'Shouldn't some of us go into the forest to find out what is going on?'

He was met with short shrift by the patrol leader.

'No, our orders are to remain in here.'

He did not feel right about this, whatever was making that sound could be heading towards inhabited areas, people could be at risk, but he had to follow orders. He went to the point in the perimeter fence that he was to guard and looked around him and saw nothing. The sound was getting further away, but still so loud. He stood there for around half an hour, by which point the noise had stopped, hoping that no one had been hurt. He was called in over the radio and returned to the mess. The officer in charge said they were increasing the patrols for the rest of the night and would investigate the forest at daybreak. He volunteered himself for this, but the team had already been chosen.

Everything had felt different this morning - not just his uniform - he desperately wanted to know if they found anything in the forest. When he returned to the mess, the team had returned.

'What did you find?' he asked one of them.

'Nothing at all, it all looked fine"

'That can't be, not with all that noise, there must have been trees knocked over or branches felled at least!'

'Mate, there was nothing out of place.'

'Have there been any reports of civilian injuries?'

'Can't help you there.'

He looked on the internet, to which they had some access, though pretty restricted, scouring it for stories from the local area, but there was nothing unusual. Before coming off the internet, he made one final search on 'legends and myths in the local area' and one thing caught his eye. The story of Sir Orfeo and the Elfin Knight and how pupils at the high school had researched this and written up a project with illustrations. There was a picture of them, with their teacher standing in the middle. 'Proud teacher, Mrs Louise Fraser, with her history class, standing in front of their exhibit of the Sir Orfeo project.' He found this interesting and read a little about the original story. One part of the story, in particular, jumped out at him. How the Elfin Knight had the power to infiltrate dreams and put people into a trance-like state. He started to wonder whether this could be the cause of the original contractors' mystery illness, but shook his head and told himself not to be ridiculous. He did not know what to think and wished he could talk to someone about it, but could not think who.

He had joined the Army when he was sixteen years old, straight out of school. He had not done very well in his GCSE exams, not actually sitting half of his exams. He knew he had the ability to do better academically, but he had grown very disenchanted with school, leading to his eventual poor attendance and disappointing exam results. Some of his teachers had tried to re-engage him, but, in his head, he was already out of there. He had supportive parents, who tried to encourage him to do more schoolwork, but all he wanted was to be able to leave school and join the Army. He had not been naive or ignorant, he knew what such a career would entail, but he wanted to get away from his home area and have some kind of adventure. His family had been upset and fearful, initially, and had tried to talk him out of this, but he would not be dissuaded. Fundamentally, he knew that his parents wanted him to be happy and had eventually accepted his career choice, although, of course, they worried about him a lot of the time, He lay down on his bed and despite all that had taken place over the past hours, he fell into a deep sleep, only to be woken by his alarm a few hours later, to start all over again.

Chapter Nineteen

Pinball

Elizabeth and Liam walked side by side, matching each other's pace. She could feel her heart hammering and her stomach was tied in knots. They did not look at each other as they walked, being completely focused on what was ahead of them as they entered the edge of the forest. She recalled the first time she had set foot in this place and how she had been both enchanted and unsettled by it, in equal measures. Before long, they were surrounded by the forest and Liam stopped for a moment.

'Let me go in front and you follow where I walk.'

Elizabeth, who would usually have bristled at such a request, agreed to this without question. It felt the same as it always had, the ground seemed undisturbed and the trees still standing, with no apparent damage. She found it hard to believe that this was a trick or an illusion on the part of the Elfin Knight, but could come up with no other explanation. She had been worried that they would fall down invisible holes in the ground or trip over fallen trees they could not see, but that was not the case.

She could see the Ash tree about fifteen metres ahead of them, as ever, standing out from the others. She stopped and said,

'Wait, can you hear that?'

'No, I didn't hear anything. What did it sound like?'

'Not much, a rustling sound.'

'Let's keep going, it was probably a bird or a squirrel.'

They reached the tree and Liam extracted the Boline from his pocket and was about to take it out from the leather sheath when they heard a shout.

'Hey, you two, what are you doing here?'

They turned around and saw a soldier walking purposefully in their direction, with his gun pointing towards them. Elizabeth gasped and looked at Liam in panic.

'What should we do?' she said quietly.

'Stay calm, just do what he says and don't tell him anything.'

As he got close, she could see he was young, maybe in his early to mid-twenties and looked as if he was of South Asian descent.

Liam instinctively raised his hands and said,

'We're just taking a walk.'

'Well, I'm sorry, but you can't do that here, it's not safe.'

Liam and Elizabeth glanced at each other and Elizabeth asked him.

'Why, what's happened? It all seems ok to me.'

'I'm sorry, I can't tell you more, but I do need to ask you to leave the forest.'

His voice was firm and he stood very square and steady, but Elizabeth could see something in his eyes that did not match this. She decided to try a different approach.

'We'll go, we didn't realise the forest was out of bounds, it's just that we heard something last night and we were worried that there might have been some kind of accident or that some trees had been damaged.'

He hesitated now and seemed to lose some of his conviction, but still held the line.

'There's been an accident nearby, we just need to keep the woods clear, while it's being dealt with.'

Liam lowered his hands and said to Elizabeth,

'Come on, let's go.'

They said goodbye to him and started to walk back the way they had come. Looking back, after a minute or so, Elizabeth saw he was still standing there, watching them and said to Liam, with a slightly hopeless edge to her voice,

'What now?'

'We have to go back to the cottage and talk to the others. We're not going to get anywhere near that tree at the moment.'

Sunil stood watching the man and woman walking away from him. They seemed harmless enough, but he had quickly picked up on their edginess. The way they had attempted to find out if he knew anything about the events of last night confirmed his suspicions that he and his unit were not the only ones to have heard whatever it was and did nothing to allay his fears that the wider community might be at risk. He would have liked to have asked them about what they had heard and what they thought it might have been, but he was too used to following orders to do so. There had been something else about them that had made him think that they were more than simply curious. He felt as if he had caught them out, that they were trying to be furtive, but not very successfully. He had immediately picked up on their accents, his clearly from Northern Ireland and hers English, probably Southern, but with a slight inflection that he could not quite pinpoint, He knew that this part of Scotland was very popular with tourists, but not so much at this time of year and this forest was quite small and off the beaten track. They had been a good looking couple, considering they must have been at least fifty. He had liked her hair and face and his pale eyes. When they were out of sight, he turned and started to walk back to the camp. He was almost at the perimeter fence, when he felt something lightly brush his back. He looked around, expecting to see a low branch or a shrub, but there was nothing there. He kept walking and felt it again, causing him to stop once more, to look around. It could not have been a breeze, he told himself, the air was pretty still today. A light caught his eye, behind a nearby tree, golden, like sunlight, but when he walked over to the tree, the light suddenly disappeared. He was starting to feel uneasy, so walked quickly back to the camp, unable to find a logical explanation for what had just happened.

As Liam and Elizabeth came out of the forest and approached the cottage garden, they could see Iain and Fred standing expectantly at the back of the cottage. They soon came rushing towards them, Iain saying,

'I am so glad to see you two, what happened in there? We heard nothing.'

'That's because of the slight inconvenience of a soldier with a gun pointing at us, near the tree, telling us to leave the forest.'

'Oh dear,' said Iain.

Elizabeth was starting to get frustrated with Iain's stoicism. She admired the fact he could remain calm in a difficult situation, but this was ridiculous.

'Oh dear? Is that all you can say? How are we supposed to deal with this now, when we can't even get into the forest without the risk of being shot?!'

As she was saying this, she realised she sounded rude and abrupt, but she found it impossible to stop herself. Iain looked at her, for once, revealing the true level of his anxiety.

'Elizabeth, I am as scared as you, possibly more so, as I think you are one of the bravest people that I have met, but it's never been my nature to show my true fear. I have always been adept at burying it and carrying on as if everything is alright and under control, even if I know it's not. If I don't, I'll fall apart and be of no use to anyone.'

Elizabeth felt horrible and much to Iain's surprise, hugged him.

'I'm so sorry, I think you're amazing and am so grateful for the way you are helping us, both of you,' looking over at Fred, who was looking scared that she might try to hug him too.

Liam took the lead and said,

'Let's go in and sit down and talk about this.'

Despite the imminent danger they were in, Elizabeth felt strangely happy to be back inside her cottage. She had come to love this place and the freedom and independence it represented. It looked as she had left it the night before, with no damage visible. The others headed for the kitchen and Liam started to make coffee, as she went upstairs. She sat on the side of her bed and took out her phone, dialling her eldest son. She got his answerphone, of course, he'll be working, she thought to herself. Her youngest son answered within a few rings.

'Mum, are you okay?'

She felt like bursting into tears at the sound of his voice.

'Yes, I'm good, I just wanted to hear your voice. How is your week going?'

He proceeded to tell her about his job and the small annoyances that he encountered there, nothing major, he fundamentally enjoyed his work. It was comforting to hear someone talking about safe, routine events and to hear that was happy and was making plans with his friends for the weekend.

'Are you sure you're okay, you seem quiet.'

'I'm fine. You know I love you don't you?'

'Of course I do. Oh, sorry Mum, I've got to go, I'm getting a call on my work phone. I'll give you a call later.'

Elizabeth had time to say,

'Bye sweetie, Take care,' before he ended the call.

She put her phone down and sat for a few minutes, then walked over to the window and looked out towards the forest. She still found it so hard to comprehend how it could all look as if nothing had happened. She was distracted by the sound of a car coming up the drive, which worried her, as the last thing they needed was unexpected visitors.

She went to the stairs and paused, as she heard car doors shutting and footsteps coming towards the front door. The door opened, without anyone knocking, but then she heard Lou's voice calling.

'Hello, Elizabeth, are you here?'

She was about to respond, but saw June walking in behind her and could not imagine what she was doing here. They started to walk towards the kitchen and before she could get to the bottom of the stairs, they had already gone in there, to be faced by three strange men sitting at the kitchen table. Elizabeth heard Lou's unamused voice.

'Who the hell are you lot, where's Elizabeth, you better not have hurt her!'

Elizabeth appeared at the kitchen door behind them.

'I'm here, I'm okay, everything's fine.'

She walked into the room, brushing part an open-mouthed Lou and said,

'Lou, this is Liam, my neighbour, Iain, his friend and Fred, who works with Iain.'

Lou looked both confused and extremely dubious at his comment.

'Where have you been today? I came round earlier, because I was worried about you and I find you gone, with the house unlocked and your handbag on the table.'

She couldn't think what to say, but Iain jumped in.

'Fred and I were visiting my old friend, Liam, today. He wanted to show us the glorious forest here. I'm very interested in trees and he suggested to Elizabeth that she might like to join us for the walk.'

'Then why was your car gone?' looking at Elizabeth.

She had never been any good at thinking quickly on her feet and was a shocking liar, her face always giving her away. Lou had known her long enough to sense something was not right and was not giving up. Iain stood up.

'Please come and sit down, we can make more of this excellent coffee.'

Lou suddenly remembered June, who had been standing quietly behind her.

'Sorry, my manners, this is June, she lives in the village and runs the tourist information office.'

June said hello to the others and took a seat, whilst saying by way of explanation,

'Lou came to see me this morning, with a few questions and asked if I'd like to come out to see Elizabeth with her.'

Elizabeth looked at Lou warily, asking,

'What sort of questions?'

It was Lou's turn to look slightly uncomfortable.

'Elizabeth, can I have a private word with you? June, are you happy to stay there?'

'Oh yes, I'm sure these gentlemen can keep me entertained.'

They walked into the hallway, shutting the kitchen door behind them. Lou went first.

'What is going on with you and that lot? I don't buy that story about a walk in the woods for a moment. I was really worried about you, when you didn't respond to any of my calls or messages and when I came up here, I got the distinct impression that you had left in a hurry.'

'Where does June come into all this?' was Elizabeth's response.

'I had the feeling that she was someone who could help me and I'm glad I spoke to her. She told me about what she had heard and seen last night. After she had told me this I felt even more convinced that something was wrong.'

What did she see?'

Lou looked at her, as everything started to fall into place in her mind.

'You saw it too didn't you? That's what this is all about?' pointing towards the kitchen.

Elizabeth took a deep breath and said,

'What I'm going to tell you is going to sound unbelievable, but please, just listen and I'll tell you what is really going on.'

Beginning with the events of last night, Elizabeth gave Lou the whole story, the Elfin Knight, Iain's specialist areas, Fred's role, their apparent ancestry and what they needed to do, ending with their encounter with the soldier. Lou didn't say a word throughout all of this, which Elizabeth appreciated must have been very hard for her, and then walked towards her and hugged her. Elizabeth fought back tears and said,

'Come on, we've left them with June for too long now, She'll be scaring them.'

When they walked back into the kitchen, Iain said,

'We've just been bringing June up to speed and she has told us about her fascinating family history. I'm extremely glad that you thought to include her Lou, I think she needs to be part of this. I'm assuming that Elizabeth has told you everything?'

'Yes, she has and I can see that it's a jolly good job that we're here, as it sounds like you need our help.'

Chapter Twenty

I'm Waiting for You

They all sat around the kitchen table, Liam had to fetch a couple more chairs from the sitting room, debating what should happen next. Lou tended to dominate the conversation a bit, the teacher in her never being too far from the surface, firing out ideas without thinking them through. June was quieter, but when she did speak, it was nearly always succinct and insightful. Iain and Fred were intrigued by her ancestry and asked her several questions about this, with Fred, at the same time, researching more about the Steward's role on the internet. Liam busied himself with keeping them all topped up with caffeine and looking through Elizabeth's fridge and cupboards to see what food he could put together. Classic displacement activity, Elizabeth thought to herself. She looked around the table, at this apparently disparate group of people, finding it heartening that they were all trying so hard to help them. By the time they had finished the surprisingly good lunch that Liam had managed to throw together from the meagre contents of her kitchen, they had a plan.

Lou and June were going to take a walk in the forest, by way of a different track, one that passed closer to the edge of the camp. June was going to pretend to take a fall, though Elizabeth secretly thought that Lou was the one more likely to do so, being incredibly prone to clumsiness, and appear very distressed. Their aim was to attract the guards' attention and draw them over to assist them, hopefully allowing Liam and Elizabeth to reach the tree. There was some initial reluctance towards this plan, particularly from Liam, who had concerns for the safety of the two women. He did not really suspect the guards would fire on them or hurt them in any way, but he did not feel completely sure about this. When he voiced these fears, June had said,

'I'm not scared to do this, what scares me is that thing being free to wreak havoc. It's my duty to be part of this,'

Her conviction made it hard for Liam to know how to respond.

'As long as you're sure and don't feel at all coerced into this.'

June shot him a look that said, 'do I look like someone who could be coerced?'

Elizabeth's main concern was with the distraction not working.

'There are several guards, they could just send a couple to deal with Lou and June and the rest could get to us before we reach the tree.'

Iain, looking quite pleased with himself had said,

'Of course, this could happen, which is where Fred and I come in. We will create another diversion, near the back perimeter fence.'

'What type of diversion? They're going to be extremely suspicious if walkers keep falling over today.'

Iain got up and left the room, returning a few minutes later, holding a metal detector.

'Fortunately, I always carry a couple of these around with me. Fred and I will just be a pair of detectorists out for the day, with a passion for Second World War artefacts. We'll have headphones on, so we won't hear them shouting at us, which will, hopefully, buy us a bit more time.'

'Sounds a little risky. What if they're telling you to raise your hands and you don't hear them?' asked Elizabeth with a concerned tone.

'I like to think that won't happen and I feel pretty confident that I will be able to bore them enough with my detectorist exploits, to convince them that we are the genuine article.'

'Am I the only person who is curious about why you carry metal detectors around with you?' queried Lou.

'A fair question, Lou,' said Iain, 'Fred and I were once called into an archaeological dig in East Anglia, where they were excavating the site of a Viking battle. Some of the people helping with the dig began to get extremely frightened, claiming to see ghostly figures in the field, at twilight. They were so scared that most of them refused to work there and left.'

'So, were there ghosts there?' asked Lou.

'There were indeed spectral presences there, of some of those slain in battle.'

Lou seemed excited by this.

'Viking ghosts? That must have been incredible. What did you have to do?'

'We carried out some rituals and invocations and the dig was troubled no longer. A fairly simple case as it turned out. They gave us some metal detecting equipment as a thank you. I'd always wanted to have one, but had never got around to it.'

'That still doesn't explain why you carry them around with you,' chimed in June

Iain's oblique response was,

'In this line of work, random items are often the most useful.'

Liam stood up and said,

'This is all very interesting, but I think we need to get this done soon.'

They all concurred and after various trips to the bathroom they converged outside the front door of the cottage. After a last minute run through, Lou and June were the first to leave, followed by Fred and Iain, headphones around their necks and metal detectors in their hands. Liam and Elizabeth were to wait for twenty minutes to give them all a chance to reach their positions. While they waited, Elizabeth paced the garden, with Liam watching on. After exactly twenty minutes, he walked over to her, placing his hand lightly on her arm.

'It's time.'

Near the perimeter fence, some distance from the tree, Lou and June stood, ready to play their part in the plan. They could not see any guards yet, but assumed a couple would be approaching soon. Lou looked at June

'Okay, give me your best fake fall.'

June, with some assistance from Lou, carefully got down on the ground and spent some time positioning herself. When she looked suitably uncomfortable and incapacitated, with one of her legs bent in an awkward manner, Lou started to shout.

'Help somebody, please help us!'

Nothing happened, so she tried again, louder this time. They heard movements nearby and two soldiers came into sight, both holding large guns. One of them barked,

'What are you doing here? These woods are out of bounds. You're going to have to turn back.'

'We can't, my mother has fallen over, she's hurt her leg, she can't move. Please help, she's in pain.'

June let out a convincing groan at this point.

The soldier approached, still on the other side of the fence and when they saw the amount of pain that June was obviously in and Lou's anguish, they softened their tone.

'Have you called for help?'

'No, there's no signal here.'

'Okay, we will use our radio to get some help. What sort of injury do you think your mother has?'

June said in an anguished, faltering voice,

'It's my ankle, I think it's broken!'

'Lie still, try not to move. We'll try to get you some help as soon as possible.'

June started sobbing, joined soon after by Lou, crouching down next to her.

'Oh Mum, I'm so sorry this has happened.'

The soldiers were talking to someone on their walkie talkies, asking them to radio for an ambulance and also to get blankets and a first aid kit to them. Lou and June were taken by surprise when less than ten minutes later a couple more soldiers walked towards them, having come through the nearest gateway in the fence. With one soldier looking on, the other knelt down next to June and asked if there was any evidence of bleeding.

'No, but she seems to have injured her ankle in some way, possibly a fracture.'

'The best thing we can do is keep her warm and completely still. The ambulance has been called and I'm afraid it will be at least half an hour.'

'Can't you give her something for the pain?' pleaded Lou, employing her best acting skills. When she was younger, before embarking on her teaching course, she had, in fact, toyed with the idea of going to Drama college.

'I can't give her anything, it's best to wait until the ambulance gets here. Try to stay calm and talk to her.'

He gently placed blankets over her. June smiled faintly up at him through teary eyes and thanked him. He stood up and said to his colleague that they should leave and get to the road, in order to guide the ambulance crew.

'Oh please, can you stay with us a bit longer?' implored Lou.

The soldier with the compassionate and gentle manner said he could not, but one of his colleagues would stay with them.

Somewhere over the other side of the camp, on a fairly open piece of land. Fred and Iain had started to run their detectors over the ground. With their headphones on, they were not aware of the guards shouting at them, from the other side of the fence. Iain felt himself tapped on the shoulder and looked suitably shocked and frightened when faced with an irritated looking soldier, with his gun pointing towards him. The soldier gestured with one hand, for them to take off their headphones, which they did very slowly.

'You can't do this here. You need to leave straight away.'

'I was under the impression that this area is open to the public. I've had no problem here before.'

'This area is currently restricted to the public, so you do need to leave.'

'We did not see any signs to that effect. That's such a shame, this area is rich in items from the Second World War. Did you know this used to be a prisoner of war camp? I've found several interesting things here in the past.'

Turning to Fred, he said,

'Do you remember the engraved cigarette tin and cap badges that we found last year? Old Arthur at the club couldn't hide his envy at us having found them. I don't think he's ever got over it.'

'Sir, you really need to leave now. I'm asking you politely.'

'Oh, don't worry, we'll be off, but can I just show you this?'

Iain reached into his coat pocket, and as he did, the soldiers aimed their guns at him and shouted.

'Keep your hands where we can see them!'

Both men placed their detectors on the ground and did as they were ordered, raising their hands instinctively.

'I was just going to show you a fascinating item that I found when I last came out here. Thought you might be interested, it having military connections.'

Judging by the look on the soldiers' faces, Iain said,

'No, probably not then.'

'Leave now or we will have to take you into custody.'

'I don't believe you have the jurisdiction to do that, but, it's time we went, don't you agree, James?'

Fred, looking momentarily confused, said,

'Yes, definitely time to go" and picking up their detectors, they turned around and walked back towards the road.

As Liam and Elizabeth reached the tree, there were no guards in sight.

'It must actually be going to plan,' Liam said, unable to keep the amazement out of his voice.

He reached into his pocket and pulled out the Boline, for a second time today and said to Elizabeth,

'Give me your hand.'

When she saw the curved blade, all she could say was,

'That does not look clean.'

'I think that an infection is the least of our worries right now. It looks clean enough to me. We have to use this knife, you remember what Iain said about it.'

Elizabeth realised this was not the time to be picky and held out her hand to Liam.

'Go on then do it!'

'You can do it if you like, It doesn't have to be me.'

'No, I think you'll make a better job of it than I would.'

'Why do you say that? Oh, I get it, because I'm some rough oil rig worker from Northern Ireland, I'm bound to know my way around a blade.'

She looked at him, keeping her expression as neutral as possible, still holding out her hand

'No, I did not mean that at all, I'm just worried I'll mess it up and hurt you unnecessarily. Please Liam, can we just get this done.'

He held her hand in his and made a quick incision on the palm. She winced and watched as he did the same to his hand.

'There's hardly any blood coming out!' Elizabeth exclaimed.

'That's okay. Iain said it should only take a few drops..'

They both held their hands close to the ground, at the base of the tree, until a few drops had fallen from each of them, wiping their bloody hands on the ground for good measure.

'What now?' she asked.

Before he could answer, they heard a low, rumbling sound, coming from below them and they felt the ground begin to shake, They backed away from the tree and as they did, the ground in front of the it, where they had just been standing, started to fall away, leaving a crater about five metres wide. They looked on in horror as the few trees and shrubs that had been standing there, fell into the crater. When the rumbling and the shaking finished, the once blue sky, with a smattering of pale clouds, darkened instantly, looking as if a deluge of rain was about to fall. The air grew even colder and they stood, transfixed, unable to move in any direction, as a dark, undefined, but familiar figure crawled out of the crater.

Chapter Twenty One

Chasing Cars

Liam, once again, took Elizabeth's hand, but not so gently this time and started to run, pulling her with him. Elizabeth had never been a good runner, but a very healthy flight instinct had now kicked in and she ran with all her might, greatly aided by Liam practically dragging her along. She looked back and stumbled, Liam's hold on her the only thing that prevented her from hitting the ground.

'Don't look back,' he told her, "Keep your focus ahead of you.'

'But I didn't see him, why isn't he following us?'

'Don't talk, try to save your breath!'

She started to see more daylight through the trees, they were nearly at the edge of the forest. When they reached it, they could see her garden wall a short distance ahead of them, but the very distinct sound of gunshots being fired made them stop for a moment. This got both of them looking back, but, still they could see nothing pursuing them. Elizabeth sounded hopeful.

'Maybe the soldiers have killed him?'

'If getting rid of him was as simple as shooting him, Iain would have supplied us with a gun. Come on, nearly there.'

They reached the wall and entered her garden through the gate, running across the lawn to her cottage. There was no sign of the others anywhere, but this was not surprising, it would take them all a bit longer to get back from where they had been. Elizabeth started to shake, letting the shock of it all start to take over.

'Oh god, what if the soldiers were firing at them? We should go back and try and find them. Maybe we should call the police and say what's happening?'

Putting an arm around her shoulders, in an attempt to ease the shaking, Liam could not hide his own fear.

'Where would we even start with the police? They wouldn't be able to do anything, we'd just be putting more people in danger.'

They heard footsteps heading quickly towards them and spotted Fred and Iain running along the gravel path that circled the house, with poor Iain extremely out of breath. Elizabeth could not hide her relief.

'I am so glad you're ok, we heard the shots and had no idea who they were aimed at.'

Iain managed to say

'Please, tell us what happened!'

Liam answered him, trying to keep his voice as steady as possible.

'When we put our blood at the base of the tree, a crater opened up and we saw him starting to come out, so we ran, but he didn't seem to be following us, then we heard the shots as we left the forest.'

Lou's car came up the drive much too quickly and she slammed her brakes on. She came running towards Elizabeth and flung her arms around her.

'You're okay, I thought you were being shot at! Did you get rid of it?'

Elizabeth watched as June got out of the car, relieved that she looked alright.

'We don't know,' and explained to her what had happened.

Iain suggested they all go into the cottage, Elizabeth said,

'Shouldn't we all get away from here. He could turn up here at any moment.'

'That's why we need to go inside. I need the Grimoire and Fred and I need to prepare.'

She turned to Lou and June.

'You two should go home, you've done enough. I don't want you to get hurt.'

Lou looked at her in amazement.

'You think I'm leaving you know?! I'll take June home if she wants, but I'm coming straight back.'

June appeared outraged.

'I am not going anywhere until this is done!'

They headed indoors, back into the kitchen. No one was in the mood for coffee, though glasses of water were drunk and June conceded that she could do with lying down for a while. Iain and Fred opened up the Grimoire and took other items out from the holdall, including some large marker pens and what looked like a plastic container of broken bits of mirror.

Elizabeth asked,

'What is that for?'

Iain explained

'The first thing we're going to do is cast a protection spell, in order to keep us safe within this house.'

The others watched as Iain and Fred left the house and they could see them from the kitchen window, walking around the exterior of the house, occasionally stopping to chant something and they appeared to be drawing something on the walls. They found out when they returned that they had drawn various symbols on the outside of the house, including eyes and the faces of gorgons. They had also hung pieces of mirror from window frames and doors. All of which were supposed to ward off evil spirits and negative energy. Iain handed Lou two necklaces, asking her to give the other to June when she woke, both with the same symbols as pendants, circular and gold with an eye engraved in the centre, with a blue gem as the iris.

'The evil eye symbol, as it's often called and the gemstone is a blue topaz, which also has protective qualities.'

Liam said,

'I found a blue stone in the woods the other day, that I'm sure is blue topaz. It looked as if it had fallen out of someone's necklace.'

Iain's responded by looking at Liam and Elizabeth and saying,

'I hope you two are still wearing your amulets?'

'We are,' said Elizabeth, 'But, I'm not feeling convinced that it would offer much protection against what I saw out there.'

Iain pulled out the chain that was around his neck, that had been hidden by his shirt.

'I've worn this for years and it has always kept me safe. This is the seal of the seven Archangels.'

It was a circular gold pendant that looked tarnished and aged, with triangular shapes dividing it into sections. Each section had some writing and various symbols etched on it.

'Each section represents an Archangel, whose powers of protection and healing are imparted into the amulet.'

'Sounds powerful, 'Elizabeth pointed out, 'Maybe one of us should be wearing that one.'

'It would be extremely dangerous if worn by an inexperienced person.'

'Inexperienced in what way?' asked Elizabeth.

'In what we are dealing with right now.'

Iain continued, this time addressing the whole group.

'I think we should stay here, in the house, for the time being. The Elfin Knight might have been affected in some way by the soldiers firing at him, not hurt, but perhaps unaccustomed to such things, so might have gone back to his realm temporarily.'

Lou could not keep the fear out of her voice when she said.

'For all we know, those poor soldiers could be lying dead or injured in the forest. Shouldn't we go and see if they need help?'

Iain disagreed and said.

'I'm sure someone managed to radio a message to whoever their superiors are, when it all started and I doubt that the Elfin Knight would have killed them all, I don't think that would be his aim.'

Lou was shocked at this comment.

'His actions don't sound very reasonable to me. The fact that he was most likely aiming to take my friend and what he did to Lady Isobel originally.'

Iain contradicted this.

'Yes, I agree, he probably is aiming to take Elizabeth, but we have no evidence that he hurt Isobel and I really don't think he would want to hurt Elizabeth either.'

Lou was just getting started.

'No, he would just take her back to his realm for an indefinite period and do god knows what to her!'

'Thanks!' Elizabeth said.

'If it would help, Fred and I will send a drone over the forest and see if we can pick anything up.'

'You have a drone in that holdall too?!'

Fred looked astonished at this comment and said,

'No, of course not, it's in the car boot.'

Fred operated the drone, flying it over the forest and the camp. Watching on his laptop screen, they saw no evidence of bodies lying on the ground, nothing else was evident apart from the crater by the tree.

'That's really not right.' said Liam. 'Where are they all? Someone should be walking around.'

Iain tried to sound reassuring.

'They are probably inside or they may have driven away.'

'Let's hope,' said Liam, 'Though would that not be unusual in this sort of situation, to simply desert the place?'

'I doubt they have a protocol for a situation like this,' said Iain.

They were all distracted by June reappearing, after her rest, feeling much better she said.

'What have I missed?' she asked.

Iain updated her and reminded Lou to give her the necklace. June said,

'I had an extremely strange dream just now, very different from the dreams I usually have. I'm sure it must mean something.'

Iain asked her to elaborate.

'It was as if I was flying, no, rather floating and all around me was this pale blue light. I wasn't scared, but I couldn't move, I was being pulled along by something I couldn't see. Then, I started to hear a voice, a woman's voice, she was singing. It was beautiful and sounded Gaelic, but it was hard to make out, though I'm sure I could hear the words 'whar ghorten han grun oarlac' or something very similar to that.'

'What does that mean?' asked Elizabeth.

'Where the harts run yearly,' replied June.

'Could you see the person singing?'

'No, the singing eventually faded out, but the blue light seemed to get brighter until it was dazzling me, then I woke up with a start.'

They all looked at Iain expectantly.

'I'm no expert in dream analysis, but, yes, that sounds interesting. Let me think about it.'

'Has anyone had any thoughts about why the blood did not work?' June directed this question towards Iain.

'Fred and I are still trying to work that out. It could be that the blood has, for some reason, had the reverse effect and strengthened the Elfin Knight, or perhaps too much time has passed and the blood has travelled through too many generations. It could even make some difference if certain bloodlines have been mixed together over the generations.'

Liam was puzzled by this.

'What do you mean by that? About certain bloodlines?'

'It's purely speculation, but if your ancestors were mainly Scottish, or at least Celtic, that would keep the bloodline stronger, but if you, for example, had some ancestors from a very different part of the world, that might impact.'

'Well, according to your family tree, my ancestors are either Scottish or Irish" said Liam, then looking meaningfully at Elizabeth.

'I suppose I could be the weak link here. I don't have any information about my birth father, apart from the information I got from the dna test I did a few years ago. My ethnic make-up came out as 49 percent Irish/Scottish and 51 percent Greek, so that's a bit of a clue there!'

Iain repeated.

'As I said, this is only a guess. There could be other reasons that the blood was not successful. That part of the original story could be inaccurate, maybe we're missing something else that should be used to send the Elfin Knight back.'

Liam, with a slight note of frustration to his voice, said,

'We need to move on from this, debating why the blood did not work does not seem helpful now. Surely, what we do next is more important? We can't stay holed up in here for much longer.'

Iain tried to reassure Liam.

'No one is expecting you to do that, but for today and tonight it's our safest option. The protection spell won't last that long and he will be able to find a way around it eventually. My suggestion is that Lou and June go home,' quickly adding, 'But come back in the morning, by which time, I hope to have come up with our next move, with Fred's assistance.'

Lou and June agreed, Lou knew that her husband's suspicions would be roused, if she stayed away too long and June said that the people in the village who knew her, might start asking questions if they saw the tourist information office shut and were not able to find her. Elizabeth felt sad when they left, but knew it was for the best. She partly wished that they were not coming back tomorrow, she would rather they were kept away from it, but knew that was unlikely with two such formidable characters. As they left the house, Iain said,

'Get straight into your car and drive the most direct route home and don't stop at all.'

They didn't question this.

When they had gone, Elizabeth went into the sitting room and sat on the sofa, with her head back against the cushions. After about ten minutes, Liam came in and asked if she would like a drink.

'Yes please, there's some wine in the fridge.'

'I had noticed. I'm going to nip back to my place and grab some food. You're a bit low on supplies.'

She looked perturbed by this.

'Do you think you should?'

'It'll be fine. I'll be very quick.'

He came back in with a glass of wine and said,

'See you in less than fifteen minutes.'

When she heard the front door shut, she felt so tense and ill at ease and found herself unable to sit down, constantly listening for sounds outside. Fifteen minutes passed and he was not back. She went into the kitchen, where Iain and Fred were and said,

'He should be back by now!'

Iain looked up at her, apparently unperturbed.

'He'll be careful. I think we can safely give him another five minutes or so.'

Elizabeth went back into the sitting room and looked out of the window and when she saw Liam's unmistakable form walk up the path, carrying a box, she rushed to the front door.

'You were longer than fifteen minutes!'

'Ah, don't tell me you were worried about me?'

She wasn't sure what she felt, it was an uncomfortable mixture of fear, anger and something else that she could not describe. As she sat on the sofa, she also felt mildly guilty, as she was not helping in the kitchen, though was coming to the conclusion that Liam was a better cook than her and seemed to enjoy it too. She wandered into the kitchen, mainly to seek out another glass of wine and was greeted by some very tempting cooking smells. Liam turned to from the cooker and said,

'Good timing, this is pretty much ready now.'

'Smells good, what is it?'

'It's only some pasta with sauce.'

The sauce turned out to be homemade and delicious and there was also salad and bread on the table. The four of them ate, all hungrier than they had realised, no one in the mood for too much conversation. Iain and Fred did not want to linger over the meal, they were impatient to get back to their research. Elizabeth insisted on washing up, telling Liam to sit down as he had done all the cooking, to which he did not object. When she had finished, she found him in the sitting room, with his eyes shut. She wanted to retrieve her phone and her glasses, so she could go to bed, but they were on the arm of the sofa, right next to him. She crept over to him as quietly as she could, but stealth had never been her strong point, (as her ex had so kindly pointed out to her,) and when she was reaching for her phone, he woke up with a jolt and grabbed her arm. This made her jump and exclaim,

'Jesus!'

Liam was a bit befuddled for a moment, but then, realising what he had done, apologised to her profusely.

'I haven't hurt your arm?'

'No, it's fine, I was just getting my phone, I want to go to bed now.'

'Yes, you should, it's been quite a day. Don't worry, we'll all be down here and I somehow don't expect those two will sleep much. When Iain has his teeth into something, he is unstoppable"

'He's impressive, and Fred too, you're lucky to have him as a friend.'

She walked towards the door, saying good night to him, as she went.

'Goodnight Elizabeth, see you tomorrow.'

She hesitated and looked back at him.

'Thank you.'

'For what?' he asked, sounding a little bewildered.

'For getting me out of there.'

'Well, I was hardly going to leave you behind, was I? Anyway, I think you would have managed on your own, just as well.'

Elizabeth was going to contradict this, but decided to leave and walked out the door.

Chapter Twenty Two

Sledgehammer

Elizabeth suddenly felt like she was hitting a brick wall of tiredness, as she reached the top of the stairs. She brushed her teeth in the bathroom and lay in her bed, not getting undressed. As she was drifting off to sleep, a poem that her father used to say to her when she was a child, came into her mind. He used to sit next to her on her bed, when she was having trouble getting to sleep or she had woken from a bad dream and say it quietly, in his soft Devonshire burr.

'Into the dimpsey you go
I'd like to follow but I know
This is one journey you must take alone
I must let you go
I see you fading in the soft mauve light
Your form disappearing
Until you are beyond my sight

I reach for you

I murmur your name

But into the dimpsey you have gone'

He had written it himself and was very proud of it. Elizabeth secretly thought that he got some enjoyment from having to explain to the uninitiated what the dimpsey was. He would proudly say, in his strongest accent, that it was a Devonshire word for the twilight, (but not just any twilight, a special one, of course, unique to Devon). Tonight it made her cry, wishing she could get a hug from her Dad right now and have him make this all go away.

Another dream; she feels cold, she is walking through trees in the dark, suddenly the ground starts falling away beneath her feet and she has to run, as fast as she can, to get away from the collapsing earth. She jumps to the side and is crawling desperately, trying to find somewhere safe. She woke up with a start, relieved it was only a dream and opened her eyes, but instead of her bedroom ceiling, she saw trees and a dark sky. She was lying on the ground, somewhere in the forest. She was too scared to move at first, worried that she was injured, but after carefully moving her arms and legs, realised that she was unhurt, just cold and extremely confused. A loud noise shocked her out of this confusion a little, a noise she had heard before, a low, rumbling noise. It was him. She wanted to cry out, but knew she could not, she had to hide. She stood up a little shakily and tried to think where to go. She had no idea where she was, so all she could do was run away from the noise. She ran, stumbling a few times, until she reached a dense thicket of tall bushes, which she crawled under. She tried to make herself as small and quiet as possible. The sound grew closer and she started to be able to make out footsteps. She had never felt such fear. Her instinct told her to leave something for the others to find, so she took off her ring and placed it on the ground next to her. She knew he was right on the other side of the bushes in front of her. She could hear his breathing and smell him, a damp, woody smell. She closed her eyes, as if that would prevent him from finding her and curled herself into the smallest shape that she was able to, waiting for the inescapable.

Liam woke up on the sofa, with an intense feeling of fear. He had not had a bad dream and had not heard anything, but still felt extremely disturbed. He walked out into the hallway, where he could hear Iain and Fred talking to each other in the kitchen, and went upstairs. He quietly opened Elizabeth's bedroom door and peered around. The bed looked empty, but he still went over to check. She wasn't in the bathroom or anywhere else in the house. He pulled on his boots and grabbed his coat, shouting to the others as he left the house.

'Elizabeth's gone! He must have taken her!'

Iain and Fred came running out of the kitchen, with Iain shouting after him.

'Liam, wait! Please don't go out there!'

Their pleas were in vain, as he ran towards the forest. He did not know which direction to head, or if she was even in the forest, but had no idea what else he could do. He had to slow down when the trees started to close in around him and cursed when his foot went down into a hole in the ground. He kept going until he knew he was getting closer to the Ash tree. He stopped, remembering the crater that stood in front of it. As he caught his breath and tried to think about his next move, he heard something, a scream, Elizabeth, he thought and started to run again, towards the sound. He suddenly felt like he was running in slow motion and losing control of his limbs. He tried to shout out her name, but nothing came out and he was falling forwards, but he never reached the ground.

Elizabeth could still sense him on the other side of the bushes, but he had not yet made any attempt to grab her. She began to wonder if he did not actually realise that she was there and the smallest amount of hope started to creep into her mind. She started to open her eyes and when she did all she could see was a pair of glowing eyes searing through the dense undergrowth. She was unable to stop herself letting out a scream, expecting an attack.

The glowing eyes disappeared, as the leaves and branches that were shrouding her, started to fall away. What stood in front of her, when her last defence had all gone, was not the dark, indefinite shape that she had seen before, he had taken on the form of a man, tall and lean, with long, flowing dark hair, very pale skin and eyes that looked black. He wore robes that floated around him and was surrounded by light, as if he had the sun shining behind him. Elizabeth opened her mouth, but could not make a sound, all she could do was look at him. He extended his hand towards her and she found herself reaching her hand out to his, unable to stop herself.

The hand that took hers was warm and felt remarkably human. As soon as her hand was in his, she started to rise up from the ground, but not to land on her feet. She felt as if she was floating in warm sunlight, through the trees, with no fear and nothing mattering to her, apart from the sensations and sounds she was experiencing at that moment. She gradually began to feel a little more awareness of her surroundings and realised they had come to the edge of the forest and ahead of them was the hill She did not understand what they would do now, go around it or over it, He turned around to her, as if sensing her concern and she looked at that pale, long face, with its dark, unfathomable eyes. His nose long and fine, his mouth a straight line. He looked like a stone carving she had seen on a recent visit, with her youngest son, to the Victoria and Albert Museum in London. The carving was originally from a Priory in Herefordshire and was meant to represent Jesus, but, to her, looked more Pagan than Christian. She remembered how struck she had been by this image, standing in front of it for so long, her son had come back to find her, wondering where she was. Looking at his face made her feel calm, the type of calmness she had never experienced before and she felt herself drifting.

When she became conscious again, if conscious was the correct description of what she was currently experiencing, they appeared to have found their way inside the hill, as if a tunnel had opened up ahead of them She could still feel his hand around hers, not pulling her, even though she was moving forwards through the dark tunnel. They suddenly stopped and looking ahead, she saw him raise his arm towards the wall of rock in front of them, which signified the end of the tunnel. As he did so, an arched entrance way appeared in the rock, with a blue light on the other side of it. He turned to her, as if to reassure her and led her through into a vast cave. It was not dark, a pale blue light gently pulsed around the walls and ceiling of the cave. Looking down, she could not make out the floor of the cave. There was a narrow walkway of stone, wide enough for one person at a time, but there was nothing but darkness on either side of it. Despite this, she was not frightened, finding herself almost revelling in the feeling of weightlessness, as he continued to guide her through the cave. Another wall of rock faced them, but this time there was a huge wooden door within it that opened as he got close to it. What she saw on the other side of it was unlike anything she had ever imagined.

Chapter Twenty Three
Everybody Hurts

Liam dreamt that someone was calling his name, over and over, until he realised that Iain really was kneeling over him, trying to get him to wake up.

'Come on old chap, there you go, welcome back.'

Opening his eyes, he slowly became aware that he was lying outside, in the dark forest. It took him longer than usual to gather his thoughts and to remember what had happened. Piece by piece, it came back to him, like the morning after a heavy night of drinking, with what you did and said the night before, coming back to you, in small drips, until it floods in all at once. He tried to stand up too quickly, resulting in him nearly falling back to the ground, with Iain's steady hands the only thing stopping this from happening.

'Whoa, not so quick!' said Iain.

He stood still for a few moments and came to the conclusion that he was not hurt, but his head felt as if it weighed too much for his body. He brushed the twigs off, that still clung to him and picked some damp leaves from his face.

'How about telling me what happened here? Can you remember?' asked Iain, finding it hard to leave the concern out of his voice.

'I'm not sure, I was running, looking for her and I heard her scream. I tried to run towards her, but I felt like I couldn't control my own legs and I started to fall. That's honestly all I can remember.'

At this point, he started to walk away, but Iain rushed towards him, grabbing his arm, none too gently, whilst saying,

'Where do you think you're going? You're not in any state to be wandering around alone.'

'We need to keep looking, she might still be in here.'

Iain lessened his grip on Liam's arm and said.

'I agree, but we need to think about where we're looking, rather than heading off in random directions.'

Liam started to feel a bit unsteady again and sat back on the ground, watching Iain, as he shone his torch on the ground surrounding the spot where he had found him, occasionally picking up bits of earth and stones.

'Have you found anything?' Liam asked after a few minutes, though he realised he would let him know if he had, he just felt so useless sitting there.

'No, but she probably went this way, look at the ground, and how it's churned up. This could have been her, or, more likely, him following her.'

Liam felt lightheaded and put his head down on his knees.

'Oh God, this is bad isn't it? We're not going to get her back!'

'Liam, I know you're scared for her, we all are, but we need to look at this methodically. Are you able to get up now?' In a tone that was now a little firmer.

He did and they started to follow the churned up earth, until they reached what looked like a dense cluster of bushes that had been pulled up from the ground.

Liam said,

'It looks like she might have tried to hide here and this was where he caught up with her.'

'We don't know that for sure, but, yes, it's entirely possible.'

Liam noticed something on the ground, partly covered with a leaf. It was a ring, a silver ring, with a pale lilac stone set in the top.

'This is hers. She is always wearing it. Clever girl, she must have left it for us.'

Iain looked around and said,

'The trail seems to end here, there's no more evidence of tracks or disturbed ground. He must have travelled from here, by some other means.'

'Well, how the hell are we supposed to find that?'

Iain put his hand on Liam's arm, in an attempt to calm him.

'Think about the original story of Orfeo, when the Elfin Knight took Isobel, they travelled through the forest and then through a hill, which led them to the entrance to his realm.'

'This is supposed to help how?' asked Liam

Iain, without replying, started to walk off ahead of Liam, turning back to him, only to say,

'Well, are you coming with me or not?'

They walked for nearly half an hour, until they reached the edge of the forest. Ahead of them, the hill started its slow incline.

'Now what?' Liam said a little more caustically than he intended. 'The hill parts before us?'

Much to Liam's surprise, Iain took out a mobile phone from his jacket pocket.

'I thought you hated them?'

'Fred convinced me that it would be a sensible idea for situations like this.'

He somehow managed to get a signal and made a call to Fred, back at the house, asking him to look something up for him in the Grimoire.

'What did you ask Fred to find for you?'

'To look for a particular spell, one that will, hopefully, help us with our current predicament.'

Within five minutes, Iain's phone pinged to let him know he had a text from Fred. He studied the message for a minute or two and then turned to Liam.

'You might want to stand back a bit.'

Iain began to recite something, in what sounded to Liam like Latin. He did not understand what he was saying, despite the fact that he had been made to study Latin in school.

'Deus magne montis, te rogamus, permitte nos ambulare intra te'

He repeated it three times and waited, but nothing happened. He repeated it again and again, until after the tenth or eleventh time, they heard a deep rumbling noise and a tunnel entrance formed in front of them, it was as if the rock had simply evaporated. Iain turned to a stunned looking Liam and said in a matter of fact tone,

'Shall we?'

They started to walk into the tunnel and as they did, the earth and rock parted cleanly in front of them, to allow the tunnel to go ever deeper into the hill.

'What did that mean, what you were saying back there?' asked Liam

'God of the great mountain, we beseech thee, let us walk within thee.'

was his reply, as if it was something he uttered every day.

It was pitch black within the tunnel, but, thankfully, Iain had his torch, although this made little impact on the sheer depth of the darkness around them. Liam said to Iain,

'Give me your mobile phone and I can use the torch on it.'

Iain handed it over to him, expressing surprise that it had such a facility The tunnel was cold and silent. Liam's fear of what might lie ahead or of the tunnel collapsing onto them, was overtaken by his strong desire to find Elizabeth and the thought of what she might be currently experiencing.

After walking for about twenty minutes, they reached a huge expanse of extremely solid rock. Iain tried the incantation again and several times after that, but nothing moved, not even a tiny fragment of rock. He turned to Liam and admitted that he had no idea what to do now and that they would have to go back. They walked back through the tunnel and when they came out, Liam said,

'Should we leave the entrance open? We might not be able to get back in if we don't.'

Iain did not have to answer this, as the tunnel entrance began to disappear of its own accord, as if a veil of grass, earth and stone had been lowered seamlessly over it.

'If you call Fred again, will he be able to find you another spell, to get us through the rock?'

Iain looked uncharacteristically downcast, when he said,

'No, the spell I was using should have worked on the rock wall too. I really don't know why it did not. I'll need to confer with Fred again, back at the cottage.'

Seeing Liam's anguished face, he tried to soften his words.

'Give us some more time and we will find another way. Please, don't lose faith Liam.'

'I don't think faith has got anything to do with this.'

Chapter Twenty Four

Jai Bajarangi

Dawn was starting to break, as they walked side by side, in silence, back through the forest. When they had almost reached the edge of it and were in sight of the garden wall, a voice called out to them, from the direction they had come from, making them jump and turn around. They were greeted by the sight of a young man, in his twenties, tall and lean, with very short dark hair, wearing a dark jacket and jeans. He looked vaguely familiar to Liam, but he could not think how.

'Hey, wait, you were here the other day with a woman, over by that tree, I was the one who said you had to leave.' This was directed towards Liam.

'Oh, yes, I thought I recognised you.'

His next question was aimed at both of them.

'Were you here the other night, when that thing attacked us?'

Liam and Iain exchanged glances and Iain said,

'What exactly did you see?'

'The same thing that you did, I'm sure, or why would you be here now? What happened to the others?'

'Which others are you talking about?'

'The woman you were with when I saw you and the other two women, the mother and daughter. The mother was claiming to have broken her ankle, but I was not convinced, although I didn't want to say that at the time. What on earth have you all been up to?'

Iain said,

'It's a very long and unlikely story. Too much to explain to you out here.'

What are you doing here and where are your colleagues?'

'They've all gone.'

Liam was horrified.

'You mean, they are all dead!'

'No, they are doing fine now, they are recovering in a military hospital, but I was unaffected and have been given a bit of leave.'

'So you decided to come back here for your break? Interesting choice!' said Liam dubiously,

'I had to, I needed to understand what it was that I saw out there. Was it some type of demon?'

Iain looked at him directly and said,

'Not exactly, but, yes, something from a different realm. If you'd like to come back to the cottage over there with us, we can explain.'

Liam shot Iain a sharp look.

'Thank you so much, I was terrified that it might go on some kind of rampage in the village, though none of my colleagues were actually hurt, they were just in some kind of trance for a while. We shot at it, as that was all we could do, but when our bullets had no effect, we retreated. Back at the mess, I realised I was the only one still standing.'

Iain looked curiously at him.

'You were the only one unaffected?'

'Yes, I'm not sure why. I'm Sunil by the way.'

Iain and Liam introduced themselves and they all walked back to the cottage.

Fred was waiting for them anxiously and this was rapidly replaced by confusion when he saw Sunil, although he seemed pretty accepting when his presence was explained, They sat down with Sunil and told him what had been going on and how Elizabeth had disappeared, They also told him what had happened in the hill and why they had come back, Sunil was a careful listener and picked up what they were saying quickly and without judgement or overreaction. They were interrupted by a car pulling up outside. Liam exclaimed,

'Lou and June! They're early. I almost forgot about them in all this. They are not going to be happy.'

Iain said,

'They can hardly blame us for Elizabeth disappearing.'

'Oh, I think they can,' said Liam with a strong sense of foreboding.

'What do you mean, she disappeared in the night? Why weren't you keeping a proper eye on each other? She should never have been left alone!'

It was hard to work out whether Lou was angry or upset, but whatever her current emotional state, she was formidable at the same time. Liam objected.

'It was her choice to go up to her room. We could not very well prevent her or go in there with her.'

'I think, in the circumstances, you could have.'

Iain, ever the voice of reason.

'Lou, I understand your frustration, we're feeling it too, but we need to focus now and think of a new way to get through to his realm.'

'And who is this?' looking at Sunil.

'Hi, I'm Sunil, we have actually met before, in the forest, when your mother fell over.'

Lou and June turned a rather fetching shade of pink and apologised to Sunil for their deception.

'That's ok, I would have done the same thing, You did a good job. I brought it, well, for a bit anyway.'

Iain and Fred went into a huddle in the kitchen, pouring over the Grimoire and Fred's laptop, occasionally muttering and pointing at something. Lou and June quizzed Sunil about what exactly he had seen, as well as asking him unrelated questions about his family and his time in the Army, whilst Liam, as usual, kept the coffee on tap. He would rather have been taking a sledgehammer to the rocks in that tunnel, but in reality, knew that was futile and that he would have to wait for Iain and Fred to come up with something.

They all visibly jumped when the landline in the cottage rang. Lou answered it hesitantly, with the others hearing her say,

'No, I'm sorry, she is not here at the moment. Can I ask who is calling?'

'Oh, I see, yes, I'm her friend, Louise, and she told me about her visit to your home and how much she enjoyed talking to you.'

'That sounds really interesting, I'm afraid she is unlikely to be back for the next day or so, but I'm sure she would be fine with me coming to take a look. Would that be ok with you?'

'That's fantastic, I can be there within an hour.'

She put the phone down and said to the room,

'That was Roderick, or should I say Earl Ross. Elizabeth visited his castle over at Strathconon the other day and spent some time talking to him and when she came back, she said it was really useful.'

'How did he get this number?' asked Liam with some suspicion.

'He said she had told him where she lived, but, come to think of it, he was a bit shady about how he got the number. You know, these aristocrats, they have connections all over the place. I don't think the methods he may have used to get her number are that important, do you? What's more important is that he has found some items that she would probably find very helpful. He said he has letters and a portrait he wants to show her.'

Liam was not convinced.

'Sounds like it could wait'

Lou was obviously not in the mood for backing down.

'I don't think it can, not if these items are connected to Orfeo and Isobel in some way.'

Iain was in agreement and backed Lou up by saying,

'If he felt it was important enough, to go to the trouble of finding Elizabeth's phone number, it could be worth following up. From the sound of it, he's happy for you to go in her place?'

'Yes, if June agrees, I'll take her with me.'

June was more than happy to do so and they left straight away, with Iain calling after them,

'Please call us if you think it could help us.'

When they had driven away, Sunil said,

'I would really like to help here, but I feel a little superfluous to requirements.'

Iain reassured him.

'Not at all, I think you are here for a very important reason. No one that you have met today, is here by accident. All of us have a part to play in this.'

'But I have no idea what mine is.'

'You did not succumb to the Elfin Knight's power, you stayed conscious, I would say that was pretty significant. Have you had any similar experiences in the past?'

'I can't say I've ever crossed paths with a mythical figure before.'

'No, I don't mean that, I'm talking about any occasions when those around have been affected by something, but you have not, or a time when you have been protected somehow?'

Sunil thought for a moment and said,

'When I was younger, in my hometown ...' he tailed off

'Carry on,' Iain encouraged

'This is going to sound bizarre.'

Liam looked at him slightly incredulously and said,

'I wouldn't worry about that, considering what we have all experienced here.'

'Okay then, a group of us got hold of a Ouija Board, I know, we should have known better, and broke into a derelict building to use it. Basically, we scared ourselves stupid and ran out of the place in terror.'

'What had you seen?' Iain asked.

'A sound like a howling wind and things falling over and windows shattering. It was terrifying.'

He stopped for a moment or two.

'Within days after, my friends were all taken ill, one quite seriously, though he did recover.'

'And you?'

'I was fine, no different. My friends were though and none of them had what I would call happy lives so far.'

'I think this is your answer,' said Iain.

'You seem to have some kind of immunity or inbuilt protection against the powers that presences from other realms might try to use against us. We need you here. Did your parents ever say anything to you about this?'

'Funnily enough, my mother always had this story, that I found hard to believe, about how when she took me to my grandmother's home in Northern India, when I was little, we visited a shrine to Bajrang Bali, a Hindu Deva, and that she prayed to him and placed my tiny hand on his statue.'

Fred had been busying himself looking up information on the internet about this and found a page regarding Bajrang Bali.

'According to this, Bajrang or Vajrang Bali was blessed by the gods with, (amongst other things,) immunity from celestial weapons, extreme speed and to be free from fears of death. He also received the eight Siddhis, which include clairvoyance, levitation, bilocation and astral projection, materialisation, and having access to memories from past lives.'

Sunil looked surprised.

'I wouldn't say I had been blessed with any of those things. I am not that fast anymore, I definitely can't levitate and I can assure you I have a very real fear of death.'

'These things are often not so literal. You could have been blessed with a very small part of this, perhaps the immunity from celestial weapons or powers.'

'My mother is going to be so happy, when she finds out that she was right all along.'

Iain said,

'Bit of a long shot, but would it be possible for you to talk to your mother and ask her a bit more about this, the prayer she said might be useful.'

'I can try, she'd be overjoyed that I'm showing an interest at last, though she might ask some awkward questions.'

Iain smiled at him.

'I'm sure you'll cope admirably with them.'

Sunil disappeared to call his mother, returning nearly half an hour later, looking sheepish.

'Sorry I took so long. I haven't spoken to her for a while, so we had a lot to catch up on. Don't worry, I didn't tell her anything about what is going on here, although she was pretty suspicious about why I was asking about the prayer.'

'What did you tell her?' inquired Iain.

'That I was thinking about her and the story about Bajrang Bali and trying to remember the mantra. This seemed to satisfy her curiosity, but the trouble now is she thinks that I am finally becoming more interested in religion. I've written down the mantra for you. She said that there are several different mantras, but this was the particular one she chanted.'

'Do you know why she chose this one in particular?' Iain asked.

'She said that she felt it was the one with the most power, as it is supposed to get rid of diseases and evil spirits, as well as giving you courage and strength. Here, I've written it down and she gave me the English translation too.'

Iain studied the piece of paper Sunil had handed him and read aloud, after apologising for any mispronunciations.

'Om Namo Bhagvate Aanjaneyaay Mahaabalaay Swaahaa Rama Priya Namastubhyam Hanuman Raksh Sarvadaa'

'What does it mean?' asked Liam.

'I bow down and surrender to Lord Hanuman, he who is the son of the powerful Anjana'

'Seems quite simple,' said Liam.

Sunil added,

'She said you're supposed to recite it one hundred and eight times, while facing East, in front of the idol of the Lord Hanuman.'

'Hmm,' said Iain, 'That might be a bit difficult here, but thanks so much for doing that Sunil. Sounds like a bit of improvisation is going to be in order.'

'One other thing I meant to mention,' said Sunil.

'Before all this happened, I had a bit of a strange experience in the forest. I know it sounds ridiculous to describe it as strange, in the light of what has just taken place, but, I don't know, it rattled me.'

'Go on,' said Iain.

Sunil described how he had felt something or someone behind him, as if they were gently pushing his back and the golden light behind the trees that had disappeared when he tried to get close to it. Liam sounded dismissive when he said,

'Sounds like nothing, the breeze or the light playing tricks,'

Sunil did not respond to this and Iain leapt in.

'That's interesting Sunil, Fred and I will definitely add it to our list of things to look into,' casting a curious look at Liam, at the same time.

Chapter Twenty Five

Ever Fallen In Love

Lou and June pulled into the castle grounds and continued along the impressive, tree lined drive that led up to it. Roderick had instructed them to ignore the public car park and drive around to the right of the castle, where they would find a security gate marked private. Lou buzzed the intercom, giving their names and the gate automatically opened for them. They found themselves in a small car park with two very expensive looking cars in it. A door in the castle opened and out came a tall, lean, very aristocratic looking man of around eighty. Lou had not been sure what to expect, although he had sounded friendly enough on the phone, but she need not have worried, as they were both greeted warmly and ushered into the castle. He led them through a long, not particularly well lit, passage, with thick stone walls, hung with pictures that they did not have time to stop and admire, eventually ending up in a room which Lou presumed was his study. It was a surprisingly cosy room for a castle, warm paint colours and rugs on the floor and thick velvet curtains. The walls were lined with books and the desk piled with even more books. There were a few comfortable chairs in front of the desk, with a small table between them.

'Please sit down, can I get you a drink of some kind? Tea? Coffee? Something stronger?'

'Coffee would be lovely,' said June.

'Ai, for me too, thank you,' said Lou.

Much to Lou's relief he did not ring a bell for a servant, as she had expected him to, but disappeared for a bit and returned carrying the tray himself, laden with cups, a coffee pot, sugar, milk and a plate of biscuits.

'Please, help yourself to coffee and the biscuits are homemade.'

Once they all had what they wanted, Roderick said,

'I hope Elizabeth is not unwell. I really did enjoy my chat with her the other day and she seemed so interested in learning about the history of this area.'

Lou replied, attempting to maintain the most neutral tone possible.

'She's not unwell, just had to sort out a personal matter for a few days. We're hoping she'll be back soon.'

He was not giving up that easily.

'Oh dear, that sounds a bit serious. Has she had to go back down South?'

'No, she's still fairly local.'

She could see he was not looking convinced so changed the subject.

'We're very interested in seeing what you have found, June and I have been speculating on the way here. We both have a strong interest in history. I'm a History teacher at a high school and June runs the tourist information office in our village.'

Roderick looked at June, with his twinkling blue eyes.

'I've always wondered who ran that office, I regret not ever having come in. You must have so much local knowledge. Have you lived here all your life?'

'Yes, I have, as have generations of my family, as far back as they can remember.'

'Sounds a bit like mine!'

June looked at him dubiously, but did not say more about this.

He got up and moved over to his desk, picking up a very old-looking wooden box, about the size of a large shoe box. It was made of a dark wood, with a carved pattern on the lid, inlaid with a cream coloured, pearlescent material. As he brought it over to them, Lou stood up and removed the coffee tray, placing it on another table. He put the box down and carefully opened it.

'This is quite fragile, though considering it is at least six hundred years old, it is in pretty good condition. I found this in one of the storerooms, one that I have not been in for many years. After my conversation with Elizabeth, something was telling me to go and look in there and I am so glad I did and I think you'll agree with me. It was extremely well hidden, but I had to persevere.'

He took out a book, an extremely old book. not particularly large, maybe around eight inches by six inches. It was bound in what looked like leather, which would once have been a deep reddish brown colour There was nothing written on the front of it, but a fairly elaborate, geometric pattern was carved into it.

'This is yet another example of my ancestors acquiring things from other noble families in the area. Perhaps when Sir Orfeo left his castle, items were left behind or I would not be surprised if they came by it through nefarious means.'

He started to delicately turn the thin pages, which were full of an antiquated and hard to decipher style of handwriting.

'It was unusual for women, in the fifteenth century, to write about anything other than religious matters, so I find this remarkable. This appears to have been written by Sir Orfeo's wife, Lady Isobel.'

Lou and June were stunned.

'What is she writing about?' asked Lou

'She writes about her child, who she adores, and her love of nature and being outdoors. She particularly loved the forest and she talked about a certain tree a lot, an Ash tree I believe. It is also very sad, she seems unhappy, as if she is always yearning for something.'

'Does she say what?' was Lou's next question.

'She just refers to 'him' a lot, but the way she writes about him is quite beautiful. It feels contemporary. Here, let me read you an example of what I mean. If you don't object, I'll put it into modern English, as all that 'thee' and 'whence' will become a bit tiresome.'

'Even when he was not with me, I could always sense his presence. No danger could ever befall me, if he was near me, he would not allow this. At the same time, I was free to run through the fields and the forests, to lie in the long grass next to the river, watching the birds soar through the bright blue sky. He was not always there, but he was always with me. Now, I feel cold and alone. Were it not for my son, I would feel no purpose. '

Lou and June sat in silence, processing what they had heard. Roderick continued,

'From this point it gets even more interesting. She recounts a story of what happened to her, when she disappeared for seven years, at least, she tries to. Listen to this part.'

'At times, it feels as if it were nothing but a dream. I fear for my memories fading, as dreams often disappear on waking. I could not bear to lose my recollections of that place, of the light and the space and, of course, of him.'

She also talks about a Steward, who she describes as holding the complete trust of her husband and how his loyalty was incomparable. She mentions how kind he was to her and how she felt he was one of the few people in the castle who had some concept of what she had been through.'

Lou looked at June.

'That must be your ancestor?'

'Yes, that's right, It's incredible actually hearing about him from someone that knew him.'

Roderick got up at this point and said,

'I've got something else to show you.'

He walked towards a picture that was leaning, the wrong way round, against one of the walls. He turned it toward them and they saw a portrait of a Medieval woman.

'I found this wrapped in layers of paper and cloth, tucked away behind some old furniture and pieces of wood. It is incredible it has not been damaged.'

She had reddish brown hair tucked under a dark blue headdress that looked as if it was made out of velvet, very pale skin, fine features and bright, golden brown eyes. Around her neck was an ornate, golden cross, inlaid with five, pale blue jewels. Lou pulled out her evil eye amulet that Iain had given to her and pointing out the blue stone in the centre of it she said,

'It looks like the same stone. Iain said this was blue topaz.'

Roderick agreed with her and turning the portrait around, pointed to some writing in the lower right hand corner, saying.

'I'm not sure if you will be able to make this out, the writing is very small, but it undoubtedly says, 'Lady Isobel Mackenzie, 1471.'

Lou and June, in turn, leant down to look at this, squinting their eyes to bring the writing into focus.

'You're right" exclaimed Lou "This is incredible, to actually see what she looked like, It's almost too much to take in. She looks beautiful here, so serene, though a little sad too.'

Lou and June spent several minutes gazing at Isobel's portrait, until Roderick interrupted them.

'Elizabeth seemed very interested in this family when she came here. Does she have some personal connection to them?'

Lou and June were not sure how to answer this and the combination of their hesitancy and the looks they were exchanging, led him to ask.

'Has something happened to her? Is that why she is not here?'

Lou burst into tears.

'Oh my dear, I didn't mean to upset you, please have this, I promise it's clean.'

She dabbed her face with the large white handkerchief she was handed, with the letters RM elaborately embroidered onto it in deep red thread. June stepped in.

'I'm afraid we haven't been truthful with you, but there's a good reason for this.'

She went on to tell him what had taken place, starting from the beginning when Elizabeth first came to live in the cottage. Roderick sat in astonished silence when she had finished. Lou, who had just about managed to gather herself said,

'So you can understand why we didn't tell you this straight away. We're trying to involve as few people as possible, but I'm beginning to think that we are not going to be able to deal with this ourselves and that we might have lost her.'

The sobs started again.

'What am I going to tell her boys?'

Roderick patted her hand and June put her arm around her, saying,

'If anyone can handle this, that fellow Iain can and I don't think Liam will give up either. I haven't met any of these people, but from what you have said, it seems that exactly the right people are working to get her back. What could the authorities do? They would have no understanding of what is at play here. They would simply treat her as a missing person.'

'Or worse,' said Lou, 'And accuse one of us of murdering her!'

June, in an attempt to steer Lou away from this train of thought, said,

'Roderick, we are so grateful for all this. You have done more than you needed to. I'm sure we have taken up enough of your time. We should be going.'

'You're right, you need to get this back to your friends, so that they can see if there is anything of use to them. You do not need to thank me. As anyone who knows me will tell you, I am generally a very sceptical person when it comes to anything supernatural, but that box was really calling to me - I find it impossible to describe the feeling - and without moving it, I wouldn't have found the portrait.'

When Roderick handed the box and the portrait over to them, June said,

'We promise to be very careful with them and bring them back to you as soon as we can.'

'No, I want you to keep them and hand them to Elizabeth when she comes back. They are part of her heritage, and this Liam's of course. One thing you can do for me is tell me as soon as she is safe and then I'm going to invite you all over here for supper.'

They loaded their precious cargo into Lou's car and were kissed on both cheeks by Roderick. Lou could see him waving to them, in her rear view mirror, as they drove away. They were halfway back to the cottage, when Lou suddenly said,

'Oh no, I forgot to call Iain. Let me pull over.'

June said,

'Don't, we'll be there in less than half an hour. He'll understand. He won't be able to figure anything out without seeing it all anyway.'

They were greeted like long lost friends at the cottage. They apologised for not calling, but Lou said,

'When you see what we've got, I think you'll forgive us. We wanted to get it back to you as soon as possible.'

They brought the box and the portrait into the kitchen and, without saying a word, took the book out and handed it to Iain. He poured over the book, handling the pages as delicately as Roderick had done. After ten or so minutes, he looked at them in wonder.

'This is one of the most amazing things I have ever seen.'

Liam was bursting with impatience to know what it was.

'This is proof that Isobel was taken, but it turns everything that we thought on its head" marvelled Iain.'

'What do you mean?' asked Liam.

'She loved him, the Elfin Knight, that is. She wanted to be with him and not in the human realm. She was yearning for him. Show me the portrait.'

Lou carefully unwrapped it and turned it to face the others.

'You know who she looks like, don't you?' said Liam

Lou was staggered.

'How did I not see that before, of course, it's Elizabeth!'

'She has her eyes,' said Liam, 'And her mouth.'

Liam studied the portrait a bit more.

'That necklace, there's something familiar … hang on a minute, I need to get back to my cottage. There's something really important in my bedroom.'

Iain was unhappy about this, but Liam insisted and dashed out of the cottage.

He returned with the piece of blue topaz in his hand.

'Look, it's the same shape as the stones in the necklace, almost identical.'

They all peered at it.

'He's right,' said Fred.

'By the way,' said Lou, 'Where is Sunil? I hope we didn't scare him away earlier.'

'He had already booked himself a hotel room in Inverness, so he decided to go back to it. I think he might have needed a bit of time to take everything in, but, fundamentally, I believe he is with us on this,' was Iain's hopeful response, adding, 'He'll be back in the morning.'

Lou and June did not stay too much longer, Lou needed to get home and they both understood that Iain and Fred needed some time to read and process the contents of Isobel's writings.

'Please call me when you reach any new conclusions,' requested Lou.

'I will,' said Iain, 'I am starting to think that Isobel's role in all that is happening here is a lot more integral than we might have realised. Of course, the Elfin Knight was stirred by the presence of Elizabeth, and, in part, Liam.'

'Well, thanks,' said Liam.

'This book is telling us very clearly of her longing for him and her desire to, somehow, get back to him. Everyone who knew the story of Sir Orfeo always assumed that she was overjoyed to be back with her husband, but doesn't appear to be the case. I feel sure that there will be clues in here, something that will help us to find a way to get to his realm.'

'If that's true, then why did Isobel not manage to get back there herself?' asked Liam.

'I can't answer that yet'

Lou, who had been looking at her phone, said,

'There's a nasty storm coming in tonight, according to the weather forecast, you all take care now. Come on June, we had best head back.'

Lou had been right, that night, powerful winds howled around the cottage and rain battered the windows. Liam lay down on Elizabeth's bed, while the other two remained downstairs and found himself breathing in her scent from the blanket. He felt tears start to prick his eyes, but stopped himself from crying properly, by telling himself not to be so ridiculous. He had always trusted Iain implicitly and assumed he would know the answer to pretty much anything out of the ordinary, but he could not stop doubt and pessimism from creeping into his mind. He lay there, listening to the wind and rain lashing the cottage. He would usually have loved this, the wildness of it, but not tonight.

Chapter Twenty Six

Such A Night

The memories of the day that she first encountered him were permanently etched on her memory. Walking with her handmaidens in the forest, on that May morning, full of the promise of warmth, listening to the birdsong, as she made her way to her beloved Ash tree, On reaching the tree, she remembered feeling overwhelmed with tiredness and her handmaidens' concern, which she cast aside, telling them to carry on without her, while she rested awhile. She sat down, beneath the spreading branches, ignoring their protests as they departed and not caring if she messed up her robe, feeling the rough bark, as she pressed her back against the strong, hard trunk. Leaning her head back and closing her eyes, she thought about her life, her husband and his kindness, how she longed for a child and how much she had missed her father and sisters since coming here, to her husband's castle.

One thing that she did not remember was the pain of the arrow, which had not even woken her from the deep slumber she had fallen into. The first thing she could recall was opening her eyes and the realisation that she was floating, on her front, surrounded by a golden light that was warm and soft against her skin. She did not understand, at first, how she was being pulled along, but soon felt a gentle pressure on her hand and looked towards it. Then she saw him, unlike any man she had seen before, unsure that he was indeed a man. She could only see his back, but was able to clearly see his height and the leanness of his frame. Long, straight, dark hair flowed around him, as did his iridescent golden robes. She tried to speak, but no sound came out of her mouth. He turned towards her, his pale, solemn face and dark eyes, grave, but not unkind. She felt something on her chest and looking down saw a small golden arrow embedded in her. She felt no pain, though tried to scream, but was unable to. He stopped and reaching out his other hand, removed the arrow from her. She expected a searing pain as he did so, but felt nothing and looking down, saw no blood, as if it had never been there.

He continued to gently pull her along, but, unable to see anything outside of the golden light that swathed them, she had no idea where they were. She knew the forest well. She liked to walk in it every day, even when the others deemed it to be too cold or wet for such an activity. Her handmaidens found it hard to keep up with her, as she liked to run as well as walk, imagining herself to be a hart, galloping through the trees. They would occasionally scold her for this, but she did not care, even when they told her husband. She would return from the forest, at times, with mud on her robe and shoes, her long, chestnut hair wild, her usually pale face flushed and her golden eyes bright. Her husband, rather than being angry with her, showed her nothing but love and admiration. He had wanted her as soon as he had seen her, at her father's castle. He had visited them as part of a large hunting party, but his true purpose was to find a bride, from one of her father's daughters. She was the youngest and whilst her sisters preened and, in her opinion, simpered a little too much, she was roaming around the woods, observing birds, having to be found and brought into the castle by her father's stern manservant. Her handmaidens tutted and exclaimed over her appearance, forcing her to wash her face and attempting to calm her hair at the same time as dressing her in a more appropriate, cleaner robe.

She entered the room where her father and sisters sat, along with other members of the hunting party. The one called Sir Orfeo bowed to her and seemed unable to take his eyes off her for the rest of the evening, though made little attempt to talk to her. The next morning, her father came to her chamber and told her that Sir

Orfeo wished to marry her and he had agreed. She cried and remonstrated with him, but to no effect and once he had left her room, ran away, into the woods and lay on the ground, beneath the trees, crying and beating the ground with her fists. She wished she could run away properly, far away, but did not want to hurt her father and would have had no idea where to go, not having travelled anywhere else before and certainly not been anywhere unaccompanied. She had no mother to talk to and did not confide in her sisters but she supposed that any mother would support her husband and be happy for her daughter to be the wife of such a man as Sir Orfeo. Her father had told her of Sir Orfeo's fine castle in another part of Scotland, further Northeast and quite far away, with much land around it. He told her that he had heard Sir Orfeo was a good man and a fair one and that he would treat her well.

Her father had been right, he was kind and fair to her and to all those who worked for him. He was well read and accomplished in many areas, including music, with his harp playing sending those who heard it, into some sort of rapture. She had witnessed this on so many occasions, the mesmerised expressions and glassy eyes of his audience, although she did not seem to be susceptible to the charms of his playing. He told her, often, that he loved her and granted any request that she made of him. She had never felt threatened or scared of him, but she could not rid herself of the longing that she always felt within her, a longing for something she could not define. The closest she came to fulfilling this need was when running through the trees, with the wind in her hair and no other people around her.

They came to a stop and Isobel attempted to focus her eyes, though she still could not see as she should, perceiving that they had reached what looked like a cliff face of rock, stretching high above them. He let go of her hand, but she remained suspended, with no control over her limbs, making escape impossible. Watching, she saw him raise his arms and as he did so, the rock parted, noiselessly. He reached out to her and without hesitation, she found herself placing her own hand in his and no longer floating, as the use of her legs came back to her. This was how she began her entry into his realm, walking next to him. They were no longer surrounded by the golden light, there was no need for this, the sight that greeted her was beyond her understanding and experience. She thought they would be in a cave, underground, and at first they were, but a cave with a ceiling so high, she was unable to see where it ended. The walls that surrounded them were emitting a pale, translucent blue light, gently pulsating at regular intervals. They walked, still side by side, her hand in his until they reached an arched entranceway, with no door, through which she could not see anything, as a thick fog seemed to hang within it. He turned to her, his eyes, once black and expressionless, seemed full of light and she did not flinch when he brought his other hand towards her face and ran it over her eyes. It was as if he had lifted a thick veil from her face, as her eyes came into sharp focus and she surveyed the world that stood beyond the opening.

This was where she remained for seven years, barely ageing and less aware of the passage of time, as she had been in her former life. She lived in his castle, with its golden walls, covered in curious and intricate carvings, with arched windows reaching way above her head, their jewel-coloured panes casting bewitching patterns of light across the floors and walls. She slept, she ate, she bathed, with others to tend her if she needed. She learnt to communicate with those around her, quickly realising that the language they spoke was an ancient form of Gaelic, with touch and expression being as important as words.

She was free to explore anywhere she wished, both inside and outside of the castle. The landscape which lay beyond the walls of the castle was achingly beautiful, with rich green fields and steep hills to roam, punctuated with forests full of incredibly tall trees the likes of which she had never seen before and rivers leaping with fish. The forests were bursting with life, from the song of birds with feathers more brilliant than any she had seen before and the sounds of deer and wild horses, moving through the undergrowth. As in her realm, there were seasons, but they were not so defined. There was always enough water in the rivers and enough sunlight for the plants and trees, but an absence of the biting winter cold and frequent rain that she had known at home.

He left her alone at first, although, she always felt his presence, it was she who sought him out, wanting to know and understand him and be around him. They would walk together, through the gilded rooms of the castle, as he told her about those who had created the carvings within the walls. He knew them all by name and held a great admiration for their skill and dedication. This was how he spoke about all his subjects, as valued and respected members of this realm, all with a role to play and a contribution to make. Yes, he was their leader, but she was not aware of their society having different layers of hierarchy as they had in Scotland, or of anyone living in abject poverty.

What she loved most was walking by his side, outside, through the courtyard and out into the fields and woodland surrounding the castle. One day, he took her hand and held it to his lips and the rush of love and contentment that she felt was how she felt every time he touched her, from that moment on. She should have been scared and longing for home, but was not, she felt more at ease than ever before and felt loved and understood for the first time in her life. She did not think of Sir Orfeo, or any part of her life before being here, all that mattered was the gentle warm breeze, playing on her face and in her hair and the soft grass beneath her bare feet and the trees that she sat beneath, listening to the birds, watching the deer run.

When Sir Orfeo came for her, she felt powerless again, she wanted to scream and shout at the Elfin Knight, to tell him to stop being so enthralled by the music he was hearing, to not offer Sir Orfeo his heart's desire. She felt betrayed and angry towards him, for letting him take her away. This was soon replaced by intense longing and despair, which remained with her for the rest of her life. She took solace in the children she went on to have with her husband, always striving to keep her sadness from them. Her time with him, after a while, felt like a dream, or rather, like a long buried memory from childhood. The only tangible thing she had left, were the blue topaz stones that he had given to her, that she always carried with her. As before, her husband was kind and undemanding of her, but did not attempt to find out about her time away from him, leading her to believe that he had used some kind of magic on him, to help him to forget. She wished he had used this on her.

Within two years of being back in Sir Orfeo's castle, they left for a castle offered to them, by his uncle, over on the west coast of Scotland. She was devastated at leaving, in case he came back for her, but had to be with her child, a beautiful boy with curly chestnut hair and pale grey eyes like his father. She had five more children, three boys and two girls, but lost one of her beautiful daughters before the end of her first year of life. She did not think that she would ever learn to bear the pain of this loss, but she did somehow.

Years later, she thought she would have to try to live with yet another loss, when her eldest son was injured in a clan battle, but he survived. He had been carried back to their home and she had remained by his bed, day and night, until she was sure he would not die from his wound. Whilst she had sat next to him, she had prayed, not to God, but to the Elfin Knight, holding her blue topaz cross next to her heart as she did so. When she had finished her prayer, she would place the cross on her son's chest. His recovery was seen as miraculous by all those around her. Their servants were mainly from the local area and had not been with the family when Isobel had disappeared. Those that they had taken with them were loyal and did not mention it, but there had always been talk and suspicion regarding Isobel, that there was something strange and different about her. The survival of her son only served to add to these ideas.

She lived until she was forty nine years old, eventually succumbing to a fever. Before delirium took hold, she requested of her husband that after her death, she be taken back to the forest next to their old castle, to be buried beneath her favourite tree. Death did not scare her, all she hoped for was the happiness of her children and that somehow, through death, she would find her way back to him. Her husband did take her body back to their old home, but did not honour her request to be buried beneath the Ash tree. He did not think this befitting of a woman of his wife's rank, so he buried her in a nearby graveyard. He did not want to completely disregard her wishes, so buried something that she had treasured beneath the tree, her blue topaz cross that she wore every day. He had never known where she had found the stones or the meaning of the inscription on the back and did not have the desire to question her about this. His loyal Steward had accompanied him on this journey back to their old home, which lay empty and requested of his master that he remain there, which was agreed. The Steward had never felt at home on the west coast, longing for his birthplace and the hills and forests there.

She waited for him to find her, caught between realms, existing in the shadows of both. She found herself being more drawn towards the mortal world, a woman, beautiful, with long chestnut hair, like her own, with a sadness inside her that she understood. She saw her, walking through the forest and stopping at the Ash tree, gazing up in awe at its branches. Then, later, came a man, with eyes that she recognised and an expression she had seen before. People had always passed through the forest, some spending longer to admire the trees than others, some with no apparent regard for the splendour that stood around them. These two felt different, pulling her towards them, filling her with sensations she did not recognise, or, at least, had not felt for longer than she could remember.

It was not long after that that she first sensed him, moving through the forest. When she saw him, she called to him and reached out, but he did not see her. The intensity of her longing for him and his realm came back as strongly as before. She could see that he was watching the man and the woman, so she stayed close to them, hoping they would see her, leaving signs for them, sensing that they would be her only way back to him.

Chapter Twenty Seven

Salford Sunday

Liam was woken the next morning by Iain, standing over him and loudly saying,

'Liam, wake up, we have got something to tell you.'

In his confusion, Liam said,

'Is she back? Elizabeth?'

'No, sorry, she's not, but Fred and I have found what we think is some useful information. Come down and we can talk about it.'

Iain left the room and Liam groaned as he dragged himself out of bed and stumbled across to the window. The wind had completely dropped now and it was not raining, though the sky was still full of threatening grey clouds. He noticed some blown over plant pots and the gate in the garden wall had partially come off its hinges. Sadly, a couple of the small trees in the cottage garden had been uprooted. It was too far away to see if there was much damage to the forest, (that is, further damage, thought Liam).

He freshened up in the bathroom, wishing he had time for a shower, but made do with borrowing Elizabeth's deodorant and toothpaste, after which he went down to the kitchen.

Iain and Fred were both sitting at the table, with Fred's ever present laptop open and Isobel's book in front of them.

'Did you two get any sleep last night?'

Fred piped up.

'Yes, we've had some power naps, so we're good.'

'So, what is it you have got to tell me?' he asked, as he helped himself to the coffee that sat on the table.

'Towards the end of Isobel's book, she starts to talk about her wishes for when she dies. She writes that she has no fear of death, in fact, she seems to welcome it, convinced that it could be her way of returning to the Elfin Knight. She said that she clearly laid out to her husband her desire to be buried back here, specifically under the Ash tree and that her blue topaz cross should remain around her neck.'

Liam asked,

'The cross seems so important to her. Have you any idea why?'

'I think I do. Her writing implies that she brought the gemstones back with her, from his realm and that she had them put into a cross and that she, apparently, wore everyday of her life.'

Liam looked incredulous, as he took the single blue gem out of his pocket.

'So this stone could have come from a different realm?'

'Yes, if we are to believe Isobel. She talks of her husband offering her many beautiful necklaces to wear in its place, but she refuses. One thing we have not managed to find out yet, is whether her burial request was carried out. I have called Lou and she has agreed to go with June to the parish church, to see if they can find anything out about this. She is well aware this could be difficult, due to the lack of records from this period, but the combination of Lou's historical research skills and her, dare I say it, forceful personality, are going to stand her in good stead.'

Fred added,

'Such a prominent local family, even from that period, should have some record made somewhere of their death.'

'That's correct,' said Iain, 'but it's all dependent on the age of the church, we don't even know yet whether the local church was the place of worship that existed at that time. Most noble families would have had their own chapel within their home, although they would have been buried in grander surroundings, such as a cathedral.'

Lou had been standing at her kitchen window, sadly surveying the apple tree that had fallen over in last night's storm. She had loved that tree, but was not surprised to see that it had succumbed to the violent winds that had lashed the house, for most of the night. Lou's heart had leapt into her mouth, when her mobile phone had started ringing and when she heard Iain's distinctive voice, she was terrified that he had bad news for her. She was relieved when he told her of his latest discoveries from Isobel's book and gratified that he had a specific task for her. She had already thought about where Isobel might be buried, when she was talking to June on the way home yesterday. June had suggested that the family members of local clan leaders would have likely been buried somewhere with grandeur, as well as religious significance. Fortrose Cathedral and Beauly Priory were a couple of the places she mentioned.

Lou remembered taking a group of her pupils on a visit to Beauly Priory, about five years ago. She would have liked the opportunity to walk around this ruined priory, at her own pace, taking in the beauty and sadness of the place, but that was not to be with thirty year nine pupils to shepherd around. If she was not stopping them from climbing on the centuries old stone tombs, she was ensuring that they did not try and write anything offensive on the priory walls. When she thought the day could not get any worse and it was time to round them up for the journey back to school, they realised that they were two pupils short, leading to a frantic search of the surrounding area. They were found after half an hour, hiding in a copse of trees nearby, the smell of their cigarette smoke giving them away. Lou had always meant to go back to the priory, alone, but had not yet managed to. June said that she had not been there for decades and could not remember any of the names of those buried there.

She was intrigued by what Iain told her about Isobel's burial wishes and the necklace and found herself trying to imagine what this woman must have experienced. How she could long to be back with this monster, after he had kept her away from her husband and her home for so long, was beyond her. The idea of Elizabeth at the mercy of the Elfin Knight was too much to contemplate and to stop her mind from wandering there, she busied herself with calling June and getting ready to leave the house. Her husband was already at work, which she was pleased about, as even though he understood what a good friend Elizabeth was, he was starting to get suspicious about why she was spending so much time over at her place. She dearly wished she could tell him what was going on, not being in the habit of keeping anything important from him, but like the others, knew that it was best to keep it as contained as possible. She was glad that she had decided to involve June in all this, as she enjoyed her, occasionally prickly, company and found her presence oddly calming and reassuring, which was definitely what she needed right now. At the same time, she felt a bit guilty at burdening her, but she quickly realised that she was a very resilient woman with way more energy and stamina that a woman of her age would generally possess.

June was already waiting outside when she pulled up outside her house, dressed in her usual neat and sensible style, with her knee length, a line brown tweed skirt, teamed with beige woollen tights and flat brown lace up shoes. She had a beige raincoat on and a fairly large, dark brown leather handbag over her shoulder. Her silver grey hair was as immaculate as ever, reminding her of how her mother and her friends wore theirs, with their weekly visits to the hair salon for a wash and set. She loved her mother very dearly, but found it infuriating when she was with her friends, gossiping and running other people down. She looked like most other women of her age, particularly those who had spent their lives living here, but it was June's eyes that set her apart, along with the way she quietly considered everything and only spoke when she had something to say that she felt was meaningful and of some value. Lou could not imagine her sitting with her friends and criticising someone for their untidy lawn or their taste in curtains. Lou would have liked to be more like that, but she was well aware that she tended to jump in a bit too quickly sometimes and could do with filtering herself a bit more. She only hoped she could be as sharp and compelling as June when she got to her age.

June climbed into the passenger seat and placed her handbag down by her feet. Lou thought she looked troubled and asked her if she was feeling alright.

'Yes, apart from not having slept at all well because of the storm, I feel fine, but I've been thinking a lot about Isobel's writing.'

'Me too, I can't get my head around why she was longing to be back with the Elfin Knight so much. After what he did to her.'

'I've been thinking about that too and I can understand, to a degree, how she could have been enthralled by him and of course, he could have bound her to him and his realm, with some kind of magic.'

'Yes, I can see that too, but, surely, when Isobel went on to have her own family, that longing should have faded?'

'I think that his magic was too strong and powerful. Even though he vowed to Sir Orfeo that he would not try to take her back or set foot on his lands again, he remained inside her head. I can't stop thinking about my ancestor, the Steward and how he must have felt about all this and whether he was aware of Isobel's true feelings.'

'Surely that would be Impossible to know?'

'I'm not too sure, I am starting to find myself convinced that he was aware and that is part of the reason why this story and this compulsion to protect has run through the generations of my family. Yes, there was the fear that the Elfin Knight might come back, but also the understanding that Lady Isobel might not be free of his power and could be looking for ways to get back to him.'

'So, your ancestor might have been mistrustful of Isobel? He certainly sounds as if he was fiercely protective of Sir Orfeo.'

'I think you're right, but, and this might sound a bit surprising coming from me, I'm beginning to wonder whether perhaps she should have been allowed to remain with the Elfin Knight. I never thought I would come round to that way of thinking, but hearing about Isobel's unhappiness and desperation throughout the rest of her life, I can't help but think this.'

'I do understand what you are saying, but we certainly can't let him keep Elizabeth.'

'Of course not, I wasn't implying anything like that. Let's go to the church.'

As they drove through the village, they could see people picking up the debris left behind by the previous night's winds, mainly wheelie bins that had fallen over and a few rogue shop signs that had become detached. They had to avoid some fallen branches in the road, as they left the village, but, other than that, the storm damage did not seem too severe. The church stood a couple of miles beyond the village. It was a simple, grey stone building, with a small bell tower at one end of the roof and arched windows in each wall. It stood on a small hill, surrounded by Yew trees, none of which had, surprisingly, been damaged by last night's storm and there was a small graveyard nearby, with a large, ostentatious, stone mausoleum in the middle of it, out of place next to the simplicity of the church.

Lou walked up the stone steps and tried the wrought iron handle on the dark, wooden door, but found it to be locked. She knocked a few times, but there was no response from inside. She turned to June.

'What now?'

'We could try to find out where the Minister lives.'

'Don't you know? I thought you'd know where everyone in the village lived?'

June said, with a slight bristle to her voice,

'You assume that I am a regular church goer and know everybody who lives here?'

'I'm sorry June, I had no intention of offending you …' She tailed off when she saw the glint in June's eye.

'I'm playing with you. Yes, I know where the Minister's house is, but no, I don't frequent this church. We can walk to the house, it's just over there.'

She pointed at a handsome, two storey, double fronted house not far behind the church. The walk down the hill behind the church was a bit muddy and Lou, wishing that she was wearing boots, rather than trainers, was a bit concerned that June would slip, but it was her that lost her footing and ended up on her backside, with June helping her up. Lou looked down at her muddy jeans in dismay. Ever practical, June eyed her jeans and said,

'Oh well, I've got a newspaper in my bag, you can sit on it in the car.'

They reached the door and, this time, June knocked.

It was answered fairly quickly by a surprisingly young man, with curly dark brown hair and gentle brown eyes. He was tall, with broad shoulders and looked as if he would be more at home on the rugby field than in a church. He was dressed in black trousers and a slightly worn, dark green jumper, with his white dog collar showing above the neck.

'Hello, how can I help?' He said in an accent that indicated that he was from the Edinburgh area.

Lou had not rehearsed what she was going to say and her words came out in a bit of a jumbled rush. He looked a bit puzzled, but said,

'You both look as if you could do with a hot drink. Why don't you come in?'

They followed him into the hallway, with its tiled floor and mahogany ballustraded staircase.

'Should I take my shoes off?' asked Lou, 'They've got a bit muddy.'

'Don't worry, I'm always trailing mud around the place.'

He ushered them into a sitting room, which looked as if it had not been changed for decades, with its yellow and green, floral patterned wallpaper and furniture that appeared to be dating from the 1950s. Lou thought how this room would be viewed as very cool and retro by many nowadays, although it was not to her taste.

'Please, sit down,' he said, gesturing towards an extremely battered and worn brown leather sofa.

Mildly embarrassed, Lou pointed out her muddy jeans, but he was unconcerned and said it did not matter remotely.

'Coffee or tea?' he asked.

They both requested coffee and when he was out of the room, they looked at the books and magazines that were resting on the coffee table in front of them. If they were expecting worthy, religious texts, they were wrong, as there were a few biographies of well-known sporting personalities, an American detective novel and a couple of gaming magazines.

He returned with a tray which he placed on the coffee table, on top of the magazines.

'Please help yourself to milk and sugar.'

He sat in the equally aged armchair opposite them and looked at them expectantly, with an open, friendly gaze. Lou began.

'We are doing some family history research and are looking for the grave of an ancestor, Lady Isobel Mackenzie. The family lived in a castle near the village, which no longer stands. They moved to the west coast, but she requested to be buried near her former home.'

'When was this?'

'Around the late 1400s.'

'She must have been very attached to the place, to have wanted to be buried back here?'

Lou and June exchanged glances and June said,

'Yes, she loved the forest and wanted to be close to it in death.'

'Why did they move to the west coast? That would have been unusual in those days, particularly if the family had a castle and significant lands in this area.'

'We're not sure about that. At the moment, we're just really keen to find Isobel's grave, to find out if she actually got her wish to be buried around here.'

'We do have parish records, but I doubt we'll find anything from that period of history. One thing that I can tell you for sure is that she is not buried here. We do not have any graves for members of the nobility. They would have been laid to rest somewhere a bit grander than the humble parish church.'

Lou mentioned the mausoleum they had seen in the graveyard. He looked mildly amused when he explained.

'Ah yes, that is the burial place of a slightly eccentric American woman, who died in the early twentieth century. Their ancestors were from around here, but left for America towards the end of the eighteenth century, like so many others at that time.. They were fortunate and became a very wealthy and prominent family over in North Carolina. This particular descendant of the family was obsessed with their Scottish heritage and ended up living back here and requested to be buried in our churchyard, but, as you can see, in a very grand manner.'

'When was this church built?' asked Lou.

'Only in the early nineteenth century, but there has been a place of worship on this site for centuries before that, supposedly going right back to Pictish times. This church was one Telford's Kirks. I don't know whether either of you have heard of them?'

'Oh, yes, I do know about them. Weren't they built by Thomas Telford, with money from the government, after the Napoleonic Wars, as a sort of thank you to God, for their victory?'

June seemed pleased that she had managed to remember that, something that she had probably been taught about back in school.

'That's right," he said. 'They were fortunate to get one in this area, as only thirty two were granted for the whole of the highlands area. Let me dig out some books for you.'

He left the room, leaving them to drink their coffee, returning with a few, large, dusty volumes.

'Our burial records don't go back far enough, but I have found something that could be useful.'

He placed the books on the floor next to his chair and picked up the top one.

'One of my predecessors was very interested in the period you're talking about and wrote this book about his findings.'

He poured over the index in the back for a minute or two and then exclaimed

'Here, this is the family name you are looking for.'

He went to the relevant section of the book and read out loud.

'The Mackenzie family lived at Coille Dorch Castle from its construction in the late fourteenth century, until their unexplained move to the west coast in 1472. Then there's some description of the castle and the grounds around it and, yes, it says here that Sir Orfeo returned in 1499, with the body of his beloved wife, Isobel, at her request, to be buried at Beauly Priory. This was where his ancestors were also buried. So, you're right, she is buried in this area. Interestingly, it goes on to say that Sir Orfeo himself, was not buried next to her, presumably buried near his west coast home. Curious, don't you think?'

Lou was unsure what to say.

'Yes, I suppose it is, but, thank you, that's exactly what we wanted to find out"

'There's something familiar about the name, Sir Orfeo, I'm sure that I 've heard it somewhere else.'

'You might have heard the old story of that name. Quite a local legend, some nonsense about an Elfin Knight,' said June

'Maybe that's what I'm thinking of. Sounds interesting, I must look into it.'

June finished her coffee quickly and said to Lou,

'We should be getting on now Lou, if we're going to get to the priory.'

They got up and left, thanking him for his help. He stood in the doorway, watching them walk back up towards the church, pondering over what he had just learned.

Chapter Twenty Eight

Bittersweet Symphony

On the walk back to the car, Lou took care not to slip over again. Their conversation with the minister had reminded Lou of the surreal nature of the situation they were currently dealing with. She could only imagine his reaction to the truth about their research and doubted that they would have been believed by him. Part of her was concerned that other people would think they were all terribly negligent and irresponsible for not reporting Elizabeth as missing and getting some help from the authorities with finding her. The thought of not finding Elizabeth was unbearable to contemplate and she tried hard to stop her mind from going there, but she had found this increasingly more difficult over the past couple of days.

They got into the car and drove along the main road through Garve, past the stunning Rogie Falls and through the small village of Contin, then picking up the smaller road to Beauly, passing through the Muir of Ord. Ordinarily, she would have loved to stop off at Rogie Falls to walk over the river and look on in awe at the strength of the water there. She remembered taking Elizabeth to see the Falls, on one of her early visits to the highlands, when they were first getting to know one another. She recalled how she had been hesitant about walking across the slightly precarious looking bridge that crossed the river, but with a bit of encouragement from Lou she had eventually done it. Elizabeth was different from her other friends, not purely because she was English, she had a serenity about her and was definitely a bit of an old soul. She was brought back from her memories by June thrusting a packet of mints under her nose and asking her if she would like one, finding herself grateful for the older woman's presence once again.

They arrived in Beauly, finding a parking spot not too far away from the priory. They were not alone there, the tourist season had not properly begun yet, but regardless of the time of year, visitors from all over Scotland and the world were drawn to this place. Today, a group of German tourists were there, being shown around by a guide, with a voice that carried, Lou wished it was quieter, she was not in the mood for being surrounded by too many people. As if reading her thoughts, June said,

'Within the priory walls will be busy, but hopefully, the graveyard area outside will be quieter. Shall we start inside?'

Lou agreed and they walked up the path that led towards the ruined priory.

Stepping through the archway where a door would have once been, they surveyed the scene in front of them. There were alcoves built into the walls, containing tombs, along with some tombs free standing on the priory floor, interspersed with graves beneath the floor, marked by slabs.

At June's suggestion, they parted ways, each taking one side of the priory, slowly working their way along, carefully looking at the tombs and the graves beneath their feet. It was difficult to make out the words engraved upon them; faded and weathered by the centuries and the elements. After nearly ten minutes, Lou called June over. She was standing in front of the largest opening built into one of the walls, with an elaborately crafted wrought iron screen shielding it. Lou, peering through the screen, into the relative darkness of the space within, could make out a number of stone tombs, each with an effigy of its occupant, carved upon them. There was a large, arched wooden door, to the side of the metal screen, which appeared to the entrance to this crypt, which was, unfortunately, locked.

'Well this is frustrating' exclaimed Lou 'We've no way of knowing if one of these tombs contains Isobel.'

June was busy looking at her phone, whilst Lou tried the door again, in frustration.

'I don't think now is the best time to be looking at your phone,' was Lou's slightly snarky comment, though, of course, she should have known that June was about to come up with something that would save the day.

'I'm on the Historic Scotland website. There's a lot of information about the priory here, including some detail about who is buried here and the dates of their deaths. It says that within this crypt are the remains of several members of Sir Orfeo's family, but Isobel or her husband are not mentioned. The minister was right about Sir Orfeo not being here, but according to his book, Isobel should be.'

Handing Lou her phone, she said,

'Could you have a look as well, in case I have missed something?'

Lou carefully studied the information on the website, before looking up at June,

'No, you're right, there's no mention of Isobel. Did you notice the number of members of the clan who were buried in 1491?'

'Yes, that date is ringing a bell in my memory. I think there must have been a big clan battle at that time. I should know this, I must have read about it at some point.'

Lou looked up information about Mackenzie clan wars and exclaimed.

'That's it. I remember now. The Battle of Blar Na Pairce took place in that year. Not far from here actually. The MacDonald clan tried to seize the Mackenzie lands, Their clan chief was known as the Lord of the Isles and was making fairly regular incursions into the area, as he felt the lands were rightly his. My pupils particularly enjoyed learning about this battle, as it was particularly bloody, ending with a large number of MacDonalds drowning in the River Conon.'

She handed the phone back to June, who went back to the information about the tombs.

'There are other dates when a larger than usual number of Mackenzies were buried, 1452 and 1488 are the ones I can see, I suppose there were battles during those years too. It's hard to imagine how it would have been for a mother like Isobel, to live with the fear of losing one of her children in battle.'

They looked everywhere within the priory walls and then moved outside, relieved to be no longer having to dodge photographs being taken by tourists. June had felt herself becoming angry with the people she observed thoughtlessly walking over peoples' grave and had to stop herself from saying something none too polite to a few of them. They worked their way around the gravestones and monuments outside, but found nothing for Isobel. Lou noticed a more overgrown area of the graveyard and suggested they look there. It was June who spotted it first.

'Lou, come over here!'

Lou found June bending over a clump of grass, clearing it away to reveal a small rectangular gravestone, very old and covered in moss.

'I can barely make it out, Your eyes are better than mine, Can you read it?'

Lou squinted at the gravestone.

'Not really, here, let me take a photo and enlarge it.'

She did so and when she had made the photo as big as possible, they could just about read the inscription.

Here lies Lady Isobel Mackenzie

Born 1450 Died 1499

Beloved mother

Am faigh thu na tha thu ag iarraidh

'What does that mean?' asked Lou, my Gaelic is very rusty.

'May you find what you seek' replied June after a few moments thought.

'Oh my goodness,' said Lou. 'He knew, didn't he, about how she felt. That's why he buried her here, away from the rest of his family, with such a small gravestone, with no mention of the husband she left behind.'

'Yes,' said June, 'It does feel like some form of revenge or that she has been ostracised in death, but the Gaelic inscription is not angry or bitter.'

Lou and June cleared away the weeds and grass that overtaken the gravestone and found some wildflowers around the graveyard, tying the stems together, with a hair band Lou had in her pocket and placed them on Isobel's grave.

'What does all this mean for trying to get Elizabeth back? I don't understand how it will help,' said Lou disconsolately.

'I don't know. We should call Iain and let him know. It might help in some way.'

Chapter Twenty Nine

Baddest Blues

After they had eaten some breakfast, Liam and Iain pulled on their boots and coats and made their way into the forest. There was a lot of damage, as they suspected there would be, with fallen branches everywhere and whole trees uprooted every now and then. Most of these trees were young and not strong enough to have withstood last night's powerful winds. As they approached the part of the forest where the Ash tree stood, they stopped dead in their tracks. This tree, that had stood for centuries. had been unable to survive the storm and was lying on its side, half in the crater that stood in front of it. The two men walked around this forlorn giant, with its massive tangle of roots that had been wrenched cruelly from the earth.

'I don't understand this,' said Iain, the shock and sadness easy to hear in his voice. 'This should not have happened to a tree like this. Last night's winds were strong, but it must have weathered worse over the years.'

'Perhaps it was diseased,' suggested Liam.

'It looked pretty healthy to me, considering its age,' was Iain's response. 'There are plenty of other trees around here that look weaker, but they are still standing. I really can't fathom this.'

Liam had no useful suggestions for Iain, he felt equally mystified and started to examine the area of ground, where the tree had stood. Iain stayed where he was, seemingly unable to move. After a few minutes, Liam called out.

'Iain, come and look, something's in here!'

He was pointing towards an object within some of the roots of the tree, that were suspended above the crater.

'Yes. I see it, do you think you can reach it?'

Liam got down on his knees and crawled forwards, as far as he could, without falling into the crater, the depth of which he had no concept of and reached his right arm out as far as he could, all the while, Iain held onto his jeans belt.

'I've got it! Can you pull me back?'

Iain dragged him by this belt, so hard, that he fell backwards on to the ground. In his hand, Liam had what looked like a clump of earth, with something metallic showing through it. He sat up and tried to take some of the earth off, but it wouldn't budge.

'We need to take it back to the cottage, we could damage whatever it is otherwise.'

They looked around a little more, but saw nothing else that might help them and headed back.

Back in the cottage kitchen, Iain took the object from Liam and submerged it in a bowl of warm water, allowing the earth to soften, allowing him to gently take the earth away.

'Oh my goodness, look at this.'

Fred and Liam stood either side of him, looking at what was unmistakably a gold cross, inlaid with pale blue gems.

'One is missing,' said Iain

Liam took out the piece of blue topaz from his jeans pocket, which he had been carrying with him, contained within a small box, since Elizabeth had disappeared. It fit perfectly.

'It's hers isn't it? From the portrait?'

'It most certainly appears to be,' said Iain.

Iain cleaned off the back of the cross a little more

'Look, there's an inscription on it, but I don't think I'm going to be able to make it out.'

Fred said

'Here, let me.'

Taking the cross, he laid it on some white paper and took a photo of it with his phone, which he then looked at on his computer.

'I have a program that can help with this, even if there is hardly any of the inscription visible.'

After ten or fifteen minutes of hyperfocus, he said,

'It appears to be in Gaelic, it says, and please excuse my pronunciation,'

'Mo ghràdh 's m' fhuil gu bràth'

'Let me just run that through the translator.'

'No need,' said Iain, who had been looking over Fred's shoulder, 'it means, 'My love, my blood, always.'

Fred and Liam looked at Iain with admiration, but he said,

'Don't be too impressed, my Gaelic skills don't stretch too far. I would certainly find it difficult to hold a conversation with a fluent speaker.'

The three of them looked at the cross in silence for a minute or two, a silence that was broken by Liam.

'This feels unreal, for us to have only just been talking about this piece of jewellery and its significance and, lo and behold, here it is. Perhaps it's not the real thing?'

'I'm not a jewellery expert,' Iain replied. 'But it looks old to me and the inscription seems to fit with everything that we have learnt so far. You're right, it all seems a bit convenient, but has it not occurred to you that there could be something else at play here?'

Liam did not, initially, understand what he was implying.

'You're wanting me to believe that all this has somehow been instigated by a spirit?'

'Liam, my friend, surely you can suspend your disbelief a little bit more, considering what you've seen recently?'

Liam sighed and said,

'I think I'm willing to believe pretty much anything at the moment, but if we have somehow been led to this cross, by a supernatural force, how does this get us any closer to finding Elizabeth?'

'We can't overlook the significance of having a personal item of Isobel's in our possession, an item that contains stones that, if she is to be believed, came from another realm.'

Iain was interrupted by his phone ringing. It was Lou and Iain put her on speaker phone.

'We've found Isobel's grave, it's at Beauly Priory.'

'That makes sense,' said Iain. 'Did you find other members of Orfeo's family buried there?'

'Yes, but her grave was separate, outside of the priory walls, in a far corner of the graveyard. It's a small gravestone, but it has a very interesting inscription.'

After she had told them what the inscription was, she asked, 'Is any of this useful? We're really not sure how it will help.'

Iain said,

'We have just found something pretty significant,' and went on to tell her about the cross.

'You might not feel that the gravestone is important, but it is. We're getting more and more confirmation of Isobel's desire to get back to the Elfin Knight and this must be integral to us getting Elizabeth back.'

Lou and June arrived back at the cottage an hour later, with, to the others' surprise, Sunil, in the back seat of the car,

'Look who we found in the village, He said he was happy to walk up here, but we insisted.'

Sunil looked a little abashed and said,

'These two are very hard to refuse.'

'We've bought lunch with us,' said Lou, as she emptied the contents of her shopping bag onto the kitchen table.

'Now, please, show us this cross, we're desperate to see it.'

Iain had cleaned it up further and it looked even more extraordinary, its blue topaz stones had such a pure, clear quality, their colour switching between pale, icy blue and a deeper, aquamarine blue, according to the light that danced around them.

'The stones make you want to get lost in them, they're so cold and empty in one sense, but if you keep looking at them, they seem to go on forever.'

Liam told them about the research he had done into the stone, when he first found his in the forest.

'There's one thing, in the light of all we've been finding out about Isobel, that really strikes me now. When I first read about it and its protective qualities, I assumed that she was wearing it to protect herself against the Elfin Knight, but now we know that he most likely gave her the stones, it must be that he wanted to protect her.'

'What was the one thing you mentioned?' asked Lou.

'Wearing topaz is supposed to draw love to the wearer, so maybe she was hoping that it would draw them back together?'

Iain said,

'This piece of jewellery is going to be key to getting Elizabeth back, but we still need to tackle how we are going to get through that great wall of rock, I don't think that this cross is going to be the answer to this.'

'Do you have any thoughts?' asked Liam

'As a matter of fact, I do,' he said, turning his attention to Sunil.

'Sunil, I have been doing a bit more reading into your deity and I discovered that those who have been blessed by Hanuman can have the ability to break down, seemingly, impenetrable obstacles and impediments. Now, I'd say that fits in pretty well with our issue here.'

Sunil looked doubtful as he said,

'I can go along with the enhanced immunity, but I can't say I've ever managed to break down anything like that.'

'It might not have been a literal wall or barrier, but, perhaps more of a metaphorical one? Do you remember anything like that?'

'I've been overcoming obstacles for most of my life. Someone from a South Asian family, whose family wanted him to pursue a more academic path, joining the Army is just one of them, so if that's the kind of thing you mean, then, yes.'

'I think you're on the right lines, but there has to be more, I'm convinced that the mantra your mother told you about is important here. When we attempt to get through to his realm, would you be willing to come with us? I think your presence is vital to this'.'

'Couldn't one of us just say the chant?' asked Liam

'No, it has to come from Sunil, he's the one who has been blessed, but it's his choice entirely.'

Sunil looked around the others at the table and said, with conviction,

'Of course, I'll come with you. As you said, none of us are here by accident. What's the point otherwise? When are you planning on doing this?'

'Soon,' said Iain, 'Fred and I have a few more preparations, but before the end of today.'

Liam's frustration rose up again.

'What else is there to prepare? We have the cross, we potentially have a way through the rock. What more do we need?'

'Liam, I understand how you feel, but we will be stepping into an extreme unknown, so we need as much protection as we can be afforded, Fred and I are going to spend a bit more time on the Grimoire and I'm also waiting to hear back from someone.'

'Who is that?' asked Lou, 'I thought we were trying not to involve anyone else.'

'This is someone very unique and usually reluctant to become involved in anything outside of her world.'

'Her world?' asked Lou, 'That sounds familiar.'

Iain elaborated a little.

'Eilidh is someone I used to work with at the university, a lecturer within my department, with a particular interest in witchcraft from the early Middle Ages onwards. I have found her to be a great source of knowledge over the years.'

'Did she actually teach that subject to the students?' asked Lou.

'Yes, indeed, she was an excellent lecturer, who really engaged the students' interest in her subject,' said Iain. 'But, unfortunately, the senior management team at the university decided to let her go, after receiving complaints from certain factions within the student body.'

'What do you mean?' asked Lou.

'Specifically, from the Christian Union, who were convinced that she was encouraging her students to become involved in Wiccan and Pagan practices. The Union started to make a lot of noise about this and the university decided they did not want to deal with the likely negative publicity, so sacked her for some spurious reason.'

'So, was she?' asked Liam.

'If you're asking if she was encouraging these students to dabble in witchcraft, I think you better ask Fred.'

They all looked at Fred, who was quietly working on his laptop at the other end of the table. He looked up and said,

'Eilidh was one of my lecturers on my first degree course and was one of the best lecturers I've ever had, (apart from Iain of course). Her knowledge of her subject is vast and profound and she had a way of enthralling her students, so much so, that you didn't want to leave at the end of the class, you just wanted to keep listening to her talk.'

'Sounds a bit intense,' remarked Lou.

'She was, but not in a sinister or disturbing way. She made you want to learn more and really immerse yourself in the subject matter.'

Iain added,

'It's thanks to Eilidh, that I started to work with Fred. She realised his skills and potential very early on and sent him in my direction, for which I will forever thank her.'

Fred looked almost bashful at this point and continued.

'What happened to her was a disgrace. The senior management were weak and too scared of some of their funding being pulled.'

'But was there any truth in what was said? Was she leading her students into witchcraft?' asked Lou.

Fred smiled in a way that could only be described as enigmatically and said,

'Only the ones who had a true interest already.'

'So is she a witch herself?' asked Lou.

'I don't think she'd like the label,' answered Iain. 'She does engage in certain practices and beliefs and her knowledge in this area is pretty impressive. She's helped me out many times in the past and I'm hopeful that she will do so again.'

Iain turned to Fred and asked,

'When will she be ready for the Zoom call?'

'She just messaged me, asking if we can give her half an hour to finish something.'

'What are you hoping to get from her?' asked Liam.

'I've already told her what has happened and she's aware of the findings we have made today. What I would really like is for her to reassure me that I'm on the right track with all this and let me know if I have missed anything.'

They ate the lunch that Lou and June had brought with them; sandwiches, pastries and fruit from the village shop. Surprisingly, their appetites were good and they fell on the food. As the time for the Zoom call came, Iain turned to the others and requested that they stay out of the camera view and not say anything.

'Eilidh can be a bit distrustful, understandably, so best if it's just Fred and I taking part in the call'

'We can leave the room if you prefer,' said Liam.

'No, I'd like you all to hear what she says; I just won't be telling her that you're in the room.'

'That's a little dishonest,' said Lou teasingly, causing Iain to redden a little.

He was saved by the familiar chime of an incoming Zoom call on Fred's laptop.

'Eilidh,' said Iain, 'It's lovely to see your face again. It's been too long.'

The voice that replied was deep, warm and humorous.

'I wish I could say the same about seeing your lovely countenances. No, seriously, it's great to you both. Now, what on earth have you got yourselves involved in this time? Iain, I thought you were going to ease up a bit on this kind of thing?'

'When Liam and Elizabeth initially arrived on my doorstep, I was intrigued and I admit, it had been a while since I'd been called upon. As I looked into this and, of course, when Elizabeth disappeared, there was no choice, I had to help. Tell me, what are your thoughts?'

She paused and then said,

'What you're dealing with here is very ancient and extremely powerful, I'm surprised that none of you have been harmed. If he wished to, he could wipe you all out, along with all those in the surrounding areas. I'm really concerned about you trying to reach into his realm.'

'We have to,' said Iain. 'Elizabeth needs to come back. We're convinced that he does not want to harm her or anyone else, as he would surely have done this by now. What do you think about Isobel being the key to all this?'

'I believe you're right, but her cross alone is not going to give you enough protection, or any of the amulets or talismans that you might be wearing. I've got something for you, that I want you to promise that you will use if you manage to get to him. It's very ancient magic and it's only to be invoked if your lives are in absolute danger and you can see no other way out. This magic is unpredictable, as Beira is.'

Iain sounded shocked.

'Beira! I wouldn't dream of invoking any of her powers. It could be catastrophic. She can build mountains and plunge us into endless winter, on a whim, depending on her mood. I don't think this is a good idea. I'm sorry, Eilidh.'

'I understand your fears, Iain. She is an extremely powerful goddess, but she is one of the few that he would fear, so, please just have the incantation with you. I've just sent it to you in a message. Promise me that you'll both come and visit me when this is over, now, I must go.'

She left the Zoom call somewhat abruptly, before Iain could make any further objections. Fred began to say what was contained in her message, but Iain made everyone jump when he shouted,

'Stop Fred! Don't read it out loud, Let me look at it.'

Iain looked at the message, at the words sent by Eilidh, which were both in English and Gaelic.

Beira, I beg you, protect me from danger and bring your wrath upon this place

Beira, guidheam ort, dìon mi o chunnart, agus thoir do chorruich air an àite so

'Wow, she was impressive,' said Lou. 'Who is Beira and why are you so scared of her?'

'She was a Celtic god, on a par with Odin, the Norse god and Amun Ra, the Egyptian god, usually referred to as Queen Beira, the Queen of Winter and viewed as the most powerful Celtic god. She had the power to control the weather and change the landscape, but she was cruel and malicious and if she felt she was not being worshipped enough, she would create mountains and turn summer into a harsh, icy winter. She could be benevolent too, but this could change on a whim if angered.'

'Okay, now I get your reluctance to have anything to do with her power.' acknowledged Lou, 'but it could be useful as a backup.'

Iain got up, without saying a word and walked out of the room. Liam followed soon after.

Chapter Thirty

Into The Mystic

She had no idea how long she had been here, Minutes and hours made no sense, she felt as if she was constantly going through time slips, suddenly realising she had lost a day, or even days at a time. Sometimes, she felt quite lucid, walking around the vast, cavernous rooms of this strange, but beautiful building. It was a type of beauty she found hard to process, as she gazed up at intricately carved, golden walls that seemed to reach up into infinity. There were figures with faces that looked almost human, that she could make out in the carvings, along with creatures that she did not recognise, some looked benign, others ferocious.

There were windows in the walls, made of opaque, jewel coloured glass, which she could not see through, which frustrated her. Whenever she felt like this, or experienced any other strong emotion, time would slip again and what had just happened was days, or was it weeks, earlier. She knew who she was, that she was called Elizabeth and did not belong to this world and that she had been brought here by him, but that was all. She could not remember anything before this, but she was filled with a deep longing to get back to her own world, but felt completely powerless to do so.

She was not alone, there were other women that came to her, to bring her food, to run her baths and dress her. They all had long, shiny black hair, worn loose, falling way down their backs and wore robes in a variety of colours, some pale and delicate, others deep and rich. Their faces were pale, with fine features and dark eyes. They did not speak to her, but were calm and graceful and did not feel at all threatening. The food they brought her was fresh and full of flavour; apples like she had never tasted before, with breads and honey and a drink that was creamy and sweet. She never felt hunger or thirst and did not mind when the women bathed her and dressed her, enjoying the sensation of them brushing out her hair and gently rubbing scented oil onto her body.

She was dressed in floor length robes, made of a material that was so light and fine, but she always felt warm enough. They were pale aqua in colour and glistened in the light. She wore no shoes, but felt no need for them. The floors were bare, made of a smooth, white stone, but not cold or hard when she walked along them. There were sounds, it was not completely silent. She could hear birdsong from outside, but not like any birds she had heard before and sometimes she could hear music and singing, in a language she had no knowledge of. The singing was haunting, but soothing, but she could not work out where it was coming from.

She sometimes knew he was there, watching her, as she walked through the rooms. He kept his distance and did not speak to her, but she was not scared of him, just aware of his presence. She did not try to talk to him, not until she came across a statue in a room she had not yet been in. The statue was made of a pale stone and was of a woman, wearing long robes, with bare feet and long, hair, rippling with waves. Her face was beautiful, with high cheekbones, delicately chiselled and a fine, straight nose. She wore no jewels, only a circle of flowers and leaves around the crown of her head. She could not stop staring at this statue and reached out her hand to trace the outline of her robe.

As she did she realised he was watching her, with an expression on his face quite different from before. He looked almost wistful.

'Who is she?' she asked.

He did not answer, but she found herself somehow being guided towards another room, in which she found more statues of the same woman, all similar, but with subtly different facial expressions. She looked at him, as he stood in the room, surrounded by these effigies and suddenly it became clear to her, as if a part of the veil across her memories had slipped. She remembered something so vividly from her life before.

'Isobel! It's her isn't it? They're all her!'

He looked directly at her, at the mention of her name and for a moment, she was scared, at the fire that seemed to burn in his dark eyes.

'I remember now, this is why I'm here, It's because I am descended from her. I understand, but I'm not her and I have a life outside this world that I really need to get back to.'

She didn't know whether he understood what she was saying, but he turned away from her and walked towards one of the windows and gazed out. She followed him, not expecting to be able to see anything out of the window, but this time, she could. She saw bright green, gently rolling hills and a wide river cutting through them, with dense woodland and steep, craggy mountains in the distance. The sky was a brilliant blue and she could see birds flying in formation. Directly beneath the window was a huge courtyard, shaded by canopies of red and gold fabric, hung from tall pillars. She followed his gaze to a small group in the courtyard, One of them looked up at the window and appeared to smile. He was young, a younger version of him, with the same long, black hair and pale skin, but his face was softer and he looked more human, almost like one of her own sons.

A lifetime of memories came flooding into her mind, overwhelming her, forcing her to kneel on the floor before her legs gave way beneath her. She cried out, as if she had been hit by something, as she remembered her children, her family, her friends, everything that she had lost. She looked up at him with her anguished face, with tears falling down it.

'Please, let me go back! I have people who I love and need. Surely you understand that? You must!'

He looked away from her, gazing towards the window again and a sudden realisation came crashing in on her.

'He's your son isn't he? He looks like you. Then you must understand how it would feel to be separated from him.'

He kept looking towards the window, his profile as still and solemn as ever.

'Imagine how your son would feel if you were taken away from him, or his mother. How could you live with that?'

She didn't even know if he could understand her, but she continued regardless. She realised she was potentially endangering herself by talking to him like this, that there was the possibility that she could anger him, but nothing he had done up to this point had threatened her or hurt her. She began to wonder who the young man's mother was and where she was in all this, but then, almost instantaneously understood. Isobel must be his mother. Could that really be possible she thought?

'It's her isn't it? Isobel, she is his mother. How could you let her go? Why didn't get her back again?'

He turned back to her and this time he looked angry and she felt, for the first time, fear grip her whole body. She stood up on unsteady legs and backed away.

'I'm sorry, I just don't understand. You didn't have to let her go back to her husband. You could have easily sent him away.'

For the first time, she heard his voice, speaking a language she did not understand. His voice was surprisingly soft and low.

'I don't know what you are saying.'

He moved towards her, forcing her back against a wall. She closed her eyes, bracing for an attack, but instead felt his cool hands on either side of her face, applying a gentle pressure. He spoke again, but this time she understood and what she heard brought tears to her eyes once again. She learnt of his deep, unending love for Isobel, how she was so happy here, walking in the forests and lying in the fields, able to do as she pleased. He told her of how she had become respected and accepted by the others around her and her innate kindness and profound love for nature. He had wanted her from the first moment he saw her, walking through the forest in the human realm, with her hair shining like autumn leaves in the light and her golden eyes. He understood that taking her from her home and her husband was wrong, but he felt sure that she would be happier here, with him. Their son had been born and he had never felt such contentment and had never adored her more.

When Orfeo had seen her and followed her, he admitted, he had been bewitched himself by his music and felt powerless not to offer him that which he desired most. When he chose Isobel, over countless gold and other riches, he had no choice but to accept this. He knew that once they had left his realm, he would be unable to get her back, without dishonouring their agreement. Honour was everything in this realm and breaking his vow would have destroyed him. His son had no mother, he could not leave him without his father. He had longed for her ever since and his son had known no other mother.

He removed his hands from her face and now it was her turn to reach out to him. Placing her hand on his cheek and looking into his eyes.

'I can see how she would have been very happy here and that even though she went to have other children, she would have constantly thought of you and her son. I was drawn to this place for a reason, but I don't think it was purely down to you. I feel sure that Isobel is still close by. I have felt a presence that I didn't understand, but now, I think it must be her, trying to get back to you.'

He put his hand over hers and closed his eyes and Elizabeth felt a rush of pure emotion, stronger than anything she had ever experienced. A mixture of joy, contentment and love, that permeated her whole being. She closed her eyes and found herself existing only in that moment, nothing else mattered.

Abruptly, he pushed her hand away and she was aware of her surroundings once again. When she looked at him, his face had changed, becoming hard and cold, his eyes as black as the darkest onyx. Confused and alarmed, she cried out.

'What is happening?'

She lost consciousness before she could hear any form of reply.

Chapter Thirty One

White Noise

Iain stood outside the front of the cottage, well out of sight of the others in the kitchen. It was not something he made a habit of doing, leaving a room in such a dramatic fashion, but he had started to feel as if the walls and ceiling were closing in on him, as his heart started to beat too fast and had to get out. He knew that if had stayed there, within a few minutes he would have felt as if he could not catch his breath and would begin to feel lightheaded and on the verge of fainting. He had felt like this only a few times before, over the past year or so, each time preceded by an overwhelming sense of doom and hopelessness.

He was a man who, over the decades, had faced up to situations that most people could not even imagine. He had put himself in the face of danger on many occasions and had experienced rather too many close shaves as a result. He could not pinpoint when his interest, or some would say obsession, with the supernatural had begun. He had grown up in a relatively stable family. His father was a Physicist, working for a research company and his mother an Artist, (albeit, not a particularly successful one, her paintings being a bit unusual for most tastes). He was an only child and had felt nurtured and loved by his parents. His preferences were for reading and studying nature, rather than kicking a football around or listening to contemporary music and he had no recollection of his parents applying any pressure on him, to conform to the behaviour of most of his peers. He remembered being quite happy when he was younger, although, looking back, he could, of course, recognise his social isolation and anxiety when thrown into certain situations. His idea of hell had been a school end of term disco, which he had attended when he was fifteen years old, as the nearby girls school had been invited and he was hoping he might be able to pluck up the courage to ask a certain girl he liked to dance. She had not been there and the lights and music had been too much for him, forcing him to leave early, vowing never to go to another disco again.

Fortunately, he had not experienced any bullying, the other pupils at school tended to leave him to his own devices. When he was around thirteen, he started to read a lot of books about folklore and mythology, from all over the world, He allowed himself to become immersed in the worlds of Scottish Banshees, the Lambton

Worm of Northumbria, the Roggenwolf of Germany and countless other creatures and demons from all over the world. He had never considered any career other than an academic one, to be able to research and write about an area that he loved and to try to inspire others to develop an interest too was enough to satisfy him.

The further he delved into mythology and folklore, the more he began to realise that it was still all around us, other realms and beings living alongside us. University, followed by a career working in Academia followed. The head of the university department he worked in, would, at times, disappear rather suddenly, for a few days, usually citing illness, but Iain always suspected that he was hiding something. On one of these occasions, he had gone into his unlocked office to see if he could find any clues. What he found in an old, leather bound journal, set him on the path that he had been on for the past few decades.

This journal was a record of the many supernatural beings, demons and creatures that he had been called on to assist with. There were illustrations and lots of written detail about their characteristics, powers and how they could be defeated. Iain had confronted him on his return and had pleaded with him to take him along next time, which is how it began.

In the months prior to Liam contacting him, he had been seriously considering giving up. Every time he was called to a new investigation, he felt it taking more of a toll than ever before, on his physical and emotional health and when the panic attacks started, he was convinced that it was time to stop. Fred could take over from him, but he would need someone to help him, which would be a problem. When Liam had turned up on his doorstep with Elizabeth, he knew he had no choice, other than to help them, even though part of him had wanted to stay at home and not become involved. He felt that he had been doing pretty well up until this point, bu the conversation with Eilidh had taken him aback, making him feel as if he could not cope and would be of no use to anyone.

He heard the front door open and saw Liam come out of the cottage and walk over to join him.

'What is bothering you?' asked Liam.

'Call it a crisis of confidence, if you like, I was feeling in control of the situation, or as much you can be when you're dealing with forces like this, but after hearing Eilidh talk about invoking Beira, it all feels a bit too much.'

Liam had never seen Iain like this, He had always been so calm and pragmatic when talking about the investigations he had been brought into. He remembered how he had been when he first met him, on the oil rig, walking around, alone and completely unphased by any potential danger. This was not a side of Iain he had encountered before and it disturbed him deeply.

'Iain, throughout all this, you have been the one to reassure me and give me some hope and optimism about what we need to do. Sometimes, I ask myself what are you doing here? You're risking your life and those around you, for a woman you hardly know, but I always reach the same conclusion.'

'Which is?'

'That, if we don't do this and try to get her back, I'll never be able to live with myself and the thought of not seeing her again, already seems unthinkable. You are the only person I know who can get us through this. I know that's a lot of pressure and responsibility to be put on you, but you have broad shoulders and all those people that you have helped over the years would agree with me.'

'Thank you for that, but if it comes to the point where we feel that we need to call on Beira, yes, that will most likely be the end of the Elfin Knight and his realm, but quite possibly be the end of us too and a lot of the surrounding area. People will die, it would be inescapable.'

Liam had no words in response to this and simply placed his arm around Iain's shoulders and gave him, what he hoped was, a reassuring squeeze.

Chapter Thirty Two

Losing My Mind

Iain and Liam returned to the kitchen, to find June, Fred and Sunil, crowded around the back of Lou, who was sitting at the table, with Isobel's book open in front of her.

'I've just spotted something really interesting in Isobel's book,' said Lou.

'I might be misinterpreting it, but in this section, she talks about the birth of her first child and she goes into a surprising amount of detail about the birth itself.'

Fred chimed in, looking a little bashful.

'I have to admit, when I was originally reading this bit, I might have skimmed the birth details.'

'What does she say about it?' asked Iain

'She had a very difficult birth, which, of course, would have been extremely common back then. She would have been fortunate to survive it. Her labour was very long, and towards the end, she talks about being unable to bear the pain and being so tired, again, not uncommon, but then she says this.'

'If only it were as easy as the birth of my first born. Then I felt some pain, but it was quickly taken away from me by the potions and the singing of my handmaidens and the soothing words of my love, which took me to another place, beyond that of pain and suffering'

'I don't know how I could have missed this,' said Fred, his embarrassment still visible.

'It was not just you, I did not pay as much attention to that part of the book as I should have, like you. I let my squeamishness get the better of me,' admitted Iain.

Lou asked,

'Is it even possible that she had a child with him? Would it have been feasible?'

'There are stories of half human half Elfin beings, throughout history. I have never come across one, but that means nothing,' replied Iain.

'Poor Isobel,' said Lou, 'It must have been desperate for her to be torn away from her child. I'm surprised she doesn't' mention them any more in the book.'

June's response to this was surprisingly sensitive and as insightful as ever.

'It was probably too painful. I imagine she tried her utmost to bury the memory as much as she could. Like a mother forced to give up a child for adoption. To think about it all the time would stop you from being able to live a life.'

'I can understand that" said Lou "But why not try to get Isobel back, for the sake of him and their child?'

'I think I can answer that,' said Iain, 'The Elfin Knight would have lived according to ancient codes of honour and vows, once made, would have been seen as unbreakable. If he had done so, he would have risked losing the respect of all those in his realm.'

'Until now,' said Liam. 'What has changed things for him to come back and take someone now?'

'Maybe just time passing, maybe the power of you and Elizabeth being here together, I don't know, there might even be a time limit on Elfin agreements. I think we should be encouraged that he kept to his word for centuries, indicating that he does have some honour and integrity.'

'This still doesn't give us any kind of guarantee that he won't hurt Elizabeth. He might be angry when he realises she's not a reincarnation of Isobel,' said Liam.

'We can't possibly know that,' said Iain. 'He might have been well aware of that when he took her.'

He looked around the table at everyone and said,

'It's time to get ready now. I propose that we aim to leave within the hour.'

Lou and June looked at each other and then at Iain, with Lou saying,

'Iain, June and I are not really sure what we will be doing when you leave. We're going to feel a bit useless and we certainly don't want that.'

'You will be coming with us, I thought you understood that? We will need you to come to the tunnel entrance with us. I'm going to give you an incantation that you will need to say while we are in there, until we come safely back.'

'How often will we have to say it?' asked Lou.

'Not constantly, but every few minutes. Are you up to that?'

'Of course,' said June, with a slight bristle to her voice. 'What will we do if someone comes along?'

At this point, Sunil could not resist saying,

'From what I remember of your acting skills, in the forest the other day, I'm sure you'll think of something!'

June shrugged in agreement at this comment.

'What about Fred?' asked Liam.

'Fred will stay here,' said Iain. 'He will know what to do if we don't come back within a certain time.'

'What exactly does that mean?' asked Liam with a great deal of suspicion.

'Let's not worry about that right now,' said Iain, firmly shutting this down as a topic for discussion.

The next half an hour was taken up with practicalities. To a casual observer it would have looked as if they were preparing for a day trip, or, to be more accurate, as if they were rehearsing a play, as most of the preparations involved reading and practising the reciting of incantations. Iain, the director, moving between Lou, June and Sunil, who were sitting in separate areas of the cottage. Liam, with no words to become familiar with, was sitting upstairs, on Elizabeth's bed, holding the topaz cross up to the light, marvelling at the way that depth and lightness fused within the blue stones. He had carefully bonded the missing stone back into the cross, a few hours earlier and it was now firmly fixed back in its rightful setting. A piece of a string was a poor substitute for the gold chain that it once must have hung from. Placing the cross around his neck, he felt a light pressure on his back, as if someone was touching him. Turning around, expecting to see one of the others, he saw nothing. He felt uneasy, but pushed it to one side, telling himself it was nothing but a draught or his imagination.

His gaze turned to a book on the bedside table, 'Glendraco' by Laura Black, which had one of the pages turned down at the corner. He read enough of the summary on the back cover to let him know that this was a sweeping romance set in the wild Highlands of Scotland, with a feisty heroine, facing jeopardy and danger at every corner. Funny, he didn't have her down as a reader of romantic novels, although, admittedly, this one did look quite good and he liked the illustration of the woman with red hair on the front, standing against a backdrop of a castle and rugged Highlands scenery. There was not much else on the bedside table, only a pen, a tin of lip balm, an empty glass and a box of tissues. He opened the lip balm and sniffed its subtle vanilla scent, but then put it back, telling himself not to be so sad.

He glanced up at the sound of the door opening. It was Iain. who had one simple question for him.

'Are you ready?'

'Yes, but I feel like I should be preparing somehow. My only job seems to be to get the Elfin Knight to see this cross.'

'There is no preparation you can do for this. We have no idea what will happen when we get through that wall of rock. As far as I'm concerned, you are the only person here who can face up to the Elfin Knight and who has the strength to deal with whatever might ensue.'

'What did you mean earlier, when you were talking about Fred?'

'I've briefed Lou and June, to come back here, if we don't return after a certain amount of time. If they do so, Fred will know what to do.'

'Yes, you said that before, but what exactly does that mean?'

'Liam, you know I would usually be completely honest with you, but this time I'm not going to be. I feel like I will be tempting fate if I tell you what I want Fred to do, in that event.'

'I thought that fate was one of the things that you didn't believe in?'

Iain looked at Liam with a ghost of a smile and said.

'Come on, let's go.'

Liam walked down the stairs behind Iain. The others were all standing in the hallway near the front door, looking expectantly up at them. Iain walked towards Fred and hugged him, saying something quietly in his ear that the others were unable to hear. Liam approached Fred after that and put his hand on his arm saying,

'Thank you for everything Fred.'

'You can thank me when you come back,' was the resolute reply.

Lou opened the front door and started to walk across the garden, with June and Sunil on either side of her, Liam and Iain following close behind. Fred stood in the doorway watching them for a minute, then turned to go back inside. Before he completely shut the door, he looked back at them and saw that they were not alone, there was a presence close to them; not a discernible figure, but a warm, pale golden light, dancing on the breeze. Fred smiled and shut the door.

Fred went back to the kitchen and sat at the table, where he seemed to have been permanently glued for what felt like a lifetime, though, of course, was only a few days. He thought back to the phone call he had received from Iain, in the middle of the night, after Liam and Elizabeth had landed on him. Iain's words betrayed a mixture of excitement and anxiety. Fred knew that he was finding things more difficult recently, Iain had never said anything about his to him, but he knew him and could see the toll, particularly emotionally, that their investigations were taking on him.

He remembered his first encounter with Iain. He had recently completed Eilidh's module as part of his degree course and he had found it more than fascinating, it had consumed him. He had always felt a bit different from everyone around him, not just because he was an introverted young man, who preferred losing himself in research to drinking all night in the student bar. It was more than that. Since childhood, he had seen and felt things in his environment that no one else could. It had scared him, profoundly, at the beginning, seeing spectral presences was a lot for a child to come to terms with. He had run, crying and screaming into his mother's bedroom and she had been so calm and matter of fact about it all, it soon became part of the fabric of his life. His mother did not see things the way that he did, but her father had and he would talk to her about what he saw and reassured her that she no need to fear the supernatural.

He did not see spirits or other supernatural presences all the time, it was only when something important or significant was happening in his life or, indeed in the lives of those around him and the wider world. He came to learn that whenever he sensed or saw something, it was like a warning. Eilidh had recognised his ability as soon as she spoke to him and had invited him to her office, after lectures, to discuss the presences that he had seen over the years to and to tell her more about his family. Not long after, he had been introduced to Iain. who had been instantly accepting of Fred, in a way that he had not experienced much before. He thought Iain had a brilliant mind and had built up a vast bank of knowledge over the years, but he had worked alone for too long and needed some help and support from somewhere, Iain was strong, he had to be, but Fred has always been able to sense his slight vulnerability and how this had ended up with the anxiety that he was experiencing on an increasingly regular basis.

He was, admittedly, more than a bit worried about them all, with the task that they would be facing, in their attempt to get Elizabeth back, but seeing the spirit presence walking next to them, which he assumed was Isobel, was heartening for him. He opened up his laptop, wondering how on earth he would be able to distract himself until they returned.

Chapter Thirty Three

I Saved The World Today - Part I

They walked through the forest, past the fallen branches and trees, carefully stepping around the churned up earth. They did not talk much, apart from commenting on the damage that the storm had done and telling one another to watch where they were walking. Liam walked slightly ahead of the rest, tracing the path that Iain and he had followed when they had tried to find her yesterday. He kept having to check himself from striding ahead too fast, knowing that June would find it hard to keep up. He longed to run to the edge of the forest, wanting to get to her as fast as he could, but he needed the others. This had no chance of being a success without them. Apart from the tree debris and the damage inflicted by the combination of the storm and the Elfin Knight, the forest felt as it had when Liam took his first walks through it after moving here. The air temperature did not drop and the feeling that danger could be lurking at every corner had dissipated, which he found ironic, considering the task that was ahead of them. He thought about how it would feel to be walking through the trees with Elizabeth at his side, admiring the light playing on her hair and in her eyes.

'Liam, slow down a bit!'

Iain's request brought him out of his reverie and he stopped, allowing the others to catch up.

Sunil reached him first and as he stood next to him, he asked Liam,

'How are you holding up? This must be really tough for you.'

Liam would usually have felt irritated by such an inquiry, but felt unexpectedly touched by this young man's question. He had not had much chance to talk individually to Sunil, but he had already got a pretty good impression of his inner strength and integrity, as well as his innate compassion.

'I'm okay, I just want to get this done as soon as possible. I can't bear to think of her in there.'

Before he could say any more, they were diverted by Lou asking them,

'Did you guys notice that light over there?'

She was pointing towards some trees to their left.

'What sort of light?' asked Iain.

'A sort of golden light, not sunlight, more like a shape. Not static, it was flickering or shimmering. I know that's not a great description, but that's the only way I can think to describe it. You saw it too, didn't you June?'

'Ai, I did, like Lou says, it moved around, as if it was following us. You probably think we're daft!'

'Not at all,' said Iain, as he walked towards the trees and looked around a bit, disappearing for a few minutes from their view. When he came back, he walked towards them smiling.

'What are you looking so happy about?' asked Liam.

'We are indeed being followed and I'm convinced it's Isobel. I saw her just now.'

'How can you know that?' said Liam.

'Liam, think about what I have done over the past few decades. I know a spirit when I see one. Of course, I can't be absolutely sure it's her, but taking an educated guess, I can't imagine what other benign spirit might have cause to be staying close to us at the moment.'

They continued walking until they reached the edge of the forest, feeling exposed after the shelter of the trees. The day was relatively fine, the sky cloudy, but not too ominous and the breeze gentle. The point where they had entered the hill before, was just ahead of them, although today there was no evidence at all of this. Iain turned towards Lou and June and requested that they stand back a little.

'Do you want me to run through anything with you again?' he asked them

'No,' said Lou. 'We know what you need us to do, isn't that right June?'

'Absolutely! Now you go and get her back.'

Iain glanced at Liam and Sunil.

'Ready?'

They nodded and Iain stood before the hill and started to recite,

'Deus magne montis, te rogamus, permitte nos ambulare intra te'

As before, nothing happened at first, but Iain continued to recite these words and after the sixth or seventh time, they started to hear something. A low, rumbling noise, as before, from somewhere deep within the hill, as the rocks in front of them started to melt away, until the tunnel entrance was revealed. This time, Iain took the lead, with Liam and Sunil following him into the darkness. Lou and June watched on in amazement, as the rocks started to form again, in front of them and the tunnel entrance completely disappeared. They found a couple of large rocks and sat down, beginning their vigil.

The tunnel was pitch black, but did not feel too cold or damp. The ground was quite dry and smooth, without obstacles to trip them up. They had a torch each, a powerful ones with fresh batteries in them. The ceiling of the tunnel was, Liam estimated, around six feet high, fine for Iain and him, but he noticed Sunil, who stood about six feet two inches, had to walk with a slightly lowered head. They continued like this until they reached the same wall of seemingly impenetrable rock. Liam reached out his hands and placed them on the rocks, which felt dry and had a warmth to them, which he had not expected. He moved further forward and placed his ear to the rock, as if he was listening to the sound of the sea through a seashell lifted to his ear, but heard nothing. He turned to Iain.

'If we get through, I'm going in alone. You won't be coming with me.'

'Of course I'm coming in with you. You don't think I would let you do this on your own!' was Iain's indignant reply. 'What are you thinking by saying that?'

'I don't want to put anyone else in danger. I think that the Elfin Knight would want me in there and me alone, considering that this was all about us being of Isobel's blood in the first place. It needs to be between me, Elizabeth and him.'

'Liam, I see what you're saying, but I honestly think that you'd be better off having me in there with you.'

Sunil, who had not said anything, to Liam's surprise, agreed with him.

'I think Liam's right, I know nothing about situations like this, though I feel I've been on a pretty steep learning curve. We'll be here, so, hopefully near enough to help if we need to, or if we can.'

'What you both are not bearing in mind, is the power that this being possesses and that he would be quite capable of destroying both you and the surrounding villages, if he wishes to. I would need to be there to invoke Beira in that situation. No one else can do that.'

'Well, let's hope it doesn't come to that. Now, are we doing this or not?" was Liam's agitated reply.'

'Liam, if I stay here, you're putting yourself, Elizabeth and many others at risk.'

'And by invoking Beira, you would be doing the same, from what I understand.'

To his own surprise, Iain capitulated and pulled Liam towards him, hugging him tightly and saying,

'You are the bravest man I know. You had better bloody well come back.'

'I will,' said Liam, 'Come on Sunil, do your thing!'

Sunil moved in front of them and raising his arms, placed both hands onto the rock and started to chant,

'Om Namo Bhagvate Aanjaneyaay Mahaabalaay Swaahaa

Rama Priya Namastubhyam Hanuman Raksh Sarvadaa'

Over and over, he repeated these sacred words. He must have said them more than twenty times before anything happened. Almost imperceptibly, the light ahead of them altered. Where there had been a solid wall of rock, was now a veil of pale blue light. Sunil gasped as his hands no longer resting on solid rock, disappeared into this light, forcing him to fall back. Liam and Iain picked him up, asking if he was alright.

'I'm fine! I don't believe that it actually worked! What is that made of? It feels warm, almost like putting your hands into water, but dry, if that makes any sense at all.'

Iain reached out his hand, running it through the blue light.

'I don't know, this is the start of his realm, everything will be strange and unknown. Liam, you need to go through as quickly as you can. I don't know how long this will stay open.'

Chapter Thirty Four

I Saved The World Today - Part II

As he cautiously stepped through the blue veil, he thought it would feel cold and wet, like walking through a waterfall, but it did not; it felt of nothing, as if he was simply walking through an open doorway. He stood, looking around him, trying to get his bearings. He was standing in a cave, which was vast, impossible to compare to any space he had ever inhabited. He could see the walls, but, looking up, shining his torch, could not see where the ceiling ended. The walls of the cave were too far away for him to touch and glowed with a soft, pulsing, pale blue light. Looking down, he reached the sudden realisation that he was standing on a narrow path, with a sheer drop into darkness on either side. This caused him to momentarily lose his balance, sending a jolt of fear, followed by adrenaline, searing through his body. He looked back over his shoulder, to find the entrance gone and a wall of rock back in its place, unable to understand how he had not heard this happen. He started to walk forward, telling himself that he would not fall off the path, it was not that narrow, as long as he was careful and looked where he was walking. He heard his grandmother's voice in his head, telling him to slow down and watch where he was putting his feet, whenever she would take him for a walk when he was a child. He was always running, trying to get to the end before everyone else, leading to frequent mishaps and grazed knees, along with the odd broken bone. He could not see where the path ended ahead of him, it seemed to go on indefinitely. He wondered how on earth Elizabeth had managed this, but then supposed that she was probably not making her own way along here. This thought made him angry and gave him the small boost that he needed to keep going. It was silent in the cave, the sound of his breathing and his heart beat his only companions. Liam had truly not expected Iain to agree with him, about staying behind and letting him carry on alone. When they had been discussing everything back at the cottage, it had seemed sensible for Iain to be with him, considering the depth of his experience and knowledge. However, as he was walking through the tunnel, Liam began to feel very differently about this, his instinct telling him that it should be just down to him to go in there and face this and not drag the others any further into it than necessary. They had already put themselves in enough danger, because of Elizabeth and him. The idea of death scared him, it always had, with no religious belief, he did not have the prospect of an afterlife to take the fear away.

His parents and grandparents had been religious, and he had attended church with them every week, but as soon as he had been old enough to decide for himself about whether he would go to church, he stopped. He knew that they had found this sad and disappointing, but he could not bear sitting in that church, listening to all that nonsense for any longer than he had to. He acknowledged that this had played a pretty large part in his decision to leave his homeland, but it was not the only reason. He had always had an underlying need to experience more of the world, an innate restlessness. Well Liam, he said to himself, you have certainly gone and found yourself enough adventure now.

He had lost all concept of how long he had been walking along this path. It could have been five minutes or an hour. He did not feel tired, as he would after a long walk and his body temperature felt the same as when he had started. Still the walls of the cave lightly pulsated with the blue light. He had to make a conscious effort not to look at this light for too long, recognising its mesmeric quality. He sensed a change ahead of him, dearly hoping that he would not meet another wall of rock. There was something dark ahead, which he could not make out. When he got closer, he saw an arched door, reaching so high, the top of it was swathed in darkness, signifying the end of the path. He touched the door, which seemed to be made of a dark brown wood and saw a black, iron handle.

He had not expected it to actually open when he tried the handle and so when it did, he was stunned. A voice inside his head was screaming that this was a really bad idea and why would this door open for him, unless it was a trap. Nevertheless, he started to push open the door, expecting it to be heavy, but it required barely any of his force. He braced himself for whatever he would meet on the other side, but what saw was like nothing he could have imagined. He was standing in a very different type of cavernous space. A room with gently shimmering golden walls, intricately carved and reaching up to a ceiling that he estimated was over three hundred feet high. It reminded him of a medieval cathedral he had seen in France, but on a scale beyond the reach of humans. The room was empty, but had windows, consisting of hexagonal panes of glass, a mixture of bright blues, greens and reds. He slowly walked over to one of these windows, but was unable to see anything beyond the opaque surface.

He saw a doorway, without a door, on the other side of this huge, empty room, through which he walked, only to find himself in what appeared to be an identical room, again, empty. He began to sense something, the hairs on his body, standing on end, his heartbeat quickening, but he could see nothing around him. Another doorway on the other side of the room, which he walked through, expecting to be greeted by yet another vast, bare room, but he was wrong, there was something in this room.

This room was full of statues, carved out of some sort of pale, rich, creamy stone, that glistened slightly in the light. Liam walked up to the one nearest to him and saw it was a woman, wearing long, flowing robes, with a slightly down-turned face, bearing a serene expression. He reached out his hand and traced one of the carved folds in her robe, admiring the beauty of her face. It took him a while to realise that this face was one he had seen before. It was Isobel, with her fine, straight features and her high cheekbones. He turned to an adjacent statue, which was definitely the same woman, but this time she was looking directly ahead, with the suggestion of a smile on her lips. His eye was caught by a movement in one of the far corners of the room, obscured by a pillar. He walked towards it and as he passed around the pillar, he saw her, suspended off the ground in front of him, as if she was floating.

He cried out, 'Elizabeth!' and tried to touch her, but she was surrounded by an invisible barrier, preventing him from reaching her. He stood, transfixed, looking at her. She wore robes, similar to those of Isobel's statues, pale and shimmering. Her long, chestnut hair was flowing beneath her and her eyes were shut. He tried to reach her again, but his hands kept bouncing off whatever was shielding her. He desperately looked around the room, trying to find something that would help him, but what, he said to himself. He suddenly remembered the Apollo amulet around his neck and removed it. He had no idea whether this would have any impact, but it was the only object he had with supposed protective qualities. He held it next to Elizabeth and pleaded for her to wake up and come back to him, shutting his eyes as if he was praying. He started to feel the air change around him and opened his eyes, in the hope it was working. Standing next to Elizabeth was a figure, nearly seven feet tall, like a man, but not. Liam instantly knew it was him. His long, black hair was rippling around his head and shoulders, as if he was standing in the wind and his black eyes seemed to burn in his long, pale face. He raised his hand and the amulet was wrenched from his hand by an invisible force and flung to the ground. Liam tried to retrieve it from the floor, but could not move his arms or legs. He started to feel himself lifting up from the floor, unable to resist the strength of his magic, feeling nothing but powerlessness and vulnerability.

It was over, he thought, all the talk and planning of how they would get her back, would end with him like this, useless. Something was happening to his mind, as if he was starting to lose consciousness, but very gradually, as if a fog was descending, thickening as it got nearer. He tried to look at Elizabeth, but could barely make her out now. He became aware of the Elfin Knight approaching him, unable to make out his face, just conscious of his looming form getting nearer. Again, he shut his eyes, he could barely think now, his head felt almost empty of thought and memory. He started to feel something on his neck, a slight pulling, which made him open his eyes. The Elfin Knight was standing right over him, looking at something in his hand, his face being illuminated by a pale, blue light. Liam started to feel the fog lifting from him and everything beginning to come back into focus and he gradually realising that he was no longer suspended, as he felt the floor beneath his feet. He glanced at Elizabeth, who was still in the same state as before, then back to the Elfin Knight. Liam could now see that he had Isobel's cross in his hand and he seemed transfixed by it. The blue light that had been

reflected on his face, now almost surrounded him. There was no hardness about his expression, the eyes that had previously burned with what appeared to be anger and rage, were now softer. Liam started to gain control of his arms and legs and backed away from him, edging towards the nearest door, but what he started to see forming stopped him in his tracks. The blue light around the Elfin Knight was now taking on a different form, that of a human, a woman. With each moment, she became more defined, and Liam started to see her long reddish hair, her pale face and her robes dancing around her. A few moments more and it was Isobel that stood before him, looking as real as him. Liam watched as the Elfin Knight placed the topaz cross around her neck and wrapped her in his arms.

The atmosphere in the room changed profoundly, as Liam experienced a feeling so pure and joyous, that he felt tears begin to roll freely down his face.

'Liam, is that you?'

He turned to Elizabeth and saw her standing before him, confused, but very much alive.

'Oh, thank god, you're back,' was all Liam could say, as he engulfed her in his arms, his tears continuing to flow..

Chapter Thirty Five

I Saved The World Today - Part III

Elizabeth felt as if she had just woken up from a very deep sleep, after a night involving too many glasses of wine. Her legs felt wobbly and unstable, as Liam held her in a fierce embrace and he appeared to be crying a lot. She could see the Elfin Knight nearby with his arms around a woman, but she could not make out who this was. The last thing she remembered was being in this room with him and the realisation of the depth of his love for Isobel and their son.

She felt overwhelmed by Liam's embrace and after she had succeeded in extracting herself, cautiously walked towards the Elfin Knight and the woman.

'Elizabeth, wait!' said Liam 'Don't go too near him.'

'It's fine. He won't hurt me.'

As she approached them, the Elfin Knight looked at her and then down at the woman, who turned her face to Elizabeth. It was unmistakably Isobel, whose face held a familiarity, not just because they looked more alike than she thought they would, but something much deeper.

Isobel reached out her hand and took Elizabeth's, holding it up to her face. She was surprised at how soft and warm it felt. Her eyes were so similar to hers, greenish gold with a reddish brown circle around her pupil. She then saw her reaching out her other hand and realised it was for Liam.

'Liam, come over here, Isobel wants you.'

Liam, after a moment of hesitation, walked slowly towards them and placed his hand in Isobel's. Elizabeth felt something running through her body, she had felt this before, as if she could feel and hear her blood coursing through her veins. As before, this did not disturb her, it made her feel stronger and more connected to everything around her.

'Do you feel that?' she asked Liam

'Yes, what is it?'

'I think it's our shared bloodline, giving us strength. She's showing us that we are all connected.'

Isobel spoke. Her voice soft, but clear.

'Thank you for bringing me back here, but you both must leave now. My beloved will let you go, but you must leave straight away. He will give you a safe passage that will take you home, but you must not turn back at all, even if you hear something behind you.'

Elizabeth knew they had to go, but being in Isobel's presence felt so right, now it was her who had tears running down her face. Isobel gently wiped away some of them away and said,

'You must get back to your sons, I have waited so long to see mine again.'

'Come on Elizabeth, we need to go.' said Liam.

'Go with him" said Isobel "Cherish each other, do not lose each other.'

Elizabeth was slightly perturbed by this comment, but said,

'How will we know which way to go?'

'It will be clear. Start off through that doorway.'

Elizabeth and Liam looked towards where she was pointing and then turned back to say goodbye, but they had both gone. Liam started walking towards the door and reached out his hand to her. This time, she took it without skipping a beat.

Elizabeth had expected another room through the doorway, but instead found a huge cave, pulsing with the same blue light she remembered from her journey here. A path ran through the cave ahead of them, with nothing but darkness on either side of it.

'This path is how I got here,' said Liam. 'If we follow it, we'll reach an entrance to a tunnel that will lead us to the outside of the hill.'

Elizabeth looked at this man, who she barely knew and asked him,

'How did you even know where to start?'

'I've had a lot of help. Iain and Fred of course, but Lou and June have been invaluable and Sunil.'

'Who is Sunil?' she asked.

'Sunil is an incredible young man, a soldier, and without him we would not have been able to get through to you here. Iain and Sunil should be waiting for us on the other side of this cave.'

'How long have I been gone?'

'A couple of days.'

'That's incredible, it's felt so long, like months, even years. How did you get Isobel to him?'

'We didn't have to do much, she left us clues. It took us a little while to work out what she wanted, but once we did … come on, let's walk, we'll talk about all this when we get out. Remember what she said, don't be tempted to look backwards.'

With Elizabeth in front, they started to make their way along the path, carefully watching where they placed their feet as they went.

'How long is this path?' asked Elizabeth

'On my way here, I found it hard to tell. It could have been five minutes or hours. As you've learned, time is so different here.'

As before, when they walked, their own concept of time became irrelevant, but eventually reached the end of the path, to be met by a wall of stone.

'What now?' asked Elizabeth.

'Sunil made a chant to open this up. I was hoping it would still be open when we came back.'

'Great!' said Elizabeth. 'I don't think they're going to hear us if we shout. Why would the Elfin Knight let us go, if he knew we would get stuck here? It makes no sense.'

'You're right, it doesn't. Here, give me your hands.'

'Why? What good will that do?'

Liam's expression told her that it would be simpler to do what he asked as she put her hands in his.

'Now, shut your eyes and will the rock to open up.'

'Are you serious?'

'Please, just try.'

Elizabeth did as he had asked and silently willed the rocks to part. She started to feel that sensation again, of blood coursing through her body and began to hear the sound of moving rocks. Opening her eyes, she was astounded to find the wall of solid rock had been replaced by a wall of blue light, which Liam started to lead her through.

'Come on, this is it.'

Passing through the light, she was greeted by darkness, quickly replaced by whoops of joy from Iain and someone who she assumed was Sunil. She was pulled into a huge hug by Iain, after he had grabbed Liam. Sunil hung back a little.

'Oh my dears,' said Iain, 'I am so very happy to see you.'

Elizabeth could hear the tears in his voice.

'We need to get going, quickly, 'said Liam. "I'm not sure how long we have to get out, but we can't hang around, oh and, for some reason, we can't look back. I'm not sure this applies to you two as well, but best be safe.'

'Who told you this? Did you speak to him? How did he communicate with you?' asked Iain, brimming with curiosity.

Liam grew impatient and said,

'We'll tell you about it when we get out of here.'

Suddenly, taking charge, he said,

'You two go ahead, then Elizabeth and I will go last.'

'Come on Sunil,' said Iain, 'Let's do as the man says.'

Sunil and Iain started to walk up the tunnel, each of them holding a torch to light their way. Elizabeth walked close behind them, finding security in their proximity, still feeling slightly dazed and taking in the enormity of what had happened to her. As she walked, she thought about the Elfin Knight; how her fear of him had so quickly dissipated and how his love for Isobel had engulfed everyone in that room. She imagined Isobel seeing her son again and how unbearable for her to have been parted from him. She longed to hold her own children, but was not quite sure how she would explain to them, or to anyone for that matter, what she had experienced. Maybe she would not tell them, although pretending everything had been fine and uneventful since she had moved to Scotland, would feel dishonest and they would know she was keeping something from them. She was extremely aware of Liam's presence behind her; this intriguing and yes, she had to admit, handsome man, who had been willing to risk everything to find her. She remembered the first time she had seen him, in the lane, and how strangely he had looked at her,

leaving her with such an uneasy and confused feeling. She wanted to talk to him and to the others, about what had been happening over the past couple of days, but she understood that now was not the time for this. No one was speaking; small talk would have been absurd and anything more serious too distracting.

She was pulled out of her own thoughts by the realisation that they reached the end of the tunnel. Another wall or rock stood before them. She heard Iain begin to speak in Latin.

'Deus magne montis, te rogamus, permitte nos ambulare intra te'

She had studied Latin at school a lifetime ago, but she could still pick out most of the words. He kept repeating these words and on the seventh instance, the rocks started to disappear in front of them and she could see daylight ahead of her. At the same time, she heard a noise coming from behind them, a low, rumbling noise, similar to that when the Elfin Knight started to appear to them.

'What is that noise?' she asked in panic.

'Try to ignore it,' said Iain. 'Whatever you do, do not turn around. We'll be out of here in a minute.'

She heard cries on the other side of the remaining rocks, as Lou and June began to see them. She watched as Iain and Sunil stepped through the entrance into the waiting arms of the two women. Then it was her being wrapped up in Lou's embrace, all her senses overwhelmed by the light and the breeze that surrounded her. They all waited for Liam to appear, but he did not.

Elizabeth called for him.

'Liam, come on, where are you?!'

Nothing. Elizabeth pulled herself out of Lou's arms and started to go back towards the tunnel.

Iain shouted after her.

'No, Elizabeth, don't go back in there!'

'I have to!' was all she said as she grabbed his torch and stepped back into the darkness.

She shone the torch ahead of her, she could see Liam, but he was moving backwards, as if being pulled. She ran towards him, barely able to keep up with how fast he was moving.

'Go back, please, don't come any further!' he shouted at her

She kept running, until she could almost touch him and yelled at him.

'Give me your hand, quickly!'

She grabbed his outstretched hand and started to heave with all her might. She felt herself being carried along with him, back into the depths of the tunnel. She had dropped her torch and could not see anything, although she became aware of the rocks falling behind him, as if the tunnel was caving in. She drew on strength that she had no idea she possessed, as she pulled back as hard as she could and felt the resistance begin to lessen. As soon as this happened, she felt herself gaining strength and began dragging him back toward the tunnel entrance. The others were right there with their hands reaching out, ready to get hold of her as soon as she appeared and pull the two of them out. The moment they were out of the tunnel, rocks started to fall down into the entrance, completely blocking it and the ground in front of them began to cave in.

'Everybody, move back!' shouted Iain.

Six figures lay on the ground, next to a crater that had opened up in front of them. One by one, they stood up, checking with each other that they were alright. The two nearest to the crater were the last to stand up. The man got to his feet first, looking down at the woman and reaching out his hand to her. She sat up and looked at him and his outstretched hand, hesitating. Then a knowing smile broke out on her face and she took his hand, allowing him to pull her up.

'You looked back, didn't you?' she said to him.

He returned her smile and said,

'How about we stick to moving forward from now on?'

Epilogue

Elizabeth watched as Liam dug a hole for the Ash sapling. When it was deep enough, she walked over to it, removed the lid from the plain, stainless steel urn she was holding and looked around at the assembled group. There was Lou, holding hands with her husband, June standing next to Roderick, Fred, Iain, Sunil and her two sons. She knew they were all waiting expectantly for her to say something, so she began.

'Isobel loved this place, somewhere that she could feel content and free from the constraints of her life. Her wish to be buried here was denied to her, not through cruelty, but through a lack of understanding about what she had lost and yearned for. She believed that she might have some chance of being reunited with her true love and her son, through death and she was right. I admire her profoundly, for her determination and her enduring love and feel so proud to be descended from her.'

Elizabeth leant over and carefully poured the contents of the urn into the freshly dug hole. She stood back as, one by one, some of the other members of the group came forward and placed their own items in with Isobel's ashes; Lou and June gave the amulets that Iain had asked them to wear, Sunil gave a red and yellow woven bracelet, a Kautuka that he wore around his wrist, Iain and Fred both recited protection spells and placed pieces of paper with them written on, in the hole. She did not know how she would ever be able to fully express her gratitude to these people, for how they had not given up trying to find her and bring her home.

She glanced over at Roderick, who was surreptitiously wiping a tear away from his eye, who had played such an important part in making today possible. He had used his contacts to hurry up the whole process of Isobel's exhumation and to enable her body to be cremated. She would not usually approve of influential people pulling strings, but was willing to overlook it this time. When it was Liam's turn, he said.

'As this was originally about our blood and our connection to the past, Elizabeth and I felt that would be our gift, so if you're squeamish, I suggest that you look away now.'

Liam walked over to the hole with Elizabeth, where she offered him her hand. He took the Boline from his pocket and gently brushed her hand with his lips, before making a small incision.

After he had done the same to himself, they both knelt down and let a few drops of blood fall into the ashes. They paused for a moment and then stood up, after which Liam started to fill in the hole with earth.

As he did so, Elizabeth surveyed the surrounding area. The fallen Ash tree was no longer there, having been chopped up and removed by the forestry commission. When they had been working on clearing up the forest, one of them had knocked on Elizabeth's cottage door and asked her if she knew anything about the large crater near the Ash tree and also the crater at the edge of the forest, near the start of the hill. He told her that they were all a bit mystified by this and could not put it down to storm damage. Elizabeth put on her best perplexed face and told him that she had no idea about the craters, perhaps they were the result of some bizarre weather conditions, such as a mini tornado. They filled in the craters and left, much to her relief. The Ministry of Defence brought in contractors to properly dismantle the old camp. Within a week, it was all gone, no huts, no perimeter fence, just an empty space. Iain had tried to find out, from his sources, what had been reported about the events there, but even he kept hitting brick walls.

The villagers remained oblivious to what had taken place, although could not help but notice what had happened to the hill next to the forest. It looked higher than before and many were convinced that the shape of it had slightly altered, the surface rocks seeming smoother and less jagged. As with most things, they simply accepted the new landscape, but still their wariness of the forest remained.

Elizabeth looked at her sons, both tall and, she thought, resembling her more than their father, with their hazel eyes and high cheekbones. When she had come home, she had called them and asked if they would come and visit as soon as possible. They sat in silence as she recounted the whole story to them. She was worried that they would not believe her and might even think she was having some kind of mental breakdown, but she did not have to worry. They were intrigued and fascinated, as well as being horrified at the danger she had been in.

Lou walked over to her and hugged her, saying,

'I hope you're going to stay up here. What would I do for adventure and excitement if you left?'

Elizabeth smiled at her and replied.

'I've no plans to go anywhere. I've become too attached to the place.'

'And the people?' said Lou knowingly.

Elizabeth gave her a mock outraged look and glanced in Liam's direction, admiring his arms as he wielded the shovel.

They all walked back through the forest, to Elizabeth's cottage, where drinks and food were waiting for them. Elizabeth had considered whether she wanted to stay here, after all that had passed, but all her instincts told her to stay. She was not remotely scared of this place and still happily walked through the forest alone, although, was usually joined by Liam now. She knew that he felt the same about the place and they had started to discuss the fact that they probably only needed one cottage between them. As she walked into the sitting room, with a glass of chilled white wine in her hand, she paused to look at Isobel's portrait, which Roderick had let her keep, hanging above the fireplace. She had attempted to return it to him, but he was adamant that she was more entitled to it than he was.

There had been much discussion between all of them, about Isobel's burial, not about her ashes in the forest, but about what would be a more fitting memorial to her, than a small gravestone hidden shamefully away in the corner of a graveyard. Again, with a little help from Roderick, they had returned to Beauly Priory, earlier in the week, to see a new inscription being engraved within the family crypt of Sir Orfeo, which read,

Lady Isobel Mackenzie

Born 1450

Died 1499

Wife and devoted mother

Bha gaol aice air an t-saoghal nàdarra agus ghràdhaich a h-uile duine a bha eòlach oirre

Elizabeth was joined by Liam, as she gazed at the portrait.

'Your eyes are more beautiful than hers,' he whispered into her ear.

She kissed his cheek and was about to say something mildly suggestive when Iain interrupted them.

'I just wanted to let you both know. Fred and I will be heading off tomorrow. I received an interesting email recently.'

'That sounds intriguing, where are you going?' asked Liam.

'To the West Country, Devon, more specifically. Your neck of the woods, I believe?' looking at Elizabeth.

'What's been happening there?' she asked.

Barely skipping a beat, Iain replied, although his eye contact somewhat betrayed him.

'I can't really say at the moment, it's just an initial investigation. It might be nothing.'

Undeterred, Elizabeth continued to press him for information.

'Where in Devon are you going?'

'Somewhere near a little village called Eggesford.'

'My sister lives near there!' exclaimed Elizabeth.

'What a coincidence!' said Iain.

'Hmmm,' said Elizabeth, 'isn't it just.'

About the Author

Kathryn Bartlett grew up in Devon, the youngest of a large family, surrounded by assorted animals and prone to daydreaming. London called, where she still resides with her Kiwi partner and numerous cats, although she would say that her heart belongs to the Highlands.

Orfeo Undone is her first novel, inspired by hearing a folk song on the radio, 'King Orfeo,' by the Scottish singer, Emily Smith.

Her next novel, 'Into the Dimpsey,' will be available later in 2024.